THE
BONE
TREE

THE
BONE
TREE

THE BONE TREE

AIRANA NGAREWA

MOA PRESS

MOA
P R E S S

Published in New Zealand and Australia in 2023
by Moa Press
(an imprint of Hachette Aotearoa New Zealand Limited)
Level 2, 23 O'Connell Street, Auckland, New Zealand
www.moapress.co.nz
www.hachette.co.nz

A catalogue record for this book is available from the National Library of New Zealand.

ISBN: 978 1 8697 1500 7 (paperback)

Cover design by Keely O'Shannessy
Cover illustration courtesy of Haoro Hond
Typeset by Bookhouse, Sydney
Printed and bound in Australia by McPherson's Printing Group

To the Captain
To Granddad
Michael Paddon Bourke

Part One

I

We left the house early to get some practice in, burying ourselves beneath our hoodies, tucking our hands in our pockets, bending at the hip and following the maze the rabbits, stoats and runaway sheep had carved through the gorse. Mum says the first of the gorse came here on a boat. Like the farmers and the old man's family. When it hooked up with our soil, it gave birth to this new kind of plant. It was still gorse, but it grew as hardy as the maunga was tall. Through heavy winds and droughts and snowfall it spread, flowering yellow half the year and spending the rest of the time sharpening its limbs, crossing its roots beneath the soil, waiting for some kid to come charging by in shorts.

Ahead of me, Black dodged the thorns with ease. I was longer, lankier and the gorse's limbs stretched every which way in the shadows. My calves always got cut. Would help if I covered them, Black reckoned, but you can't manu in pants.

The kid was named after the All Blacks. Apparently, the old man won big on them the night before Black was born. Dad might've been taking the piss when he said that, though. Who could know for sure? If not the rugby team, the kid could've been named for the gang. The old man did have a fist tattooed on his calf. I guess neither of us really know too much about him. His life before us anyway. Drinking, smoking and blowing up over this, that and everything.

We stripped down to our shorts and shoes on the other side of the gorse, shaking out our hoodies and plucking spikes from our clothes. I spat on my fingers and cleaned the fresh cuts below my knee. Old Māori medicine, Mum reckoned. Nothing like a little saliva to stop the bleeding. And they were only scratches anyway, barely drawing blood.

Once we were sorted, we chucked our clothes back on, climbed the steel-wire fence that bordered the hills of gorse, and gunned it across the ballhead's paddock. Fella was hard-case – a straight-up nutter. Lucky for us, he hardly ever came this way so early. Was most likely still hosing down the cowshed. The kid sprinted, leaping every ditch and mound, while I powerwalked with all the grace of a koro without his cane. My shoulder was buggered from one of Dad's blow-ups so I couldn't run too good.

A chatter of magpies watched from a broken trough, their whare nestled beneath a slab fallen from its concrete base. They're why this paddock was abandoned. Not even the ballhead was nutty enough to stick his stock near these taniwha. They were violence incarnate, protecting their turf like they were prospecting for a patch.

By the time I'd cleared the final fence, the kid was in the water, his hoodie, socks and sneakers thrown over the rocks. Black's cheeks were soft, his arms gangly, his stomach distended. The top and sides of his head were cut short and the locks at the back were long and brown in the water and curly and ginger in the sunlight. Handsome, half-caste and ranga though he was, he couldn't manu for the life of him. Boy's body came out of the water redder than the behind of his head.

He floated in the belly of the river bend, doggy paddling 'til I approached, then ducked underwater. The bend was wider and deeper than the rest of the river so the water moved slow. I waited on the grass, searching for him and he exploded out of the tide, eyes rolled back into his head, tongue stretched out across his chin.

'Pūkana!'

The water swallowed the kid again and I bit my tongue until he resurfaced. 'You're an idiot, aye.'

'Nah.'

'Yeah.'

'Why?'

'I saw all that water you swallowed.'

'So?'

'So you're an idiot.'

———

This bend in the river was our own. We'd discovered it like Kupe. No whitebaiters, no whalers, no cows shitting in the water upstream. For that, we were grateful for the gorse. It kept everyone away – even Mum and the old man, when those two were still walking 'round.

I've always done all I could to keep the kid away from their drama. From Dad's going at the old lady when his temper got the best of him. By saving Black from all that, I reckoned I could trick him into loving his daddy. It's hard work hating a parent, hating every piece of them you find inside yourself. And anyway, the old man has been better the past couple of years, his blowing up more a monthly mistake than an every–other–day thing like it was when I was little.

The river bend was bordered by a pair of cliffs, the side nearest our house partially collapsed, creating a sketchy ramp up and down. There were trees and flax and toetoe and masses of stone spotted about the place – a tribe of little ones at the water's edge and a few giants ones, the chiefs, cooling their feet in the river. You couldn't jump from all of them; still, me and the bro were always finding new places to manu. Our latest favourite was a tree that'd half fallen over to become a diving board.

That's where I taught the kid the technique. You squat, you pop, you stretch while you swing your legs, then just before you touch the water you fold your body into a V, arms over your puku. If it sounded like a gun going off, you'd fucken nailed it.

'Give it a go, aye, and I'll watch from underwater.'

I let out the air in my lungs, letting my body sink into the river. The kid's silhouette danced above the ripples, the boy leaping into the air and breaking water with the small of his back.

'Was that it?'

'Nope.'

'Was it close at least?'

'Close enough for today, I reckon.'

Where the water was shallow, you could see the critters darting backwards and forwards between the rocks, a greenstone hue concealing anything further than a few metres from shore. Where it was deep, you could feel you weren't alone, the occasional monster brushing against your feet. The best of the lot were the ducks; the kid and I were their friends. Every day, they would float by us, snapping at the tide, and every day, we would call to them.

'Haere mai e ngā rakiraki.' They were Māori ducks so Mum reckoned we had to call to them in Māori.

It was a waste of time. Weeks went by and the ducks never turned their heads. Eventually, we'd asked Mum if there were any other words we should use and she told us to take some bread down. 'No Māori, man or woman or rakiraki, would turn down a good feed.' After that, we were off to the races. The ducks wouldn't leave us alone. They followed the kid while he doggy paddled and watched me while I manu'd, and they tore up the bread the moment it hit the water. They didn't share, so the kid and I fed them separately. It was one of our river rules.

We'd made all sorts of rules to look after this place. You had to bring bread and you weren't allowed to fish and you had to say thank you before you left; you couldn't come alone and you weren't allowed to drink the water and if you needed to pee you had to go up and do it on the ballhead's fence.

After a few more manu, we said thank you to the river and drip-dried on the biggest rock, where the rising sun had left it warm. We never brought towels. Drip-drying was another one of our rules; the time the kid and I would talk, trading questions and spitting in the cracks in the rocks, watching the saliva bubble. It wasn't that we ignored each other at home, just had enough going on between the house and the old man that we didn't talk much.

'Better head back before you get burnt, aye, Black?'

'Soon.'

'You like that name? Or you reckon we should get you another one?'

'Nah.'

'Nah to you liking your name or the other thing?'

'I like it.'

'Yeah?'

He screwed up his face, sat up and poked his tongue at me. 'It's better than yours.'

I laughed. 'You reckon?'

He rolled onto his stomach, where the rock was dry and still warm and rested his head on his hands. 'Yeah, no-one even knows how to spell it.'

'K – a – u – r – i. Kauri.'

'That's not how Dad spells it.'

'That's 'cause Dad hates the reo.'

'What does that mean?'

'It means Mum wanted me to have a Māori name and the old man wanted me to have an English one. So Mum called me Kauri after the tree, and Dad called me Cody after the bourbon.'

'What's the real one?'

'Dunno.'

Dry everywhere except our undies, we brushed the dust from our bodies and got dressed, and started on our way home, pulling at our jocks sticking to the insides of our legs. We used to take our undies off and stow them in our pockets until one day the kid's shorts caught on a thorn in the gorse and he had to walk home with his buttcheek out. Boy had no shame but I was embarrassed for him. That day, we started a new rule: undies, whether soaked through or damp, stayed on. Washing the old man's every other night was more than enough ass in my life.

I helped Black through the fence and scaled it myself to cross the ballhead's paddock one last time, the kid sprinting as fast as his wet jocks would let him. The ballhead must have spotted us down at the bend because as I stepped foot on the field I heard an engine roar, and that no-hair-having muppet came tearing through three sets of paddocks towards us.

Ignoring him, I walked on, edging myself as close to the gorse as possible in case things kicked off, buying some time for the kid to get ahead. The ballhead pulled his ute up beside me and watched the kid disappear, his engine idling in first gear, rolling only a little faster than I was. Then he put his foot down, swinging the vehicle in front of me, cutting me off.

'Up to, sir?'

'Wondering what a little shit like you is doing on my land.' His face twisted into a snarl. 'I had a quad stolen the other day. You wouldn't happen to know anything about that, would yah?'

'No.'

'What about that old lady of yours, she know anything?'

The fire grew hot in my hands. 'Get stuffed.'

If I got anything from the old man it was his quickness to explode in anger.

'You cheeky fucken Maari.' I must've looked to the ballhead like the kid looked to me. A lanky little half-caste boy – the only difference being my hair was less a Māori mullet than a mop without a bucket. 'You disrespect me again and I'll shoot you like a dog. You ever read that thing?' He pointed with his eyes to a red and white sign strapped to a gate. 'It says if anyone steps foot on my farm, I'll put a bullet in 'em. You know why I put it there?'

I didn't answer. The heat in my hands disappeared on me and I was a coward again.

'Because one day, when I'm sick and tired of my shit being taken by a bunch of no-good fanatics like you and yours, I'm gonna load my shotgun and scream bloody murder.' He hoicked a load of snot and spat at the grass in front of my feet. 'And when the cops come to clean up the mess, I'm going to kick back on my La-Z-Boy with a cup of tea in my hands and answer every question of theirs by pointing to that there sign.'

A chorus of cicadas sung in the background, the ballhead's rage an insult to the softness of the world around us. A light wind blowing, the lunchtime sun radiating warmth.

The redness in his eyes eventually settled. His frame dwindled and he re-revealed himself. A harmless stick of a man taking his stress out on the only one in range. Still, I didn't reply. Didn't square up or bark back. I watched the man un-puff his fur and slowly regret what he'd said. Farming was a hard life, I knew. Hours like that will make a young man old, a fat man thin. A good man paranoid the locals were plotting to take back what they both knew should never have been taken.

Mum almost never talked about this side of things — the confiscations. It slipped through only when she told stories about famous fighters. Wiremu Kīngi and Tītokowaru and those kind of guys. Even the old man liked those stories. Ancestry aside, he must've seen himself in them. Fella was might-makes-right down to the core of his being.

The ballhead swung his ute around, told me to get the fuck off his land, and drove into the distance. For a moment, I stood still. Unable to move. It wasn't 'til the kid popped his head out of the gorse and hurried me on that I got to walking again.

I scaled the fence, pulled my hoodie over my head and buried my hands in my pockets and followed Black through the gorse maze. He stopped every now and again to check that I was still there. When at last we popped out the other side he said, 'All good?'

I nodded, my tongue swollen in my mouth.

'Don't worry,' the kid said. 'He's a fricken racist.'

The sun took his seat atop the sky. The maunga called it from the horizon, a snowcapped summit bordered by a family of ranges hardly tall enough to be seen above the rolling landscape. The fields of the other farmers. Mostly quiet types. Men never seen without a whip. A tractor or a motorbike. Always somewhere to be, something to do. Black used to wave at them. Dickheads never waved back.

Our own paddock sat at the bottom of a small basin, our house at its heart, a full kilometre from the road. We were caged in by fences, number 8 wire and chicken mesh and boxthorn, the southwest hillside alive with gorse. The fences guarded nothing, could not guard anything given their state. Each munted in its own way. They boxed a no-man's-land, no crops growing nor sheep nor cattle grazing. The whole area was a dump. Our family – what was left of it – a lonely island floating among the rubbish.

The dirt was littered with stone, the dry earth every shade of yellow and green. The soil was unfriendly, supporting only the hardiest plant life, weeds and a single tree. Back in the day, that tree was the guardian of this place. The only thing beautiful here. It used to bear berries that could keep for ages. Life has left it jack but a mound of bones shaking and rattling with the wind, warning any would-be visitors back the way they came.

When we first moved out here, people used to come by all the time. Always men. Always in shirts and dress shoes. They came with legal spiels and reams of paper, insisting that Black and I attend school. Or else.

Else what, the old man would say. And that was that. No cop cars. No bad guys with baseball bats. They waited longer and longer before each visit and then one day stopped coming. Who knows why? Maybe Dad finally scared them off. Scowled at them and they went running. Maybe Mum wrote one of her letters, telling them how she was teaching us the old way. Probably they were just over it. What's another couple of country bumpkins fallen through the cracks? Got enough to deal with in the city, they must've thought, let alone driving all the way out here only to get nowhere with this lot again.

Don't blame them, to be honest. I'd have done the same. Fuck dealing with the old man if you had any other option. Fella was a monster: another shade of nutter. Like the ballhead went at me, the old man used to go at Mum, threatening violence and, when he didn't get his way, making good on it. Of course, I got my fair share too – nothing like what she got, though. The difference was I was quick to cower. Mum would bow to no man.

Dad was built like a bull in his day. Small and mighty, short and muscled. His face was pale and his shoulders broad and when he marched the streets men would open up to him like the parting sea. None risked crossing him. His presence warned all passers-by to keep their distance. But, like the old lady said, everyone's made soft in the end. Same thing that raises them high slowly and suddenly cripples them.

He was an old man now, lying alive and lifeless in the centre of the lounge – lost in a sort of purgatory. Fella has lain like that for nearly a fortnight, his chest shifting, his bottom lip quivering and the rest of him fading away.

We don't know exactly what happened. Mum left us six months ago and the old man moved into the lounge, never sleeping in their bed again. After that, every day it was the same old: go get wasted in the city, walk back well after midnight, coma out on the couch, jacket and boots still on, jersey reeking of cheap piss and cigarettes. Bourbon and blues. Then finally, the weekend before last, he didn't wake up. Wasn't the first time he slept through the day, so Black and I weren't too fussed. When another two passed, we knew it was over. The old man on the way out.

We haven't called an ambulance yet. And we don't plan to. The old man was the only one keeping CYPS away, stopping the kid from being taken. If they found out Dad was dying, no doubt they'd come again.

I don't reckon the doctors could help anyway. We tried before, with Mum. A fat lot of good it did. Too much time in the books made them know-it-alls, too clever to listen to a bunch of snot-nosed Maari worried about their health.

———

One day, the old lady's stomach started to conspire against her, sharp pangs of pain knocking her to her knees. Months went by, and the pangs came and went, the old lady collapsing every time they struck. There was no predicting when they'd come, morning or night, doing the washing or reading or growling at me for picking on Black. Then it was like the old man hit her, Mum folding over in an instant, clutching at her middle, the book or the washing or the rest of her growling spilled all over the floor.

The first two or three she ignored. After the fourth, she called a doctor 'round to check on her. I took Black to the river bend to give the old lady some space and when we returned she was wild, storming through the house, performing her chores with violence, muttering to herself. The next time the doctor came around, I hung out on the porch, eavesdropping, pretending I was hanging the laundry.

'How've the cramps been, ma'am?'

'I've told you this . . . they ain't cramps. It feels like my stomach's trying to burst through my ribcage.'

'I understand—'

'I don't believe you do, actually. This ain't lady stuff. Something's happening. I can feel it. My body's warning me.'

'If the pain is getting worse, I can prescribe you some analgesics.'

'I'm not asking for painkillers. Hika mā. I'm trying to warn you that something is up. More than cramps. I've had them. Whakarongo mai: This – ain't – them.'

'Let me be frank, ma'am. I am listening and your symptoms are entirely consistent with menopause. Everything you've said to me, I've heard it before. You've been going through it for a fortnight; I've been dealing with it for years. Now I might come across like some overeducated white man but I'm actually quite the expert. I can offer you painkillers to keep you comfortable and this here handout, which will go over what you should expect going forward. Now if nothing's changed in six months' time, then we will look at exploring our other options. Until such a time, this will be your bible.'

There was a pause in conversation. The old lady must have flicked through the handout the doctor had given her.

'If you have any questions, you call that there number at the bottom of the page. Okey-dokey?'

'Āe.'

'Good as gold. Now take a couple of those,' he must've pointed at the pills, 'and get some rest. Trust me, history has shown the whole world your people are a hardy stock. You've been through a lot; you'll get through this too.'

Mum passed away a month or so later. Woke up dead.

———

When we arrived home, I checked Dad and the kid mucked around outside. Black never watched me look after the old man; he was still in denial.

Caring for Dad was like caring for a child. I relied most on my nose, checking he didn't need a wash or a change of jocks or a new pair of pants. There was no mess I couldn't handle with a rag, a towel and a soapy bucket. All he needed after that was a shave and water and painkillers: two pills dissolved into a quarter-cup, three times a day. Breakfast, lunch and dinner. Lucky, the old lady had heaps left over.

The ghosts of his past used to wake in his sleep. I could hear his grumbling through the walls, his tossing and turning. The pills seemed to keep his nightmares away. No clue how that worked. It's almost beautiful the way he sleeps through the days. His face pockmarked and his jaw square and his ears cauliflowered. His hands frozen as a half-fist and his knuckles scarred and his nose permanently broken. There was no anger on his face anymore, no pain. He'd found peace. Nothing so far has been as strange for me as missing his violence. I thought it was burned into my brain but its memory has faded and begun to feel far away.

His eyes sunk inside his skull and his stomach wrapped itself around his ribcage, the old man looking more a skeleton day by day. His breathing happened at uneven intervals, his lungs fighting to draw breath. That was the last of his warrior spirit. I'd got the sense when I watched him that he welcomed an early end like this. Fella had no idea how to look after me and the bro in Mum's absence.

He wanted to get out of the way. Burn the old bush and make room for new life.

I grabbed a razor and a pottle of conditioner from the bathroom and sat the old man halfway up on his couch, his only reaction a long pause between breaths. In every pause, I anticipated his death, stopping every time to listen with a paranoid intensity. No-one in this house knew what death looked like when she comes and goes away. The clean-up, we knew well enough. But the rest: jack-shit.

With a rag, I wet the old man's neck, patting him so as not to be too rough. Then I massaged the conditioner into his skin, the poor man's shaving cream. The razor was blunt and pulled at his hair, still, with short strokes and a fuckload of patience it did the job. Lastly, I tidied the hair growing over his lip with a pair of scissors, wiped him down and dried him off and spit on my thumb to clean the nick I'd cut over his Adam's apple.

Fella was a vain man. His head always shaved. His beard always groomed. The old lady used to cut his hair on the porch. An artist with a straight edge and a pair of scissors, trimming everything even and precise with only a look. It was the only thing the old man didn't do himself. The only act of intimacy I'd ever witnessed with my own two eyes.

The old lady loved to work. She would mop and brush and scrub and make the house pretty. It was run-down and falling apart, but because of her it was beautiful. She would sponge the timber floors and change the towel that kept the front door closed and straighten the books that decorated the shaky desk that concealed the hole the old man had made with a thrown plate almost a decade ago.

Mum was pregnant when he did it, two weeks into a bout of morning sickness, the music of nausea carrying through the house. Tissue-thin walls keep no secrets. The old man, pissed off either by the prospect of a second child or feening for a good night's rest, was acting more a nutter than usual. As often as she'd gun it to the bathroom, he would fall into a frenzy. He was never a stable man, but he'd never been this big a psycho. Curses polluted the house and threats of war reigned. Motherfucker was a poet in a fury. Like the prophets of old, he made a weapon of his words, wrapping speeches around the necks of all he meant to make suffer.

Would've been about this time when Nan first came to visit. The first and last time, I reckon. The kid and I were off on an adventure when it happened but I heard the old man and Mum arguing when we got back. Apparently, Nan came to take Mum away, move us into the city with her. The old man wouldn't have it. They traded a few words, a few insults, and when he'd had enough, he clenched his knuckles at his side, set his eyes upon her and let Nan know exactly what would happen if she ever came back. If Mum ever ran away again. (This story, I'd never heard.)

Earlier that day, not knowing what happened, I accidentally locked eyes with the old man. Fella had been crying. Embarrassed, he told me to fuck off back into the gorse and rested his hands on the kitchen bench, fixing himself there until the house filled again with the music of Mum's morning sickness.

He swung an arm. Threw a plate. Put it through the wall.

———

Mum was a tiny woman, pounamu always hanging from her ears and a whalebone koru around her neck, the taonga grainy like wood, wrapping around itself so it looked more a wave than a fern. She never wore shoes or make-up or lipstick. They were hōhā, she reckoned. Got in the way. Dressing up instead meant a cardigan thrown over her nicest t-shirt not in the wash and a pair of jeans. The rest of the time she would march around like she was ready for a hunt. Long-sleeves and track pants no matter the weather.

'Done all that pretty stuff in my day,' she told me once. 'Coats, dresses, scarfs, wedges. I tell you what, my boy, you wouldn't recognise me. No time for any of that out here. Too much mahi to do.'

We lived in the wop-wops. A mean walk, over an hour, from a city with two names. One Māori, one English. I couldn't pronounce the former for the life of me – that might've been true of everyone minus Mum, the only person I'd heard use it. My mouth made a mess of heaps of kupu. My blood was Māori but my tongue was as Irish as the old man. When I was young, the old lady tried to teach me the reo. I managed only a half-bucket of words before Dad threw a fit. Mum kept trying to teach me, of course, but I wouldn't let her. Not worth the risk.

'That language do you any good?' he said, standing over the old lady. 'What about your ancestors, it serve them well?' She bowed her head. 'Then why the fuck are you burdening the boy with that shit?'

When at the end of his tirade, he took off, went to calm himself down with a ciggy outside, Mum looked long and hard at me. 'Don't ever become your daddy, my boy.'

2

The kid shouted for me from outside.

'What's up, Black?'

'There's a goat.'

'A what?'

'He's eating the grass.'

Goats are freaky looking animals. Their eyes are sideways and their beards hang like ponytails from their chins. Even the way they chew is weird, their jaw rolling around in circles, grinding the grass to mush.

'You know where he came from?'

'Nope.'

'You sure?'

'I saw a rabbit run under the porch and I was looking for it and when I turned around it popped up out of nowhere.' The kid crossed his heart. 'Honest.'

I searched the bottom of the porch for any signs of a rabbit and saw none. If there ever was one, he was hiding well and good. Wouldn't be able to get him out with anything short of a long stick or a small dog.

'You think we can keep it?'

'Keep what?'

'The goat.'

How fast I'd forgotten. 'You wanna keep this fugly thing?'

'Don't talk about Dag like that.' He turned to face it. 'Kauri's just jealous he's not as cute as you.'

The kid was always getting into mischief, going where he didn't belong. This wasn't the first time I'd turned my back and he showed up with some kind of animal to adopt. There was the lamb he snatched from one of the neighbours and the dog he lured home with a pottle of peanut butter. He'd never shown up with anything this big or ugly, though.

'Just checking, Black, I'm gonna ask one more time. You know where it came from?'

'Well . . . I saw him walking over there,' he pointed to a winding track that ran from the house to the road. 'And I called him over. He sort've came but got distracted by the grass.'

'And that's when you called me?'

'Yup.'

'You're a crack-up, fella, you know that?'

The day was as late as the old man coming back from a quick trip to the TAB, the birds beginning to settle and the insects ceasing their song. I walked the length of the track looking for the goat's owner and, the track being empty, decided we'd keep Dag for the night; return him in the morning.

It took us three attempts to catch the goat. Black lured it with grass and I tried to wrestle it to the porch. The first time the goat shook me off and walked away. The next time he bucked and kicked, missing my bad shoulder by an inch and sending me into the dirt. I wiped my face with my shirt, spitting on my thumb to clean the scar Dad had left like a gift under my right eye. Third time lucky, the kid fed the goat grass while sneaking his other hand inside Dag's collar.

We tied him up to the porch with a length of rope from behind the house, the kid filling a bucket with water and another with grass and dandelions, leaving them next to Dag, and asking one more time if we couldn't keep him. 'Not ours to keep, bro,' I said.

We ate and the kid cleaned the dishes while I changed the old man's jocks and fed him the last of his medicine for the day. He didn't shit anymore; that stopped after the third day. Still peed a little bit here and there, nothing more than a few drops, which meant I didn't have to change his pants except when they reeked.

Dad managed his whole life to be an island, only to become this at the very end. A leaky waka. And here I was, his least favourite thing in the world, wrist-deep in his waste, working like hell with little more than my bare hands to delay the inevitable. His bastard boat decorating the sea floor. In my weaker moments, I wished he'd die already. If there was anything left of him, no doubt he'd want the same. Whatever was left of his life wasn't worth clinging to. Better to go quickly into the next one. Dive head-first. Let this bullshit go.

The kid said nunight to the old man and threw a blanket over him and I tucked Black into Mum's bed. He loved her bed. I s'pose he had every reason to. He didn't see the old lady lying dead in those floral sheets. They held nothing but fond memories for him. Rocking in her arms, falling asleep to her lullabies, awaking in her doting gaze. Some nights I thought I could hear her songs carry through the house, her voice playing in the wind.

'Hey Kauri?'

'Yeah, bro?'

'You think we could leave the door open a lil bit?'

''Course. You all good?'

'Been having bad dreams the last few nights.'

'You want me to stay 'til you fall asleep?'

'Only if you want to.'

I sat myself against the wall, watching the kid close his eyes and nestle into the mattress, tossing backwards and forwards until he got comfy.

'Hey Kauri?'

'Yeah?'

'Dad's gonna be all right, aye?'

I looked the old man up and down through the parted door, the blanket hugging his frame, his head and shoulders the only part of him I could see. His skin was discoloured, a spooky shade of white, the eyes beneath falling away from each other, rolling towards his temples. He breathed long, loud and uneven breaths, his lungs scrapping with death and losing. Whatever he was, it was not all right.

'Go to sleep now, Black.'

———

The kid was still in bed when the old man and I found Mum. Dad had crashed on the couch after a night out in town and I accidentally woke him having a wash from a bucket outside. He stumbled onto the porch, half-cut from last night's adventure and asked where the painkillers were. Reckoned he had a bitch of a headache.

'Dunno,' I said.

He scanned the horizon, probably guessing the time of day, and he realised something was off – Mum was still in bed. For the first time in her life, the old lady'd slept in. He turned and marched into her bedroom. I towelled off, chucked a pair of shorts on and followed him. Any other day, I wouldn't have been so brave, but something in the air made me check on her.

Her room smelled rank, the scent attacking me as I opened her door, watering my eyes. I wiped them on my shirt and then I saw her. I don't reckon I'll ever forget the way she looked lying in her bed. Black and stick-thin, the pain in her puku having long killed her appetite. If I felt anything at that moment, I don't remember. My feet glued themselves to the floor and refused to move. A full minute passed and I watched her, until the old man lifted Mum from her bed. Her nightie fell off one shoulder. Dad shoved me out of the doorway with his elbow, carrying his missus into the hills. To her final resting place. An unmarked grave.

When he came back, he didn't come back to the house. He walked that departing dirt track he'd carved into the earth with boot and spade. He stayed away that night. Then every night after, returning only in the early hours. I never learnt where he went in the city, only what he'd done while he was there.

I figured I'd follow him one day. Find out what was more important to him than his own kids. Where he went to numb the loneliness the old lady had left like a shiv in his side.

Dad fell sick before I had my chance. Still, I knew life would take me there. When the time was right. 'Til then, I had a dying man to care for and the kid to raise. They each left little time to daydream about that world away from this one. And yet, deep in the night when I couldn't sleep, it invaded my mind. Called to me like flax calls the tūī in the summertime.

———

I fell asleep on the old lady's floor and woke up to the kid missing. The birds were silent, every door except Mum's swinging in the gentle breeze of the morning. I called for Black but the house stayed quiet.

Room by room, I looked for him. The early orange sun pierced through our frayed curtains, the wallpaper peeled and torn, and the ceiling dipping from water damage. Some part of me reckoned something had changed. Maybe it was the silence. Or the missing kid. Either way, I knew, and tried to deny I knew it.

Between the colour of the veins that wrapped 'round his throat and the stillness of his chest, Dad looked a younger man. If it weren't for his limp hands, I might've thought he was getting better. He wasn't. And now, couldn't. Some time in the night, he left us. Gone to that place that dead men go.

My heart beat against my chest and my lungs struggled to draw breath and my legs shook, and yet, I felt jack. Not sadness, not relief. I felt I was watching myself, seeing my shaking legs and feeling divorced from it all. Dead. Even when the moments became minutes, the nothingness stayed with me, underneath it a swelling guilt. I'd wished for this and here it was.

The wind blew, whining as it found the gaps in the windowsills, the fading scent of ash still burning in the back of my throat – the neighbours must've burned boxthorn in the night-time. A chill was in the air. Fucken cold, the old man would've said to no-one in particular. I laughed to myself and my hair stood on its ends and I said goodbye. 'Laters, Dad.'

The kid was on the porch, petting and feeding the goat. He turned away from me and I knew he'd found the old man already. He must've snuck out of the old lady's room, seen Dad and run not so far away, distracting himself with his new bestie. I stood over him, and he ignored me, flinching only as I sat beside him. 'Dad's just sick,' he said. 'Needs our help. But when he's better, things will be good again. Everything will be.' He reached for my hand, and I pulled away. (Why did I pull away?) 'It's all good, Kau. Everything will be all good.'

He turned towards the house. Only the old man's feet were visible, his woollen socks propped up on his leg rest. The rickety door swung to and fro in the breeze, concealing and revealing his feet. Black fell silent, running his fingers along Dag's side, the goat's shadow moving over him as he rocked backwards and forwards.

'Everything'll be all good – aye?'

I messed the hair behind his head with my hand. What was I s'posed to say? Nah, bro. Old man's dead.

3

Black and I carried the old man into Mum's room. We cleaned him up and lay him on her bed and wrapped him in the oversized quilt the kid slept on as a baby. Dad's skin darkened and his eyes sunk deeper into his skull.

The sun limped across the heavens. It was rare in the wops that he didn't race across the sky, the days out here shorter than the nights. In the afternoon, he would shine through the blinds – they were no more than a thin sheet hung across a windowpane – and the room would warm and the old man would have to find something else to complain about. The best of someone survives their death. Mum's songs and Dad's sense of injustice.

The kid asked if this meant we were keeping the goat, using loss like a gangster uses a gun. I laughed.

'Whole house could burn down, bro, and we'd still have to return it. Fugly thing belongs to somebody else.'

'You don't know.'

'He has a collar.'

'What if his parents are gone like ours?'

'For real?'

'For real.'

'Well . . . then you could keep it, I s'pose. Would be yours to look after, though.'

'Can we go look for them then?'

'The owners?'

'Yeah.'

The kid said the goat came from that way, pointing to the fence that marked the edge of our paddock and the beginning of another never used. Every seventh or eighth post was munted, the top half suspended in the air by chicken-wire mesh and the rest of the battens barely holding on.

We untied Dag and the kid pocketed some grass to lure him with and we marched out, checking over our shoulders while we tracked through the fields in case we stumbled across the paddock of another nutter. I could guess well enough what fields were safe to walk based on their condition. If they were thistle and gorse free, you weren't free to cross. There were no guarantees, though. Even if the paddocks were pakaru, their owner might happen to drive by. Most would wave you away, tell you to bugger off. Others would shoot you as soon as they saw you.

Eventually, the field led to a road and we followed that road until the numbers on the letterboxes started to resemble the number on the goat's collar: 8568a.

The road was made of loose gravel and there were no cars to be seen. Every now and again we'd come across an abandoned shed or cottage. Black got the heebie-jeebies, but I was curious and went to explore while he stayed on the road with Dag.

The structures were painted neutral colours, the paint peeling worse on one side than the rest, the roofs rusted through, collapsing inwards. Occasionally, the doors were locked, meaning someone'd left something they wanted to protect. Whatever treasures these shacks hid, I didn't find them. All I could see was rotting wood and exposed nails and mould huddled in the corners. Stumbling through, I wondered if this was how Mum and Dad wound up in the wops. Probably they found our house abandoned and set up shop. How the water and electricity worked, I didn't know. Maybe you can claim abandoned houses or maybe they really did own our shithole, buying it outright between the money Mum made from welfare and the rare riches the old man would stumble upon. I didn't know the details, but Dad had 'steelen & deelen' tattooed on his back among a mess of other misspelled words and poorly penned pictures stretching from the bottoms of his feet to the front of his neck. Heartie. That stick and poke of a clenched fist on his calf. Fuck da wrld. Straight outta State Care.

Judging by the paranoid way he'd watch the dirt track if we ever heard police sirens, I figured those tatts were a kind of life story carved into his skin. If that were true, I s'posed the last one explained why he went so hard at CYPS. Fella wasn't so much protecting us but taking his revenge on those motherfuckers who made him what he was.

The kid and I walked a while longer, stopping every hundred metres or so for Dag to chew a pretty patch of grass, the goat refusing to be budged.

After a heap of stops and starts, Dag picked up the pace, abandoning the roadside completely and bowling through a gap in a boxthorn hedge. Black kept a tight grip of his homemade lead and was dragged along and I shook my head and tailed them both, hoping the fugly thing knew where the hell it was going.

It wasn't long before we came across a pair of corrugated-iron sheds, one small and triangular and the other fit for a family. A shirtless bloke rested against the bigger house, his hair grown over his face and his beard down to his chest. He held a thermos in one hand while the other was folded over his belly, his skin tanned and leathered. The kid waved to him and he didn't wave back. He was deep in a daydream, stirring only when Dag butted him with his head.

'Come on, girl, you know not to rark me up when I'm resting.'

'She's a girl?' Black asked.

''Course she's a bloody girl,' the bloke replied, climbing to his feet and brushing the dirt from his butt and legs. 'That's an udder, not four willies, you drongo.'

'What the heck's a drongo?'

'Those ears painted on or Dad didn't send yah to school?'

'My dad's gone.'

'Gone or gone gone?'

'Gone gone,' I said, my voice weak, the bloke seeing me for the first time.

'Well, bugger me. That's my bad. Wife always said I was too quick to kick off.'

'You got a wife?' the kid asked.

Fella laughed, taking no offence. 'Donkey's ago, I had one. Did her like my old man did Mum, though, and farked it all up.' His smiled disappeared from his face. 'I hated the bastard all my life and then what do I go and do?' He scratched at his beard. 'Anyway, she kicked me out and took half the farm. The half with the house on it.' He chuckled and I s'posed he felt like he deserved it. 'The b to this here a.' He flicked the goat's collar. 'Speaking of ol' Betsy, how'd you wind up with her anyway?'

Black recounted what happened. Dag turning up out of the blue and me trying to wrestle her and the kid baiting her with grass; him asking if we could keep her and me saying we had to return the fugly thing and the long walk over the fields and the road and the boxthorn to get here. The bloke asked why we called her Dag and the kid said because her fur was clumped with dry poo. They both laughed and I bowed my head, knowing the kid's fun would be short-lived. The old man's body waited for us at home.

As a thank-you for returning his goat, the bloke offered us some cheese. We told him to keep it. No way in hell we were taking food from a divorced dude living with a goat in a pair of rusted metal houses. He thanked us again and we said laters and made the long walk home, the day growing darker, streaks of orange, pink and yellow exploding from the horizon.

The whole walk home I thought about becoming the old man, growing up to be that same violent piece of shit. I already had his temper; a fire in me that exploded to the surface when things didn't go my way – how long would it take for the rest of him to find a place in me?

———

At the house, I fed the kid and put him in his own bed – our bed. It'd been a long day, he was knackered.

While he rested, I thought about what to do with Dad. I had to get rid of him before CYPS could catch me lacking. They even got a whiff he might be gone and I was screwed. They would up and take the kid to who knows where.

Getting rid of the old man wouldn't solve the problem, I knew. But it could buy me a visit. Could fake he was still around and steal some time to figure things out. And anyway, he couldn't lie on that bed forever. Death was soon gonna take everything his addictions had been good enough to leave him. He'd carried Mum's body into the hills and lay it down deep enough into the wops that it wouldn't be stumbled upon. Black and I didn't know where; we never asked. I couldn't carry him that far. We'd have to do something closer to home.

I paced on the porch, watching a vision of the old man come and go, a younger him marching into the distance and an older drunker him stumbling back home, getting caught up in his own feet and falling over himself.

The evening grew late and I visited him in Mum's bed. Dead as a doornail though he was, his cologne remained: piss and cigarettes from the city with two names. I got to thinking it might finally be time to tail the ghost of the old man there. Always did plan to. And anyway, how else was I gonna move on?

I raided Dad's drawers for his jacket and Mum's for her photographs. His were a mess. Gears thrown all over the place, nothing folded. A pair of jocks next to a single white sock next to a shirt I had never seen him wear. The old lady's were packed convent–style. Everything rolled up and colour-coded, the only exception a pair of plush lambs buried in the corner of her bottom drawer.

Neither the kid nor I appeared in any of her photos. They only caught the early years – Mum and Dad's hooking-up. She smiled and nestled her head into his neck, and though he never smiled himself he showed his love more subtly. Allowing her to be close to him. This went on year after year until her stomach swelled like the kererū's and the photos stopped.

Her collection was bookended by a mass of negatives. Two long rolls of film. No camera to be found.

Nothing obvious jumping out at me, I ran through the collection a second time and took a shot in the dark, nabbing a picture of Mum and Dad outside a pub. If there was anything to know about the old man, I figured I'd find it in a place like that. They looked happy, I thought, looking one last time at the photo before I pressed my ear against Black's bedroom door, checking the kid was still sound asleep.

With his every breath, my stomach twisted tighter around itself. Poor thing was about to be abandoned in the wops with only his dead father to keep him company. It was all for the best,

I assured myself, though there was no ignoring how outside the gate I was about to go.

The maunga and his ranges were invisible in the night-time. The rocks in the dirt caught the moon's glow and glittered. I went on, wrestling back my racing heart. The world was quiet again. The wind had ceased. The tree stood on edge.

At the track's end, I nodded goodbye to the munted letterbox, a rusted steel thing packed with bills, leaning on rotted wood. How long, I wondered, before they cut off the power? How many months had the bills stacked up high? The truth was I could probably pay them. The old man always had a load of cash and coins stowed beneath his bed. I just had no idea how to. And so, I crossed onto the gravel and asphalt, regretting my bare feet, and a pūkeko in the distance screamed into the darkness, its pitch haunting. Erupting out of the quiet and quickly fading away.

———

After over an hour of walking by the light of the moon, a storm of flies welcomed me into the city – a steady drone in the glow of the streetlights. The city's kaikaranga.

I looked over my shoulder and wondered if I was right to come here. The wops were dull but at least they were honest about it. The city was different. A part of me understood this difference. It takes all kinds. The rest of me was afraid of it.

Anxious, I went on. Somewhere in the stomach of this place, I reckoned there was a pub that held all I needed to know. The photo from the old lady's collection, worn by the waves of time, remembered its double doors and stained-glass windows. I didn't know where it was exactly, but I was ready to search. It was time to send the old man on his way.

The deeper I journeyed into the city, the more the steel and concrete buildings reached for the sky, funnelling the streetlight and pushing back the darkness. There were offices with glass windows stacked like crates of beer, poorly lit takeaway shops with menus as long as the walk to the wops, burnt-down businesses and boarded-up businesses and businesses guarded by sliding garage doors. Only the takeaways were still open.

The deeper I journeyed into the city, the worse the state its inhabitants were in. A starved man slept a sickly sleep on a bench. His feet were bare and his jersey holey and his lips blue. By the stillness of his sleep, I s'posed it wouldn't be long before the cold robbed the man of his life. I thought about waking him, but when I moved, my shoulder burned with the memory of the old man's violence, and I knew it wasn't my place to interfere.

I'd made that mistake only once. Two weeks after the old lady passed. He kept leaving, drinking and looking worse by the day. One night, I put a hand on his chest, asking him not to go. I was trying to keep him from killing himself. We lost her. Didn't wanna lose him too. I should've guessed what would happen next. The scar on my cheek, the crooked set of my shoulder, stopped me from ever getting in his way again.

4

A woman sat at the foot of the door to a junky apartment building, holding a pair of faux-fleece slippers in one hand and a half-smoked ciggy in the other. She was definitely a weirdo, but she looked harmless enough, and I wanted to ask her about the old lady's photo. When I approached, however, her eyes filled with panic, and she gunned it up the stairs and inside, forgetting her slippers in her hurry.

My parents used to argue about the city. The old lady calling this the land of cops and criminals. Some would rob you on sight, she reckoned, and the others just as quickly chuck you in chains. Dad would call her paranoid. In their never-ending war of words, a person could've found every reason to fear this city. Unable to separate the fire from the smoke, I brushed it all away as a mother's worry. Now, struck by the porch-lady's panicked haste, I began to think I'd got it wrong. My body seized up and my throat went dry. I considered turning and running. Fat load of good finding the pub would do if it got me killed.

But when I tried to leave, I couldn't. I couldn't bury the old man the way he'd buried Mum. I'd know that when it came down to it, I was the same unfeeling piece of shit he was. I left the lady's off-brand slippers at the foot of her door and continued into the night, prepping myself for both the cops and criminals.

A scruffy brown dog followed me for a short distance, his limbs thin and his belly bloated. He walked with a cagey gait, his eyes watchful. I paused and called for him; I got low to the ground and clicked my fingers and whispered words of encouragement. Come here, bro. Come on. You can do it. Just wanna pet you. Don't you wanna be petted? Come here, bro.

I made my voice softer and I made my voice warmer and I made my voice higher, imitating the kid. Everybody loves Black. The old man, the old lady, the goat. All the same, the scruffy brown dog didn't trust me. Black and I were cut from a different curtain. And so the dog's eyes stayed dark and wet, his fur clumpy and his tail dragging when he walked. There was nothing angry 'bout the dog, nothing scary. He was just cautious. A scruffy brown cautious stray in a cold quiet city. I got to my feet and took off, and he didn't follow, watching me all the way into the distance.

I crossed another stray dog and a cat, a flock of birds that didn't fly as I crossed their middle, broken windows, broken bottles, rusted cars without tyres resting on cement bricks, cardboard doors, cardboard homes, cardboard signs sellotaped to streetlights.

———

After a long while walking, I came across a block party, men and women drinking in the street. They wore vests and jackets, scanning each face that crossed their path. There was an air of humour about them, but only from a distance. When I approached, everything fell silent, the music they were blasting was turned down low.

I tried to pass them by, I didn't wanna scrap. A hand came down on my shoulder from behind, and I turned to see a stoner crooking his fingers at me, as if asking for something. He was dressed in an oversized pair of track pants, their bottoms tucking beneath the heels of his feet, the material torn, the concrete eating away at it. A knitted sweater hung over his shoulders, the cloth falling over him like a blanket.

I stood my ground and tried to hide the cowardice swelling inside me. With surprising speed, the stoner stole Mum's photo from my hand.

The man seemed blazed out of his mind, his eyes half-closed, the whites a deep shade of red. Still, he gave me bad vibes. Shaved head. Fingers and face tattooed. I knew I would be no match for him, so I waited while he looked over the picture, saying nothing, trying to get a sense of who was watching us. The patched-up stayed about their dealings, turning their backs to the stoner and me. I tucked my chin and tensed my jaw. Anticipating violence. If my old man had taught me anything, it was how to take a shot.

The stoner's eyes flicked between the photo and me. Then he returned it and pointed down a side street, probably pissed off he let this dirty kid and this ratshit photo interrupt his buzz. He didn't speak, just flicked his fingers and went back to the joint he'd left in a younger man's hands, the speaker going back to full blast.

The man's pointed finger led me exactly where I needed to go. Keeping my head down, I crossed two blocks and the old lady's picture sprang to life, the double doors and stained-glass windows bursting from the city block the same as they did in the photograph, only with more colour. The pub was alive with time-forgotten songs, bringing up in me the faded memories of Mum. She used to dance and spin from room to room, leaping and landing and singing songs just like these.

Like the warriors of old, I set myself to storm its gates.

As I pushed open the door, I was hit by a wall of smoke; it filled the room and blurred my vision. Then a stale chill slapped me across the cheek. And finally, bitterness; the smell of body odour and spilled beer washing away the old lady's sweet memory.

5

A broken man crept behind the bar, time having pulled his head into his chest, and six others spread about the room, none looking much better. The pub appeared to be a refuge, an escape into the past. I scanned the punters and s'posed they were slashing and burning, running out the clock on their lives. I could see the old man in all of them and wondered if they could see him in me.

I rested on the counter, watching the broken man move and trying to draw his attention. He ignored me; he was running a rite that wouldn't be interrupted, his arthritic fingers moving slowly across the counter, wiping and rewiping stains that looked as old as he was.

The scent of ciggies, piss and submission eventually overwhelmed me, punching me in the nose and making my eyes water. I squinted and blinked and could not clear my vision. I shook my head and bit my teeth and could not clear my head.

I turned to see a woman smiling at me, her face aflame with the fire of the drink. I saw her joy and her drink and I wondered if it would bring me the same comfort. When the broken man resumed the bar service, I tried a second time. ''Scuse me, matua,' I said, and he showed no response, and I repeated myself and he stayed the same, counting and recounting the till.

'Pae kare,' a gravelled voice called from across the room. 'You don't see his hearing aid or what, boy? Use all the manners you want, that old bugger couldn't hear you even if he wanted to.' A pisshead waved me over with a flick of his wrist.

He sat in a corner of his own, smothered in a veil of smoke. From his cigarette throne, he watched the room with a wasted look, smoke circling him as he scanned the booths and tables. The pub seemed to shrink as I heeded his call, each step bringing the walls closer and the ceiling nearer to the ground. The whole place seemed to fall in and focus on the out-of-it guy at the red-stained table.

'Nau mai,' the pisshead sang in a soft voice. 'Nau mai rā.' The man nodded upwards, his eyebrows raised, his mouth duck-lipped. 'Everybody's welcome in palliative care, te whare whakamomori.' He laughed.

I paused and tried to speak and didn't speak and watched the shadowy man wait for me to say something.

'Used all the manners when you spoke to the old bugger,' the pisshead said. 'Rangona koe e au. So what, I ain't worth the same courtesy? That it, boy? I'm too old? Too black?' He laughed again and broke into a fit of coughs. 'Aroha atu. I ain't laughing at you. Laughing at myself. Mum always said I was too quick to snap . . .

But what does she know? Ain't lived this life.' He breathed heavy through his nose, half a laugh and half a sigh. 'How'd you wind up here anyway? Haven't seen a face as young as yours in this place in ages. This whare's a magnet for the old and decrepit, but the young, kāo, they never come this way no more.'

He laughed and continued. 'Don't even drink, do you, boy? Far out. Really is something out-of-it going on. You looking for someone? Running from someone? Hiding?'

He continued to speculate, throwing out and throwing away wild histories. Ousted from a church or a gang or your brother pushed your father into the sky. E Rangi e. Going to prison or just got out or your brother summoned five great waves to drown you and your father's whale. E Rua e. Lost your job or your house or your partner or your brother hacked maunga into your prized fish. 'Bloody Maaris, aye,' he joked. 'Always beefing with their whānau over something.'

The pisshead cast stories like spells, and my guard grew weak, my distrust dissolving like the night into a dream. He was so committed to his performance he didn't even notice the cigarette burn out in his hand. I lay the old lady's photo on his table and he studied it, his brow furrowing and his eyes jumping between me and the film in his hand.

'Ko wai?' the pisshead asked.

I didn't reply. One: I didn't understand him. Two: 'Cause of men like the ballhead and Dad, it took me ages to relax enough around strangers to run my mouth.

'Don't speak the reo, boy? Never mind.' He combed a hand through his hair. 'This couple. They your olds?'

I nodded.

'Look at you, aye, Kauri,' he said, using a name he had no reason to know. 'White as my bare ass but Māori just the same.' He drew on his ciggy. 'So, your olds, boy, you looking for 'em?'

I shook my head and fixed my eyes on the old man.

'Him, huh?'

I choked on his question, holding back the water in my eyes. Needing no reply, the pisshead went on. 'One of the OGs. Always here. Night after night. Though, to be straight, not seen him in a little while now. If he has . . . disappeared . . . should leave it alone. Let someone else find him. This place's rep ain't for murder, if yah know what I mean. Only so much shit this city can shovel on a man 'fore even an OG packs it in. He taniwha ia.'

The more the pisshead spoke, the more the room lightened. The smoke clearing.

'Not looking,' I said, finally working up the courage to speak and unable to form a full sentence.

'Already know what happened, huh? Stoked I don't have to tell it then – yah know, how it tends to go in these parts. Can't have manuhiri crying at my table. Would ruin my rep.' He straightened on his chair and combed his fingers through his hair. 'Figure I know what you're here for then. All right, whakarongo mai. Won't tell it twice.'

The pisshead lit another ciggy, the last one in a packet of greens, and continued with his knowing-too-much talk, with his switching between the indigenous and the colonial tongue, with his marrying of worlds. Words. Languages. He described Dad in heaps of detail, his praise describing a man I didn't know and the opposite one I knew too well. He claimed to have admired the old man and I couldn't help but think that Dad was being misremembered. The dead are always more handsome, more brave, better liked than they were in life.

When the pisshead had finished, I asked him if he knew the old lady and he hesitated, and he said he knew her but hadn't seen her in a decade or so. No reason why. One day she was in the pub and the next she was teetotal, never to be seen here again. 'Was a beautiful woman,' he said. The 'was' threw me for a loop. It implied he knew something he shouldn't. Although, thinking about it, the old lady's passing must've been obvious to everyone in the pub. Dad visited this place every night after. If the old man never said why, the pisshead would've guessed. No too much that'll make a man an alcoholic overnight.

The pisshead paused to suck smoke from the new ciggy burning between his fingers and I asked him what he thought I should do.

'With what?'

'Him.'

'Your old man?'

'His . . . you know.'

He removed the cigarette from his lips and watched the smoke rise. 'Aroha atu,' he said. 'Fella was a modest man; wanted nothing flash and would want no ceremony. Fella was his own man; prayed to no god and followed no faith.' He paused a long pause, squinting his eyes and turning his ciggy over in his hand, watching the smoke dance skyward. 'Old man was a man at the end of the day. And as I see it, boy, a man should lie as he lived.' He snuffed his cigarette and ran his hands through his hair. 'Ana. Should lie as he lived.'

When his speech settled, a wave of emotion struck him. The pisshead's eyes grew wet, and though he didn't cry, he went quiet and turned his face away from me. I turned away too. I figured I could, at the very least, allow the pisshead the dignity of privacy, imaginary as it was.

———

The pub was old school, a world away from the urban ugliness outside its gates. The floor was lined with dull brown timber the same shade as the walls and the bar sat as a square ring a fraction from the centre of the room. A small island lay in its middle, dressed neatly with layers of tall bottles bordered with upturned glasses, none placed too low or too far from the broken man. Some strategy was involved, he or another character decorating this place to work within his limited range. The lights were dim and the room was dark and three TVs lined a wall, all of them broken. I couldn't spot the speakers, but music carried from every corner of the room. The Howard Morrison Quartet and Engelbert Humperdinck. Water-stained tables lined the floor, and on every other one an assorted set of stools and banister-back chairs collected dust. In the corner, an old-school fireplace stayed cold: a black steel beast with no face.

The pisshead smoked and drank and stayed silent, never again looking in my direction. He turned to the bar with increasing haste, calling for drink after drink with a wave of his smoky wrist. I watched him, frozen in my place, unable to move, until he buried his head in his hands and slept. Fella wasn't the first to fall under such a spell. Of the original six punters, only two remained upright.

Before I gapped it, curiosity got the best of me and I pulled his drink across the table and sniffed at it. The fucken thing reeked; I could feel the muscles in my face tensing and my eyes beginning to water. Half of me wanted to throw the stuff across the room, decorate the pub in glass. No wonder, even after all these years, the piss could still knock a pisshead out cold. Most of what was left of me just wanted to run, to get as far away from this poison as possible. And yet, despite it all, my eyes reeling and my legs ready to go, there was a part of me, a thing deep inside my bones, that craved the stuff. I had to taste it, to reckon with the power that buried even the old man.

I checked my shoulder to make sure nobody was watching, wrapped my hands around it and threw that shit back as fast as possible. It was only a quarter-cup and still my throat convulsed and the drink threw me for a loop. I had to whip my head backwards and forwards just to settle myself. Fucken thing tasted worse than it smelt and hit even harder. How bad did you have to hate yourself, I wondered, to drink this stuff on the daily?

I stood, preparing to gap it. As I stepped from the table, the pisshead clutched my jacket. His hand was stiff with the piss and it took all my strength to pry it open. His arm fell away and his jacket fell off his shoulder. And I saw a gun tucked into the waist of his pants.

I had visited the pub with one question and left with a hundred more. Of all the places, why'd the old man drink here? How could he soothe his grief among such ratshit company? Who were they and how did he know them and what happened after they fell asleep? Did they wake at their tables in the morning, or were they dragged outside and dumped on a bench like the blue-lipped man? And the pisshead, how'd he know my name and more than that, my face? Who was he to the old man, to Mum? And why the fuck did he carry a gun?

—

The city came alive with screams, the sound of laughter and a concert of sirens. The wasted filled the sidewalk and, 'round them, many policemen laid in wait. They watched the street with a passion, their cheeks red and their eyes pinging. Over two blocks I counted twelve of them, uniformed and under quiet instruction, ready as if at any moment chaos might erupt. They stressed me the fuck out, though none looked twice in my direction. To them, I must've looked harmless, messy-haired and unmuscled, more a mutt than a dog. A boy up past his bedtime.

The piss began to take hold of me, dizzying my head, and I watched the world like a film – like Whiro had turned the volume down. At long last I got it. These fellas didn't drink that stuff to drink that stuff. Life had shit on them like it'd shit on me and this was how they swung back at the bastard. The piss was a coat on a cold day, sugar in a sour drink, medicine for a miserable life.

Let that stuff punch you in the face, they must've said, and watch your worries melt away. Ain't no problem the piss can't solve – or let you forget for a little while anyway. I s'pose, 'round here, that's the best you can hope for.

Worried by my lack of worry, I turned from it all and ran, driving with my arms and pumping with my legs. A bus slammed on its horn as I gunned it into an intersection. A tanker gave me a wide berth on the narrow strait into the wops only for the driver to make sure I could see the big fat fuck-you middle finger he punched out the window. I paid fuck-all attention to these, or to the ache in my feet and the sweat on my lips and the cattle whose breath could be heard above my own huffing and puffing. I thought only of the piss and the old man and the kid, the whole time, refusing to look back. And at last I made it home.

6

The house was quiet and the night was dark and I dumped the mail on the kitchen table, arranging them in piles of importance. Bills on this side: gas and electricity. Junk mail on that one: the local paper and the occasional flyer of a business so desperate for a customer they advertised all the way into the wops. The piles eventually toppled under the force of their own weight, half of the mini-mountain of paper falling into one big blended mess and the other half decorating the floor.

What could be done about the bills, I still had no idea. The gas was gone already. Not that it mattered; the oven didn't work anyway. But no electricity would screw us. We'd be left with candles.

On the bright side, there was nothing from CYPS. Fucken bastards of an organisation, the old lady reckoned. (Dad's words were much choicer.) Only time, my whole life, I'd heard her curse. And, for all that poor woman went through, she had every excuse to swear up a storm. Abusive husband. Cold house. Ungrateful kids. And yet, despite a hell of a life, it was only CYPS that set the old lady off.

'What do they know, huh? These are my kids. My bloody kids. I gave birth to them, fed them, taught them right from wrong. And what, I don't send them to their schools to get their culture beaten out of them and now they wanna investigate me. And why? So they can take my babies away and ruin them like the rest of the rangatahi uplifted. What kind of word is that anyway? They don't uplift. They take. He momo kē o te muru me te raupatu. They take Māori kids away from Māori whānau and make their lives a game of hot potato. Here, then there, then whoever will have them for a week or a month. They're fucken bastards. That's what they are. Absolutely clueless. They don't know us. They pretend they know, but they don't. So kāore. I'm not sending my kids to their schools. Let them ruin somebody else's. Mine are my own. They're all I have. Nobody's taking them. Not while I'm around. Ko au tō mua. Ko rātou tō muri.'

———

I lay beside the kid, my back to his back and my feet to his feet. As close as we'd ever been. A dream had taken him far away.

My eyes closed and opened to the new day's sun shining so much light into the room the shadows could hardly breathe. Last night's clothes clung tight to my frame, and they were rank, smelling of piss and the pub. I turned to see no sign of Black; he must've woken first and gone on his way. By the smell of the city, he would've known I'd left him. I should've been up early, in time to wash the smell away. How could I be so careless?

The house was empty, except for the old man's body. As I paced the deserted porch, panic rising in me, I caught sight of a shadow atop a nearby hill and breathed a sigh of relief. In truth, the hill was more a mound than anything. The earth rising like the sun at the top of our basin, forming a kind of hump with no weeds or gorse. The old lady had called it Papa's chest. The ancestors – our tūpuna – reckoned the whole earth was a woman and that was the name they gave her. Papa.

The kid turned away as I approached the mound, glaring into the distance. He was pissed. But when I climbed up to sit beside him, he spoke quietly. 'You left me all alone,' he said. 'Mum's gone. Dad's gone. And when I woke up last night, you were gone too. I had a nightmare that you died. That you fell off a cliff. Then I woke up and looked for you, and I couldn't find you.'

My stomach wrapped around itself. 'My bad, bro.'

'Where even were you?'

I bowed my head. 'The city. Didn't go to drink or smoke or do whatever else the old man used to do; though. Nah. I went there for us. Went to figure out what to do with all the crap the old man has left us.' I had rehearsed this answer during all my walking through the house, this suspiciously sentimental story flowing from my lips like the lyrics of a pop song.

'What crap?'

'Everything, I s'pose. His body, his gears.'

'You should've told me.'

I nodded and I said I should've told him. I know I should've. I didn't mean to break his trust.

'It's not broken. I was just scared you were gone and you weren't coming back. That you ran away without me or something.' He rested his head on my shoulder and, resisting the urge to push him away, I nudged him with my elbow. 'Don't ever leave me, aye, Kauri.'

I told him I wouldn't, then made him promise he wouldn't go anywhere either. He promised and we bonked our heads together and I told him about the city. The tall buildings, the quiet, the smoking, the drinking. He listened intently, his eyes widest when it came to the pub and the pisshead. I decided to neglect a few of the darker details – the panicked lady, the blue-lipped man on the bench, my giving the piss a go – focusing my story on the punter's connection to the old man. Some things were better left unsaid.

The kid leapt to his feet. A ball of energy. He began to act out all that I'd told, stumbling across the mound, taking dramatic swigs of piss and drawing deep breaths of smoke into his lungs, pushing them out through the side of his mouth. He paused his acting only when the story most captured him – when the pisshead called the broken man an old bugger, when he comatosed at his table – returning again to his play when the story moved on.

We skipped our way down Papa's chest and along the dirt track. I'd always felt connected to the track. We shared a sort of kinship. Both being shaped by the old man's anger. When I was young and the kid was still a baby, the old man spent countless hours outside in the heat carving this godforsaken thing. With boot and spade and all his mortal rage, he hacked at the earth's crust and lay this dirt track a kilometre long, uphill the whole way.

The path had changed this last month. It used to be clean and smooth and straight, the same from start to finish. Smooth right the way through, from the feet of the porch to the gravel edge of the road. Dad was the real deal. Heartie. Since his long sleep, the dirt track had fallen apart, its border had become hazy, weeds clawing to claim their piece. Its soil was pockmarked with sticks and stones, and overgrown grass had made the track wind, and its surface was wrinkled by me and the bro's footsteps, bits of earth padded down and bits of earth kicked up.

The bone tree shook unchanged in the breeze. It showed no shame for its missing fruit nor the leaves lost to the wind. That thirsty thing seemed to welcome this new fate, even call for it, night after night bathing in the darkness and twisting into something almost unrecognisable.

'I reckon we should bury the old man,' I said.

The kid nodded.

'Should do it by the tree then. Mum loved that thing. Would be like they're together there.'

7

With my father's boots and spade and shovel, I dug deep into the earth and lay a hole as deep as the kid was tall.

We planned to bury him with the moon. She would be her biggest tonight and we were used to him leaving in the night-time. Two seeds would be his gravestone. And we hoped, eventually, a new tree. The old lady saved the seeds ages ago; she knew that mound of bones would not flower forever. Finally, to finish it off, the slash and burn, we'd set the bone tree alight and send the old man off in the smoke. He was not a good father, not a good husband, not a good man. But he'd have a good tangi. It was too late to wish for anything more.

When the evening grew late and a chill took the air, Black and I carried the old man from the house. No casket needed. When he was alive, he'd scoffed at this tradition and the men who followed it. I remember back in the day he'd heard of some rich Maari buried

in a box of rimu, carved with koru and everything. He laughed
and called it a waste of good wood. It's my only memory of him
laughing, grim as it was. To save him this hypocrisy, we carried
the old man in no more than the quilt and the clothes he died in.

I hooked my arms in the corners of his and pulled his back
to my chest. The kid scooped our father by his swollen ankles,
avoiding looking at him. I was grateful a month on the couch
had made the old man thin; if he was still the bull he'd been, we
would have needed more men. As it was, it took three attempts to
carry him to his resting place. My arms were weak from digging
and the kid couldn't keep his grip. By the end, we were exhausted,
knackered beyond caring, getting low down beside that dead thing
and pushing him into the earth, his body rolling into the hole,
his body turning as he fell, the old man at last lying twisted like
a speed racer around a streetlight.

The fall had closed his hands – had made them fists again.
The bone tree shook overhead, cheering the old man's grit, and I
couldn't help but chuckle, and Black couldn't help but scowl at me.

———

The edge of the old man's grave was crooked, its border like broken
glass. The soil was a mess of colour, veins of yellow braiding through
its flesh. Its crust was dense, the roots of the grass stretching inches
into the dirt. No shovel alone could pierce it. A spade was needed.
Its tongue a taiaha.

Through the soil, the children of Whiro crawled. Itsy-bitsy
beetles and worms. No wonder our ancestors used to hang their

dead from trees. Wrap them up in sheets of flax and leave them 'til they'd become only bone. Used to sound crazy to me. I reckon now I got it. Anything to save them from these creepy little bastards.

A better man would've said something at this point in his old man's memory. I couldn't stomach a single sentence. I'd said jack to him in his lifetime, so to say anything now would only be performance. In the place of a mihi, the kid scooped a handful of earth from the dug-up dirt, muttered something and let it fall. Keeping the same rhythm, he repeated himself. Silent. The earth fell first upon the woollen socks of the old man. Then from his feet, it piled upwards. As it approached the neck of his jersey, I clutched my brother's shoulder.

His eyes were wide with heartache, his breath was shallow, and my grip tightened as I felt his heart race. He looked the old man up and down and swallowed all the air he could. The kid lifted another handful of earth, stretched his hand and held it a long moment, his arm trembling, tears of soil falling from his palm. We each looked one last look, committing the old man to memory. The kid then turned his hand and let the soil rain.

The old man had at last been buried, the earth settling over his withered frame, his whole body wrapped in a loose blanket of soil.

'All good, bro?'

The kid did not smile. 'Yeah.'

'Not long to go.' I nudged him with my elbow.

The sun fell over the hills and the sky filled with colour, and the kid and I filled the remainder of the old man's grave and packed it down with our feet. Black collected two glasses of water, one from the house and the other from the river, and – having already buried the old lady's seeds – we poured the water over the soil. I thought I'd feel something. A release. A wash of emotion. And I didn't. I asked myself if I even loved the old man.

'Mum's waiting,' the kid said. 'She's been waiting ages. We'll be all good. Go see her.' He closed his eyes and his voice began to shake. 'Love you, Dad.'

His courage failed, and the kid crumbled, one knee then the other collapsing into the earth. He buried his head in his hands and cried. I wanted to hold him, to wrap my arms around him and take his tears away. Held back by what could only be described as an inherited aversion to intimacy – shot, Dad – I combed his hair off his face.

The kid's body convulsed, the muscles of his back tensing as he struggled to breathe through his tears. I patted him and he cried harder and I stood back, feeling further away from my emotions than ever. I knew they were there, pulling at secret strings inside me. I just couldn't recognise them.

When the kid's crying settled, I raided the old man's corduroy couch on the porch, running my hands along the stitching beneath its faded cushion. We'd dragged the couch from the lounge before the day grew dark.

The old man would hide his lighter in the torn stitching on the corner of this couch, feigning a stretch of his arms as he resumed his place on his cord throne, tucking that prized thing where it wouldn't be stumbled upon.

The rectangular silver shell was older than the old man, its inscription half-concealed by rust. All that remained readable was the bottom half of a sketch of a fist enclosed within two rings. Defence force stuff or gang shit. The latter fit him best but who could know for sure? His life was a mystery and both stereotypes applied.

I spun the lighter in the dying brightness of the day, struck by the way its shine raced along the border of the house. This was the first time I'd held its sacred steel. Our father used to caress it like a lover, circling its surface with the fleshy middle of his thumb.

With a flick and a pull, I found its flame. It seemed so long watching the old man had given me his talent. I got down beside the kid and carried him to his feet. 'Almost dark now, aye. Better get on with it.'

Black threw his head to the heavens, swallowed the breeze and wiped his face with his shirt. 'Okay,' he said.

8

The old man's grave hung like a mist over the whole of the wops. The world was still and soundless. Even the owl that watches over this place had ceased to call its name. Ru-ru. And though it wasn't cold, an eerie chill possessed us, our breath visible in the night's light.

My hands shook, my vision blurred and I watched a silhouette of the old man smoke behind the bone tree. One last ciggy before the journey to the maunga – to that place that dead men go. Haere haere haere atu rā. I readied the tree for burning. It was dry and rife with deadwood, but we had to be sure. Using a hatchet and a bread knife, Black and I shredded the old man's couch into long thin strips easy for burning. Then with boot and blade, we broke down its frame and rebuilt it as a tent at the base of the bone tree, packing it full of its own hay, cotton, kindling and shredded cloth.

It looked a mess in the glow of the moon. Warped, contorted, twisted. It matched the old man almost perfectly.

The kid touched it with an open hand, pressing his palm flat against the barren tree's bark, spreading his fingers wide. He bowed his head and closed his eyes and breathed long and deep, putting his eyes back on his hand only after the breath had long come to an end. It was as good a goodbye as I'd ever witnessed.

'Good to go?'

The kid ignored my question. 'Reckon the old lady's watching?'

'If she could be,' I said.

The hills and the house were silver and blue and the bone tree every shade of black, no inch of its frame lighter than the night behind it. It must've known its fate, I thought, watching the darkness fall over it.

I left the kid and kneeled beneath the tree and with a flick and a pull set the cotton alight. The fire shot up, leaving me only enough time to skip one step backward. The couch bonfire leapt and retreated, its black and yellow and rosy flames lashing at the sky. Me and the bro watched with our mouths wide open as its heat ate away at the darkness, swallowed up the mist.

A gentle wave of colour rolled across the wops, illuminating the paddocks like the last hurrah of Mahuika, the whole of the earth alight with her passion. There were no farmers out tonight, no-one at work on the land. Surely they had felt the change in the air and placed their own kind of rāhui. If this were true, there'd be no greater honour. Time itself might as well have stopped for the old man.

The grass at the feet of the fire retreated, a burnt border reaching out from the base of the tree. Black stayed frozen and I inched away from the fire, wary that the old man might take one final swing at me, the couch spitting fire in my direction or the whole thing coming down on top of me. If visions of the dead could visit us and our ancestors see us in our dreams, who knew what Dad might do?

You want something to cry about, boy? the shadows said, imitating him. Hell, I'll give you something to cry about.

It almost made me laugh. What a fucken tribute. You better watch out, Whiro. Ain't no trait the old man didn't have you equalled in. Fella was just as mean, as stubborn, as cruel. Man was so small he couldn't even let his lover love him as much as he loved himself. Couldn't let his kids hate him as much as he, in his lowest moments, must've hated himself.

The bone tree released the old man's smoke like pollen, its petals opening, his stream of smoke catching the still breeze and floating skyward. A thousand embers escorted him, spinning and dancing upward and outward. In flight they glowed a dreamy glow, shading the silver earth in shadows red and orange. The bones of the tree, made black inside the blaze, crumbled and fell away. The might of the fire grew as that dying thing collapsed.

It was a wild final show. A display of colour unlike the old man had ever shown in his lifetime.

9

The kid fixed his eyes on the base of the tree. It was lit up red by the blaze. We stayed a half-hour, watching it burn. When the night grew late, I led Black to bed, his feet heavy, awkward and slow.

I fed the ebbing flames with what little the old man owned. The kid and I had decided it was for the best. Was mostly clothes, after all. We kept his boots and his tools and his leg rest and his coat (for my sake), and the old lady's collection of envelopes, which I koha'd to the kid and he stored somewhere discreet. (The ones with photos aside, they were empty). When the fire had consumed the old man's memories, I lay in bed too. Black's body was soft with sleep, his eyelids flickering with a dream. I shut my own and hoped for the same and a thousand thoughts visited me. I couldn't hold them nor keep them away; in waves, they came upon me, and in waves, they passed me by.

What was left of the fire crackled outside. Nothing but embers, ash, blackened bark and seared fabric. The rest of it carried as smoke in the gentle wind of night.

In time, sleep took me and then a dream. My body was carried through the ceiling and dumped in a paddock, dry grass, a thousand shades of yellow and brown, rolling across the hills, secret tracks sweeping through them. Whoever roamed here had fucked right off and whatever it was they left behind was nothing like it used to be. I walked a while though nothing called to me; I rambled through this lost land, casting my eyes over all that time had not yet swallowed. The paddock: the lives carved into the earth.

It wasn't long before the whole thing had lost my interest, but I didn't stop walking. Just paid less and less attention to this pakaru place, hoping more and more to wake up.

'This it?' I asked the sky father, Rangi, my voice straining. 'After everything I've been through, this is all you got to fucken show me?'

I'd waited years for a dream's wisdom, for the voices of my ancestors. And this was it? This assortment of fuck-all? Did it not know I had just buried my father? Did it not care to help me raise the kid and become a man and find my way in the world?

Rangi did not reply. The dream faded, feeling further and further away, like the slipping of a hand. When I woke, the old man still burned and the kid still slept, and I wondered what I'd do when morning arrived. I lay in bed 'til the new day's sun rose, watching the kid, hoping the night had brought him more peace than it had brought me.

———

I woke again with a splash of water from the rusted bucket we kept in the kitchen and set myself to cleaning the house. It'd been a long while since it'd been washed. Beginning in the old lady's room, I stripped her bed and threw her linen over my shoulder and, in the still of the morning, made my way to the stream. It was a decent walk away, a kilometre beyond our basin, down a dirt road, a gap between two dairy farms.

The road was teeming with life, the chatter of magpies harmonising with a tūī nestled among the poor man's toetoe – pampas grass.

Rangi held the sun and moon in the same sky, the latter white and without her jewellery, and the hills aflame with light, a soft orange glow decorating their peaks.

The river bend ran down from the maunga; I had no clue where this stream flowed from. It moved slow, rising and diving no more than two feet from its bed. Despite the drought, the stream endured, reflecting the sky, its reflection twisting as the tide moved, making four of the sun and two of the moon. I left the old lady's linen atop the neighbouring bank and piece by piece, from lightest to longest, soaked them in the river and wrung them dry, repeating myself twice and thrice and four times over. Inspired by the stream, I continued 'til my arms grew tired and my lungs grew weak and my beating chest forced me to lay down.

A pūkeko paraded the hill opposite, swaggering upstream, its chest a proud blue, its head blood red. The old lady reckoned there used to be heaps of manu here. Don't see too much 'round anymore. Nowadays, this land's reserved for farm animals and lifestyle blocks for the wealthy. The locals had all been moved on. With guns and volunteer armies wherever necessary. But so it goes 'round here. Men first and the land afterwards.

No point getting cut up about it, I s'pose. Just was what it was. Like the old man, those who run this shit have always been might makes right. Passive only until they didn't get exactly what they wanted. After that, as Mum tells it, it was shoot and kill and confiscate. Enemies, allies, innocents. Everybody got fucked in the end.

Back at the house, I laid the old lady's linen on the porch railing and chilled there until the sun reached its peak and bad weather crept over the horizon and the kid woke and joined me outside. Rubbing the sleep from his eyes, he forced talk of the coming clouds, trying and failing to feign a sense of ordinariness. The air smelled of the old man's tangi.

I punched the kid's shoulder, killing the conversation, and led him to the kitchen. The open fridge stood tall, acting more as decoration than anything useful. What was left of the high cupboards nursed a stale half-loaf of rēwena bread, four cans and a glass jar of peanut butter that had been scraped down to nothing with a knife and thoroughly cleaned with what could've only been a child's fingers. We ate, leaving only enough for tomorrow, and decided to venture into the city the following day. I knew only one store. One I'd visited once or twice as a young'un. Before we moved to the wops, ten years back. Before the kid was born.

It was run by a hard-case lady. She'd be old now. I didn't know if she still mahi'd there.

The sun slowed and we chilled outside, watching it limp across the sky. I half-tried to draw the kid into conversation. He took off and went about making neat the old man's grave. As he walked, his feet sunk into the earth, his t-shirt hanging over him like the black feathered cloak of mourning.

IO

I flipped the linen on the porch. Then I fixed the bed in my bedroom, making and remaking it 'til each crease had been flattened, and then I sourced a raggedy top from the bottom of my drawers, soaked it in one of our rusted buckets and scrubbed every steel tool in and outside the house. At last, I dusted and swept and mopped the floor, and straightened the books that decorated the shaky desk that hid the hole the old man had made.

I collected all three buckets from around the house and carried them to the stream. My bad arm was strong as long as I didn't swing it too fast. One by one, I rinsed and washed and filled the buckets. When I returned, I was welcomed by a shepherd's sky.

Beneath it, the kid sat at the foot of the old man's grave; he hugged his legs to his chest and rested his head atop them. To protect him against the coming cold, I stole a blanket from the porch railing and draped it across his shoulders. Committed to his grief, he ignored me. Some things are best suffered alone, I assured myself.

I served a small portion of food for dinner, no more than a quarter-can to share, and ate my portion alone at the kitchen table. The kid joined me soon after, sitting at the table's head, as far from me as he could sit. He ate slow and didn't care that I was watching him, keeping his sunken eyes glued between his fingers and his plate. He wasn't so bright-eyed this evening. Poor thing looked on the verge of sickness.

Slowly, spoonful by spoonful, he carried his dinner to his mouth. All the while, I bit my tongue, waiting for the proper time to talk, not wanting to kill his appetite.

When he finished, I stood up and stacked the cutlery. The kid rose too, his chest puffed and his fists closed. 'You said jack-all,' he said. 'He looked after us our whole lives and you said jack.'

'He—' I tried to answer, but the kid continued.

'He looked after us. He was good. You should've said something.'

I tried a second time to answer him and a second time he interrupted me. I slammed my fists on the table, the plates nearly falling to the ground. The kid flinched and stood out of range, his eyes alive with fear. How fast I'd filled the old man's place, succumbing to anger when I didn't get my way.

'My bad,' I said, massaging the ridge of my hand, the flesh throbbing. 'I didn't mean to . . . I just . . . my bad.'

The light in the room darkened as a family of clouds trailed across the sky. The kid slunk around the table and patted me on the back. 'It's all good, Kau. I was being mean.'

'Being honest.'

'I just wished we'd said something for Dad, you know?'

I asked him if he had anything to say now. He shook his head. And I asked him if there was anything he wished he'd said at the old man's tangi. His face took on a serious expression, though he didn't say anything more.

'Go on then. Never too late, I reckon.'

I didn't believe the old man could hear him. He was gone, away in the smoke, still climbing the maunga. And yet, this wasn't about the old man, just as it wasn't about me. The kid's words would be for himself. A kind of healing.

'Maybe that he matters. That I remember. That – I miss him.'

'Say it then,' I said.

'You think he'd wanna hear it?'

I paused and thought on my reply, Black's still-red eyes fixed upon me.

Overcome by impatience or sensing an answer he didn't wanna hear, the kid continued. 'Dad,' he began, and went on to say what he needed to say.

It was a beautiful moment – and yet I found my mind drifting, thinking about my outburst, my heart heavy in my chest, thinking about the city, somewhere I could escape this fucken feeling of tightness around my throat. The streetlights, the steel buildings, the pub – what would they care if I blew up or broke down?

I I

The rest of the day passed quickly, the sun moving swift across the sky. It reminded me of a story the old lady used to tell the kid, of an ancient sun that dashed across the sky and an ancient man. Imagining this story with my eyes closed, I always saw Dad – who, frustrated by the day's shortness, caught that blazing thing and beat it down, giving the sun a limp. This is why that poor thing travels so slowly, Mum used to say. He's cripple and couldn't run across the sky even if he wanted to.

I used to wonder if the sun would ever recover, get healthy and dash again, run across the sky like it did when it was little. It was a silent wondering; I never asked the old lady. Almost all my wonderings were unspoken, the old man unpredictable and Mum burdened enough.

When that poor thing set, the kid scooted off to bed. He was gonna sleep in Mum's bed. There was no goodnight – we were together in the lounge and then we weren't. I might've gone to bed too, if I thought I would sleep. Restless instead, I wandered the house hoping to find some work, imagining how the old man would've heard the kid's farewell. He always showed a strange love for Black, never striking or shouting at him. That is except the one time the kid clutched him. From us boys, he never tolerated any act of intimacy. S'pose he thought it weak.

The old man's love was never anything obvious, no word of encouragement or pat on the back. I remember watching him watch the kid one time. Black had posted himself by the sink, scaling a chair to reach the basin – Mum had asked him to do the dishes for her. He turned the tap and ran the water (back when our taps had pressure) and scrubbed the dishes with soap and steel wool, making a mess of it, spilling water all over the place. On himself. On the floor. All the while the old man stood like a shadow watching him, out of sight, his forehead creased. Fella was gripped. Unmoving until Black began upon his last cup then disappearing before he could be caught.

The kid never pissed him off like I pissed him off and so maybe he didn't so much as love the kid as hated me. He would have every reason to hate me, the biggest being my interfering in his rows with the old lady, leaping to my feet whenever a fist was raised in anger or a dish thrown across the room. I never said anything, never cried out or raised a fist myself. Just leapt to my feet or charged into the room and stared him down, my eyes wet and my fists clenched and my knees weak. A feeling that felt more like me than the very bones beneath my skin. Then one day, for a reason I don't recall, maybe feeling that my interfering only made things worse, I stopped. From then on, the old man stopped raising his fists at Mum and stopped needing a reason to rain hell in my direction, the old lady quick to kill his violence by throwing herself over me like a korowai.

Who knows why that sack of shit switched up like he did? Maybe he was disappointed in me. Maybe deep down he hoped I could stop him from blowing up, rein him in like Māui reined in the sun – wreck his shoulder like he wrecked mine. Tame the taniwha.

I suspect even a broken arm would not have eased the old man's raging heart. Rid his face of that always-there scowl. Maybe this late in his life, violence had become a feature of his character. A kind of addiction. Its frustration burning in his hands like withdrawal, its fire forcing his fists to clench and to raise and to rain down. In the end, he did slow down, I s'pose. I wonder, though, if he really was getting on top of his addiction to anger or had simply grown old and tired.

By the time the kid was old enough to keep a memory, the old man had completed this change. I reckon he had no mind for the old man's violence. He certainly saw the old man raise his fists at me, whatever fist was less a wreck that day, but that was always explained afterwards. I made sure of it. Taking full responsibility whenever the kid asked, Why? I wanted him to have a father he could love, aspire to, a man he would think a man and be happy to become himself. It was different then; I didn't know I'd take his place. I figured that short and wide and wrathful thing would live forever, his savagery making him deathless. How can rage die? Where would it go? Because of this, I got the kid's distance. He mourned Dad as our ancestors mourned a chief.

———

The sky was swallowed by a growing darkness, Rangi adorning the clothes of mourning. There was no other who would know the old man as Rangi would've known him. That father most famous for crushing his kids.

Black was fast asleep and so I wrapped the old lady's duvet 'round his little frame and tried to sleep myself, all night lying in my own bed and all night turning and all night waiting for the sun to rise again.

The ruru was back, her song carrying over the sounds of the night. Floorboards squeaked and the walls creaked and the children of Whiro crawled over glass, which rung in the night like an old woman laughing. No wonder the farmers thought this place was haunted. And that ain't even mentioning every reason our tūpuna had to stick around. To put off climbing the maunga and making their way home again. To the place our people came from.

When morning came, I was neither rested nor ready to begin the day. My back ached, my head throbbed, a dull pain rang inside my shoulder. If not for the growing light outside, I would've sworn I did not sleep at all.

I woke with a splash of water from the rusted bucket and watered the two seeds at the head of the old man's grave. The kid skulked around the chicken-wire fenceline, bounding towards me when he saw me come outside, stopping only a step away. I could've hugged him. Could've kissed his forehead. It's what he wanted. What Mum would've done. Instead, I punched his shoulder and went inside to prepare breakfast, more food from the cans in the kitchen cupboards. Aluminium tubs of baked beans and spaghetti, most of them without a label, identifiable only by the swishing they made when they were shaken. A dented can was half price. The unlabelled ones were practically free.

12

The kid, still in his PJs, stripped and dressed himself in a pair
of corduroy shorts, fumbling as he tried to feed his little feet
through the legs, falling on his side and rolling onto his back and
pulling those corduroys over himself with all the grace of a beached
whale. I made the call to leave for the city early; I thought a change
of scenery might do us well; I needed a break from the constant
reminders of death; I wanted to see the taniwha in the daylight.
The kid threw a grey knitted vest over an off-white collared shirt
two sizes too big and threw made-up karate moves in the air.
Spinning strikes, jumping kicks, what could only be described
as a patu hand. I helped him with his buttons – when he stayed
still long enough for me to do it – and fixed his collar and rolled
his cuffs. He looked halfway presentable, that pint-sized warrior.
Nothing could truly rid him of the mark of poverty. He would
live with that forever.

'You reckon I look strong, Kauri?'

'Like a businessman.'

'Oh what? I wanna look like a fighter.'

'Why?'

'So no-one'll fuck with me.'

I looked the kid up and down, wondering where this energy came from. 'Bro, watch your language, aye.'

'You swear.'

'And you wanna turn out like me?'

''Course. You're strong as. Like Dad.'

I rubbed my eyes with my thumb and forefinger, trying to drum up a halfway decent response. 'Just don't swear. 'Kay, bro? It's a bad habit.'

'Like smoking?'

'Yeah, like smoking.'

A tīrairaka followed us down the dirt track. It was brown and tan and white and tiny. Its little wings thrashed as it floated, the sweeping bird flying in a pattern of waves, up and down and left and right and every which way in between. Imitating it, the kid hopped and skipped, trying to keep on its shadow. I watched them, trying to figure where the bird came from and where it was going. The grey above made me fear what the weather had planned for this wee critter.

We left the path and the bird and began upon the gravel road to the city, the kid's face filling with wonder, his mouth agape, his eyes darting. He did all he could to take it in. He'd seen this place before but only enough to increase its effect on him. Its magic. And to him, there would be no better way to describe it.

In all honesty, I was jealous. His lightness made me feel heavy. Life had got its hooks in me. And like the great fish was pulled up, I was being pulled down. My fists were closing. My fingers becoming wooden. The pisshead flashed in my mind and I wondered if he knew what had made the old man this way and what I could do to save myself from the same path.

Black ran on ahead, waving his hands and calling me forward. 'Let's go. We're so close. We're almost there. Come on, Kau. Run. Let's race. I'm older now. I'm fast. I bet I could beat you.'

I dashed towards him and the kid broke into a sprint, his thin arms flailing and a joy filling my spirit, a smile edging in the corners of my lips. Then the pain in my shoulder shot upward and forced me to a standstill. I tried again to run and could not. The pain was too great. The kid continued into the distance, never looking back.

This is why that poor thing up there travels so slowly, the pain in my shoulder said. He's cripple and couldn't run across the sky even if he wanted to.

The gravel road was neighboured by a spotting of trees, yellow or orange or leafless, their limbs sweeping up and outward. And a pair of boxthorn hedges, each guarding fields of flattened dirt. There used to be maize there. It had been cut down. Turned to animal feed. Kept the animals plump over winter. The soil was unwell, dry and cracked, dependent on fertiliser to do its thing. Pig shit and the like. The air still tainted from the last bout of manuring.

I nursed my shoulder in my opposite arm. Only a whisper of time passed before the kid returned, stopping to look me up and down.

'You all good?'

'Yeah.'

'Was it your shoulder?'

'Yeah.'

'That's okay, Kau. I'll walk with you, aye.'

The concrete city burst from the sidewalk, and I slunk forward, taking the lead, guiding us down many deserted side streets. It seemed the city was still asleep, more dull than damned. This energy did not sit well with me; the fact a place so dangerous could appear so meek made me uneasy.

Soon enough, we saw an elderly couple strolling hand in hand. They were dressed in straight-legged pants and bulky jackets, one maroon and the other black, their shoes round and comfortable, the woman wrapped in a fleecy scarf, dwarfing her frame. The kid watched them with wide eyes, the elderly lovers smiling as they approached. 'Kia ora, e hoa mā,' the couple spoke in turn. The kid flashed them a meek grin, and I nodded my head. 'Tēnā kōrua.' I watched them in my periphery as they passed us by, their faces shocked a boy as pale as me could speak even a little reo.

These were the times I remembered I didn't look Māori, the elderly couple the shade of the earth and me more like the moon. I asked Mum about it yonks ago: being white and Māori. She laughed and said, 'Heaps of Māori things are white. Your koko's hair, the tūī's chest, the maunga, heck, even my taonga.' She wrapped her thumb and forefinger around her whalebone necklace. 'Anyone say this ain't Māori, I'd knee them right in their pounamu. And if anyone says you ain't Māori, my boy, I want you to do the same.'

'What does that mean?' the kid asked.

'Does what mean?'

'What you said to those old people.'

'Just said hi.'

'Tē-nā kō-rua.'

The sidewalk glittered, dinky specks of stone shining like pāua in the concrete. False promises, I reckoned. A lopsided banner posted above two giant framed windows, remarkably spotless, read Corner Dairy. Whatever was written before it had been painted down to jack. The old lady said there was a name there once. I asked her what it read. She never told me. Māori often outgrew their names was the most I got. More was revealed by the way she said it, the emotion in her voice. I can only remember my reaction. The way it struck me. The memory of a memory.

A small woman strolled inside the pretty little store with a steel grocery cart, stacking and restacking shelves, pulling every old item forward and placing every new one in the back, wasting no movement, aligning them and facing their labels forward. She squared every row with every column and left everything in her absence perfect. The small woman wore a long black dress, bulging around her belly, and a flour-stained apron, her skin clinging tight to her arms and leathering above her collar, the crease where a silver chain disappeared beneath her dress. No movement was rushed; she didn't notice us outside the store, all of her focused on her mahi.

A silver bell on a silver chain rang to announce our entrance. The small woman ignored it. The kid stood off behind my shoulder and watched her work. With every movement, the muscles in her arms swelled against her skin, tensing and twisting. She had to have been sixty or seventy.

The sound of the lightbulbs overhead buzzed through the store, long fluorescent tubes shining a warm yellow light on a shitload of stuff sitting on steel shelves or closed behind glass sliding windows or stacked in plastic crates. The floor was white lino, a single rug placed at the entrance and the till. There was no ice cream, no lollies. In their place was a mass of seed packets, hand-labelled and divided into three sections.

Huarākau. Huawhenua. Rongoā.

The kid and I didn't rush to fill our arms; we roamed the aisles breathing the whole store in, every shelf and row revealing a variety of flash new stuff. My eyes were drawn to all the colour, and my brother tugged at my arm, drawing my attention to anything I missed. Then, suddenly and to my surprise, he darted away, skipping over and across three aisles. Approaching the small woman as if she were his nan.

'Tēnā kōrua,' his soft voice carried across the store. I couldn't help but laugh.

The kid called for her attention with a tap on her hip and she welcomed him with a rustling of his hair. He replied with great passion, puffing his chest and flexing his muscles. 'The top of the head is sacred,' he said. One of Mum's wisdoms. The small woman showed no surprise at his comeback; she bowed her head in apology and allowed him her full attention. I tried to look busy, keeping them in my periphery, watching the kid talk and wave and laugh and the small woman return to work.

Hidden behind the cold metal shelves and a row of spaghetti, beans and corn, I turned a can and turned it back, surprised at the joy in such a simple thing. Having control. This feeling spread then quickly faded, turning to grief as I remembered Mum and her organising the house. I turned the can from its perfect place and retreated down another aisle.

Eventually, the small woman touched the kid on the shoulder, said her first words to him, and disappeared behind the till. I waved him over and he smiled and ignored me, pacing in the opposite direction. He stepped and skipped and leapt, criss-crossed and strode, tripped and recovered and went on as if nothing happened. I watched him from across the store, trying to make sense of it all. What was he doing? Where was he going? What had she said to get him to play like that?

He collected two loaves of bread from behind the glass, wrapped in a clear plastic film, and carried them like a crate of beer to the till where the small woman met him with a brown paper bag, which she folded and secured with a strip of sellotape.

'Two more loaves, little one,' she said with a wink, the kid rushing off to fill her order.

I went and offered everything I'd taken from beneath the old man's mattress, a scrunched mass of multicoloured notes.

'Waihotia,' the small woman said. 'Keep it.' She ran her fingers over the rope beneath her dress. 'You two need it more than me.'

I swallowed the choke in my throat. What had my brother told her?

'Kia rongo, e tama,' the small woman continued, noting my embarrassment. 'This is a koha. You know what that is?'

I nodded.

'Then you know it would be an insult not to accept, aye?'

I nodded again.

'Rawe.' She wiped her hands on her apron, and she wiped her hands against each other, and she rested on the counter. 'Now tell me, and be honest because I'm old, so I know a lie when I see one: You need a ride home?'

'I've got money.'

'I know you've got money, e tama. This isn't about cash and coins. It's a pick-me-up. Something small for two tānes having a rough go at it. Now, anō, you need a ride home? The neighbour owes me more than a few favours.'

'Tēnā kōrua,' the kid interrupted, returning with two loaves of takakau.

'Ngā mihi,' she said, greeting him with a wink. 'Now, back to business,' the small woman turned back to me, brushing her hands against each other. I shook my head, at last answering her question, and she smiled and went on, waving away my money. 'Well, I better get back to work and you bony little things better head home. Get some kai in you.'

13

A letter hung on the front door, stamped and addressed to Mum and Dad. I pocketed it before Black could read it, pretending it was just another desperate attempt at drumming up business.

'Out-of-it fellas probably spread this stuff as far the maunga. Waste of bloody paper, I reckon.'

The kid shrugged his shoulders and skipped into the house, using a chair to pack the groceries away in the cupboard, pulling the old food to the front and tucking the new stuff behind it. He'd had to get a chair to reach the high cupboards, the kid up on his tiptoes, pushing the bread as far back as he could, his tongue folded between his teeth, his head turned sideways trying to get the most out of his arms.

I disappeared into my bedroom, pressing my back against the door, buying just enough time to skim the letter, hoping it wasn't CYPS.

It wasn't. They were turning the power off. Too many bills unpaid.

Part Two

Part Two

I4

For three days, the sky father grieved the old man, crying an ocean of tears over the wops. The god of wind cried too, the house trembling, its walls shaking, its bones creaking, the front door exploding open, pushing and pulling and flinging the towel that kept it closed across the carpet, that soaked-through thing lying twisted in the centre of the lounge.

On day one, the kid and I played games to pass the time. Hide and go seek, tag, and the floor is lava. It was the first time in our lives we'd played inside without getting a growling. The old lady had little patience for our mucking around, always stressed we'd break something. No doubt, she was right, the kid getting carried away in the kitchen, bumping into the cupboard and knocking the peanut butter from the high shelves and smashing the jar. Cutting his foot.

I snapped at him, my worry erupting as anger. 'The fuck are you up to?'

Quiet tears ran down his cheeks.

'Come on, bro,' I said, quick to change my tone, to try to comfort him. 'You're all good. Just a bit of blood. Anei,' I handed him a tea towel. 'I'll make it better, okay?'

He whimpered, wiping his face in the crook of his elbow.

'Ko te mea tuatahi, you gotta hold your breath. Hold it real hard.' One of Mum's tricks – her exact words too. Nothing stopped tears like a set of full lungs. 'Tuarua, I'm gonna spit on my hand and clean it. Might hurt a little but promise you'll be good as gold after. Lastly, you've got to push on it with the tea towel 'til the bleeding stops.' And that's what we did, spitting and cleaning and pushing 'til I could find a clean tea towel to wrap the wound with, and a brush and pan for the glass.

The last two days of rain sucked, the kid sulking, and the storm growing, the screaming and howling of the wind ceaseless through the night. Letting the kid be, his cut slowly getting better, I mahi'd whenever possible and spent the rest of my time on the lounge floor, watching the ceiling leak and fixing the towel whenever it was thrown across the carpet, reflecting on the old man's legacy – his spirit on the way to the maunga, his anger finding a home in me.

The old lady never spoke of mākutu. Like the devil, I guess, you invite it in when you speak its name. Still, I knew it well enough to recognise it; some fella wrote about mākutu in a book on the bookshelf. What the old man left behind had to be that. Probably he crossed the wrong person in the city, steelen and deelen, and they stuck him with this magic. Him and Mum and me and Black.

I thought long and hard about it. The anger. My jealousy at the kid running so freely towards the city. My snapping when the kid cried. How long would it be before I raised a fist or put a plate through a wall? Something had to change. And it was me who had to change it. That's the way it was in our ancestors' stories. When Wahieroa, a famous chief back in the day, was slain and his bones were used as decoration it was his son who made it right.

The story goes that every day Wahieroa's bones stayed there, the tribe was more disgraced, their mana bleeding. So it went 'til Wahieroa's oldest son was grown and his journey began. He left home and walked the forest and sat in the company of those who knew his old man and learned all he needed to learn. Soon enough, he was ready, seeking out the people who slew his dad, a thousand in number, and cut them down. One by one. Returning what was stolen. Putting an end to the mākutu on his old man's bones.

———

The rain had put a stop to all mahi on the neighbouring farms. No bike nor truck nor tractor ran across the hills. The gates that were closed stayed closed and the animals huddled against the highest fencelines of their paddocks. In the blur of the storm, they blended together, a heap of white and black.

Black sat in the dark in Mum's room, cuddled into a blanket, the light switch on and the lights off. The power company did not play games. I tried to speak with the kid and he wouldn't have it.

'Storm won't last much longer, I reckon.'

'Uh-huh.'

'Lucky we went to town early.'

'Yep.'

'Your foot good?'

'Mm-hmm.'

'You know I didn't mean to snap at you, aye.'

''Kay.'

I lit two candles, one in Mum's room and one in the lounge, and watched a pair of bulls in the distance patrol a lonely paddock. They could've been cousins of the old man. Stacks of compressed muscle. The only humanity in their eyes. The remainder of them carved from stone and steel.

In the same way, I reckon Wahieroa's son and I were cousins, both named after trees. Me after the legs of Tāne and him after the Māori Christmas tree – the rātā. We were probably only half-cousins, to be honest. We only shared one name and I had two. I wonder if my other one made me a cousin to the pub and the punters. Bet that tribe loved their bourbon. Would probably haka if they knew my name was Cody. Mind you, the pisshead knew and I got no more than a wave of his smoky hand and a brief history of the old man.

Thinking about it, maybe Rātā and I were closer than I first thought. When his old man died, he had to leave home and hunt down those who knew him. It was the only way to stop the bleeding. Maybe I needed to do the same. To leave the wops and see the pisshead and ask all I needed to ask. He knew about taniwha, maybe he knew about mākutu too.

I checked my shoulder for the kid and he was still wrapped in the old lady's blanket, still wanting nothing to do with me. Though I said I'd never leave him, I was having second thoughts. Better to be a liar, I reckoned, than stay and rark him up. Rātā had to leave his tribe too. When his old lady lost his dad, I bet he said he wouldn't go either. Mākutu is mākutu, though. Sometimes you gotta do what you gotta do. Break a promise. Kill one thousand of the enemy tribe.

15

When the kid was well asleep, I took the old man's coat from the kitchen table, fed my arms through its sleeves and pulled the hood over my head. Though my lanky limbs swam inside its shoulders, I felt a man in it. No rain nor storm nor blade nor bottle could pierce its rugged hide. I was invincible.

There was no pūkeko this night. It'd do him no good calling anyway. No song, no matter how beautiful, would call a bachelorette bird into this weather. Better to save your voice. Wait for it to pass.

The cattle and the sheep were not so fortunate. With nowhere to hide, they huddled in tight packs, their hooves chomping at the grass, digging up the earth, turning their fields (and their kai) to mud. It wasn't much better for the horses. Though they were most the way covered with coats. Dark nylon blankets wrapped around them, protecting everything but the ends of their faces.

The smoky pub looked the same in the rain. Through its dreary doors, the same six punters dwelled within. This time, none but one took note of me, the others drinking their drinks and blowing their smoke as if I were their seventh.

'If it ain't the poai,' the pisshead shouted from across the pub, calling me forth with a familiar flick of his wrist. 'Nau mai,' he said. 'Nau mai rā.'

I walked and paused and meant to order myself a drink, hoping the broken man might break from the stain he was wiping. The pisshead hurried me with a look, his eyes more pink than white, unsurprised, as if he'd spent his whole evening waiting for me to show up. He sat as far away from the entrance as he could sit, his only company a half-drunk drink and a glass ashtray and a glowing fireplace and a mostly smoked ciggy held between his teeth. His cheeks collapsed as he inhaled, his skin wrapping 'round the contours of his cheekbones, the scars on his face spelling out a life not strange to violence.

The speakers blasted 'Ngoi Ngoi' by the Pātea Māori Club, one of the old lady's jams, and the fire threw red light and shadows about the room, decorating the punters and their slow fall into unconsciousness. Drinking and sighing and smoking. Licking their lips and blinking their eyes and shaking their heads. Clenching their fists and clenching their jaws and losing themselves to the drink.

'Piss is cold, and the fire is raging.' The pisshead laughed as I joined him. 'On nights like these, it ain't half bad being a boozer.'

He paused to suck the smoke from between his fingers. 'Ain't half bad at all.'

I sat across from him and put my back to the fireplace. Its smoking wood settled my nerves and I removed the old man's coat and folded it over the nearest counter's corner. The fire crackled and exploded and sparks leapt from the burning wood, floating like the trickster fairies that roamed the woods. I saw the embers and the fire and the smoke and I thought of the old man and I remembered why I'd left the wops tonight.

'Can we talk?' I asked.

''Course.' The pisshead let the smoke from his lungs into the air, furrowing his brow and squashing his cigarette.

I nodded and choked on my next words; I parted my lips and said jack.

'Hardly said a word last time, boy,' he said with a laugh and a smile, swallowing a fit of coughs before it could erupt. 'Figured you were about to make up for it. Hei aha. Most fellas never shut up. Nothing wrong with a boy who listens more than he runs his mouth . . . And it's Tears by the way. Most just call me Tea. Sorry excuse for a Māori I am. Didn't even introduce myself.'

I stayed silent and roamed the room with my eyes, Tea following them as they moved. The broken man dried a mug with a rag, sealing the glass and twisting his covered hand in its insides until it was dry, and a fat woman sipped her last drop of beer and a hulking man traced the rim of his ashtray with a finger and two others shared a table, neither drinking nor smoking nor speaking to each other. They just sat there, legs crossed, staring at their table, avoiding acknowledging the other at all costs, maybe tired of talking, listening, maybe tired of their company.

'Straight up,' Tea said, his eyes looking sad, 'I fucken hate this place. It's a scourge. A taniwha inside a taniwha. Hell inside a hell. Don't know why you've come back, to be honest. You've too much life in you, yah know.' His eyes looked sad. 'This place ain't like other places. Something strange about it. More nights I spend here, more real it seems.' He pulled a new ciggy to his mouth, readying to light it then hesitating, resting his hand back on the table. 'Visited last time searching for your old man. I get that. You can't keep coming back, though. This place'll wreck you. Make it so you can't live without it.'

He lay his ciggy down and straightened at his table, mulling over something, rolling and unrolling his fingers in and out of a fist. A half-minute passed and his thinking stopped. He combed his hair. Cleared his throat. And leaned over the table, setting his eyes on me.

'What're you still looking for anyway? Old man's gone. What else is left?' He paused and lost himself again to thought. Then, shaking his head, he continued. 'You got a reason, don't you, boy? Don't tell me you've come for jack. This ain't the place to muck around with.

'Look at these people,' he said. 'Ain't nothing good here. Kaua e wareware. Nothing for a boy like you.'

The fireplace lit the pub with a raging glow. Tea kept the same face, speaking softly as he lit another ciggy and a sinister something in his eyes overcame him. He leapt to his feet and reached his hand across the table. 'Come,' he said, and he led me to the entrance of the pub, leaving two notes for the broken man and pushing me into the street.

Tea burst through the pub's entrance and stumbled forward as if about to fall. He buried his just-lit ciggy into the side of a steel trashcan missing its inner lining. The rain had stopped. What was left of it ran down the side of the pub and into the sidewalk. The sidewalk let it into the street where it flowed and flooded the border between them.

Two men a way down the road drank from the same bottle and watched a car float downstream. Neither of its headlights lit the road, the wreck relying on the charity of the streetlights. A siren penetrated the quiet, sounding as if it was still. The cops must've found whatever they were looking for. Tea paid neither the siren nor the car nor the men no mind.

He was a different man tonight. His feelings shone through his guard and his speech was straight up. The pub and the drink and the smoke took a toll on him, this much was sure. Still, there was something sober 'bout him. Tea flicked his wrist and guided me from the pub. 'Kia tere,' he said. 'Moving'll keep you warm.'

Where in the night did he mean to take me? Could I trust him beyond the eyes of the punters? What power had overcome him, forced him from his throne of nicotine, liquor and self-loathing? These and a thousand other questions filled me. A thousand and three questions and no clear answers; no path to them except doing as he asked, travelling with him deeper into the city, later into the night.

———

I followed him, and he flashed me a smile and I caught myself in
the reflection of a window behind him. I looked much older than I
remembered looking. Looked knackered. I looked in a strange way
like the pisshead before me – we looked like two peas in a pod.

'That coat at the pub,' he said. 'Was your old man's, aye?'

Trying to hide my panic, I looked down at my arms. How in
the hell did I leave that thing behind?

'Fella wore that thing every goddamn day. Never wore anything
else. Military boots. Those faded jeans. That coat. If I didn't
know him better, I would've swore he lived in 'em.' He chuckled,
telegraphing his joke. 'Probably buried in 'em.'

'Everything 'cept the coat,' I replied, speaking my first words
since the pub and startling Tea.

'Pono? Would've made him . . . He'd be stoked. For real. What'd
you do with your old lady? Yah know, when you . . .' He stumbled
over his feet. 'She was one of the good ones.' He paused and looked
me in my eyes. 'She get a tangi?'

I shook my head.

'Loved all that traditional stuff, aye. Being Māori. Christian.
A damn shame, yah know.'

16

A young girl sat atop a set of apartment buildings, her feet hanging over their edge, the whole of her dressed in an over-sized hunting jacket and her feet in a pair of gumboots, her body leaning into the street, her head between her legs. She let globs of spit hang from her mouth, letting it fall as far as she could before losing control. Sucking it all the way back into her mouth. Whipping her head to gain that last bit of oomph.

A few storeys below, her brother watched, his feet on a chair, his body hanging out of a window. 'That was mean.' 'Ewsh.' 'Shot, sis.'

So it went, 'til the young girl sailed too far to sea, unable to catch the glob falling from her mouth, the line of saliva breaking, the mass of spit falling, smacking her brother right between the eyes. He wiped his face and checked his hand and sent a middle finger back in return. 'I'm gonna punch your fat nose in.' The young girl shrieked with laughter, its shrill sound fading as she boosted it across the rooftop, her gumboots making a ruckus as she went, the last thing heard a jab. 'What'd you think would happen, you stupid idiot?'

Tea ran his fingers through his hair, self-soothing as he stumbled through step and speech. The streetlight, reflecting from the still-wet concrete, shone on him from above and below.

'Crook as this city is,' he said, scanning the world around him, 'ehara i te hanga. It can be striking. Ana. But I'm a sentimental man. Raised as I was raised, it couldn't be helped. Church teaches nothing better than it teaches awe.

'Was a time in my life, ages ago, where Sunday was the high-light of every week. Straight up. Was the only good thing in my life, yah know. Used to share a pew with your old lady. Right up the front. The pae. And if you know your tikanga, boy, then you'd know it was a goddamn honour. So there we'd sit, your old lady and me, way up front, feening for the Good Book. I used to watch her legs shake like a dog's just waiting for things to kick off. Was out of this world.

'Got to remember, she was young. Both were. Now I'm old, heaps has changed. Life does all kinds of things to move a man. Shows him things, yah know. Nowadays, the whole thing looks fucked. Imagine, hulking dudes in clerical dresses.' He chuckled. 'Aue. And they used to be my favourite part.' He laughed another laugh. 'When I close my eyes, I can still see all that stuff. Can go back and live in it. Knowing what I know now, though, it ain't the same. Makes me angry, yah know.' He looked sad. 'Makes me want to throw hands. All the songs. The promises. Bullshit.'

Three young men tore past us on their bikes; they pulled hard on their handlebars and sailed down the street on nothing but their rear wheels. The last of the three was shirtless, his young body thin and unmuscled, leaning recklessly for the leverage to keep his front wheel afloat. The other two were larger boys, making the same movement easy, sitting back on their hips and letting their chain-and-sprocket steeds do the work.

'Your old lady was the real deal,' Tea continued, speaking endlessly, jumping backwards and forwards across times and peoples and places. 'Not even they escape the shovel, if yah know what I mean. Was a time when she wound up in that pub of ours. Was younger than you are now. Back when that place was happening. Used to drink with her and smoke and . . . We were young, playing up. Teenager stuff, yah know?' I shook my head. ''Course you don't. Never knew your old lady did that sort of stuff, huh? S'pose none of us really know our parents well. Their history, I mean.'

The steel buildings grew taller and I felt their tops narrow like the closing of a jaw. It wouldn't be long before those unbreathing beasts swallowed the sky entirely and rid the street of the night's silver light. I wrapped my hands 'round my arms and made myself small. The cold had made my fingers numb.

As if reading my every thought, Tea swung an arm and wrapped his jacket around me. The speed of his movement and the strength of his clutch implied not an offer but a command. At my hesitation, he added, 'Liquor keeps my blood warm, boy.' I nodded in the place of a thank-you, scanning his waist and seeing no gun, and fed my arms through his jacket, stunned by the quick generosity of a man without a shit to share. There was no thinking it through, no internal reasoning. Fuck-all. He saw a need and he filled it.

Thinking back, he'd done the same twice now in the pub. Seeing me waiting there and calling me over with a flick of his wrist and doing all he could to hear and to help. Maybe it was sympathy that made him help, seeing a mutt of a man so far afield. Or maybe he just saw the old man and my mother in me, and so his help was a favour for old friends.

'Kia tere,' he said. 'We're close.'

I walked on and Tea bowed his head and the streetlight flickered black and bright and the gentle wind caught me in the crossroad and his jacket fell neatly over my frame.

17

Tea and I stumbled on a lull in the steel and concrete. It was, then with the crossing of a street, it wasn't. Two rows of no more than two dozen houses stood as a monument to a time gone by. Every house was made and crafted from the same handbook. Timbered, neat, modest. Between every centred gap of every plain picket fence and blue metal letterbox, a short concrete path led to a set of small concrete steps led to a white six-panel door marking the entryway to every house with a bare cross.

A grand brick building towered above it all, its frame listing. At its rightmost edge, a red-tiled steeple reached for the stars, now revealed and shining down a soft light. The silhouette of the city dwarfed the grand brick building, and yet, it didn't dwarf its beauty. Open-mouthed, I breathed it in. Tea scratched at his beard and walked on. 'Where even are we?' I asked.

He waved his hand. I stood my ground and asked again, 'The fuck is this place, Tea?' I don't know why I made such a stand; still, I committed myself to it. Tea turned and revealed an anger burning on his face, a sober fury, raising his palm and shaking his head, a physical you-need-to-stop. He checked I got him and went on again, leading me to the heart of this place. The fading silver of the moon lit the grand brick building and revealed it as a church.

The gates were open and inside twenty rows of sculpted pews bent before a lonely pedestal. Two teenagers swept the floor with black-bristled brooms, each focused on their mahi, refusing the cold and the darkness that swallowed the world outside, the strange men watching them beneath the glow of a streetlight.

'Old lady and I spent every Sunday here,' Tea said. 'Used to sit up front. Share a pew. Sat straight and proper and all that other stuff a good kid does. Ana. Used to sweep too. Every Saturday. And used to pray.

'Should've seen it, boy. Old and young dressed up flash. Rocking up early on a Sunday morning. Just sitting. Listening. Used to go on for ages. Whole church packed. Your old lady and me on the pae. We were stoked, aye. Felt like rangatira.'

Tea surrendered himself to silence and watched the faithful servants sweep. He surely saw himself in them, and I couldn't help but do the same, my vision blurring and the servants growing thin frames and grizzly faces.

'That's enough,' he said.

'But I—'

'Kia tere,' he interrupted, his tone stern, his face frustrated. 'Seen all you'll see tonight. Nothing more for you now. We'll catch up in the morning. I'll show you all that's left then.' He cleared his throat and spat into the sidewalk. Whether it was disrespect for the church or the genuine clearing of a smoker's throat, I didn't know. 'If all goes according to plan, boy, I reckon you'll learn all you need from this place.'

We parted ways, and Tea insisted I kept his jacket. 'He kaitiaki tēnā,' he said. 'Will protect you from the cold.' I swore I'd return with it in the morning. 'Hoki atu ki te kāinga,' he added. We each left without looking back.

———

A cop car followed me down a side street. I pulled the hood of Tea's jacket over my head and walked on, feeling the eyes of the men inside looking me up and down.

'You know how that lot do it in the city,' Mum warned the old man over and again, 'they love to chuck a man in chains.'

The car mounted the curb, the rims scratching against the gutter and echoing down this city corridor. A door opened then slammed and I stood still, anticipating a call to stop. Two sets of footsteps approached me from behind, the first stopping before I could see him and the second walking into my line of sight.

He was more a stereotype than a man. White as the night is long and his sideburns as thick beside his ears as his moustache was across his lip. I checked my shoulder and the man behind me was his clone, both dressed in blue from top to bottom. Hat and coat and shirt and pants and tie.

'Everything all right, brother?' The officer in front of me, fifty years old though he must've been, spoke with a twang, trying to put me at ease. 'No good walking the streets this late at night, aye. Might get yourself into trouble.'

I avoided the officer's eyes; I wasn't gonna play up.

'Or maybe that's the whole reason you're out in the first place.' The other officer was younger and questioned me wild-like, positioning himself so as to cut off any easy exit. 'Comms have reported a number of break-ins around here. Smash and grabs. You wouldn't do anything like that, would you?'

I shook my head and could feel him stare through me.

'You alone?' The first officer picked up where the other one left off. 'How old are you, fifteen or?'

'Nineteen,' I said, surprised my lips could make the words.

'Small for nineteen,' the other officer said. 'You sure you're all grown up?'

My hands burned hot and I turned to meet his eyes. There was a smile in them. He was trying to work me up, give himself an excuse to drag this out.

'Where you heading off to anyway, brother?'

'Home.'

'From?' the other officer asked, his partner shaking his head.

'The church.'

There was a pause in the questioning, both cops doing the math in their heads, figuring where was I in relation to all the churches here.

'Well, then, there's probably not a whole lotta reason to speak with you,' the first officer said. 'I guess I guessed you were still a young'un. You see, we get a lotta youth running through the street, some of them ratbags, the rest just trying to get out of the house – many for good reason – and play up and have some fun. But that's not you, is it, brother?'

He looked me up and down and, feeling set up, I shook my head.

'Everyone needs a tribe at the end of the day. You and me, him and everyone else. Heck, that's why we got to carry this radio here. For back-up, aye, Ed.'

Ed stared at me, refusing to acknowledge the first officer's speech.

'Never mind him, brother. He's a prick at the best of times.'

Ed laughed.

'Anyway,' the first officer went on, 'unless there's something you need to say, that's us.' He paused a moment, probably hoping he'd coaxed me into coming clean – into confessing my smashing and grabbing, steelen and deelen, my needing his help. 'I guess that's it then. Shot for speaking with us. And sorry 'bout the hassle. Stay safe now.'

The first officer took off and Ed stayed staring at me a little while longer and I wondered if Tea was back-up enough for me and the kid.

18

I woke to the same scene I'd fallen asleep to, my brother lying still. I nudged the kid with my elbow (checking if he would wake), rose and dressed myself in Tea's jacket.

I knew what I was up to. No pretty lie or performance could disguise it. Tea and the city and the grand brick building called to me. I prepped a serving of bread for the kid, left it covered with a tea towel on the kitchen table and visited him one last time before I took off. He looked yellow and grey in the early light, the skin around his eyes dark, his lips dry, his nose half-blocked, his bedroom folding in on him like a casket. A wave of guilt washed over me. The kid must've had a rough night.

'Won't be long,' I said. 'Got stuff I need to do.' I heard myself imitating Tea and paused. 'I'll be better when I'm back. Won't ever leave again.'

I believed what I told Black. In my head of heads and heart of hearts, I believed it. I had to go to the city. To see what the pisshead meant to show me, to stop myself from ever becoming the old man. I knew no other way to cut him out of me. Dad and his anger.

I left the house and began upon the dirt track. Three days of rain had muddied its edges. I paid it little mind and continued, stepping and skipping the ditches and puddles.

When I entered the city, I spotted a girl not much taller than a toddler, sitting criss-cross applesauce in the shadow of a burned-out apartment building, her hair parted in the middle, one half bunched with two oversized hair claws, the other half most the way braided, her back pressed against the shins of a much older woman – one of the nannies – the little one's eyes neutral, pleasant and unmoving, a look that made clear she'd been there a long time and intended to be there a lot longer. The nan, tiny and toothless, sat on the first step of a set of spalling concrete steps, her eyes aged most the way closed and her lips folded inside her mouth and her hands making music of her moko's hair, pulling and turning and folding and twisting and setting a crown on one half of the little girl's head. Remembering the porch-lady with the faux-fleece slippers, I ducked around a corner before they could catch sight of me, not wanting to upset this magical moment. A testament to the city's range. A place not entirely lost to glass bottles, ciggies and police sirens.

I walked on, imagining the nanny's music, and didn't allow myself any more detours. I didn't wanna keep Tea waiting. Besides, there was no real reason for caution; the city was quiet, nothing out of the usual going on. One man dead asleep on a bench, a helicopter overhead, a middle-aged couple arguing in a parked car, engine still running, and a child playing in the street. None but the child inspired much in me.

He stomped up and down the asphalt, revealing and concealing the contents of his hands. His gait was mean, his arms starved, his eyes fierce. He looked to be 'bout nine years old, same age as Black, although his rugged wee frame made such a measure more a guess than anything else. He was a child with all the features a child cannot escape. His cheeks were soft, hair flowy, his body so slightly out of proportion. There was no-one else in sight. No parents, no siblings. He was alone and lonely, marching the city streets armed, ready to war. I moved to speak to him and he warned me away, turning and reaching for his rear pocket, his instincts fast.

To ease him, I smiled. It only provoked him, his lips twisting into a snarl, so I let him alone and went on my way, careful to check my shoulder in case he meant to follow me. He watched me all the way into the distance, his hand never leaving his pocket.

How different his life must've been from the young girl with the half-crown of hair. I wondered what wild shit had made such a young thing so restless, so ready to defend himself. I wondered and I heard Tea say, he taniwha ia, and I knew all that needed to be known. No exact history, I'm sure, but something like it. A kind of conveyor-belt life a quarter way to turning this poor thing into a violent one like Dad.

Tea sat resting against a building one street removed from the hood we visited last night, rubbing his eyes with his hands. The window behind him was blacked out, long sheets of newspaper taped to its glass, its text no longer readable and the white background now a shade of grimy yellow. It looked to have been some kind of takeaway shop. Someone's dead dream, no doubt.

'Tea,' I said approaching, struggling to make any sound at all. He didn't hear me. I walked on with smaller steps and did what I could to speak louder. 'Tears.'

'Mōrena.' He blinked his eyes a few times and propped himself up on the building at his back and he rose to his feet. 'Jacket looks good on you, aye.' He cleared his throat and combed his hair and rubbed his eyes again. 'Aroha mai. Didn't sleep too well. Didn't sleep at all, to be honest. Too used to the piss and the smokes, I reckon. Enough of those and you're out like a light. Hoi anō: Ended up being just one of those nights, yah know. Lying there all night long. Staring at the ceiling. Thinking.' He paused and scanned the grand brick building from tip to toe.

His voice was distant. His movements laboured. He looked anxious, like he feared what was to come. He watched the grand brick building with the red-tiled steeple like the kid watched the old man's fire, and yet, he didn't hesitate.

'Kia tere,' he said.

I nodded.

Tea crossed the street and walked the path opposite the church, and I followed, stopping occasionally to watch small groups of men, women and children drip beyond its wooden gates. They walked tall with their hands at their sides, their wrists wrapped with watches and their necks with ties.

In the gold light of day, the church looked even more impressive than it did in the dark. Its fiery colour, more orange than red, looked magical against the ugly urban forest behind it. So too did the stained-glass giant painted halfway between the street and the steeple. He wore a neat white robe and a crown made of sticks, the whole of him protected by an arched frame. His aura was otherworldly, his emaciated arms stretched wide. Like I had two names, this stained-glass figure had two sides to him, this difference most obvious in his eyes: one wide and round, the other uneven.

'Poai,' Tea said, interrupting. 'Careful now. Some out-the-gate stuff hides in there.'

'Like what?'

He didn't answer me and we crossed from sidewalk to sidewalk and started towards the church, Tea's jacket still blowing on my frame. (I'd had to roll its cuffs to make any use of my hands.) Tea was dressed in a black beanie, fleece tee, and a pair of faded jeans, the dark circles 'round his eyes telling of his lack of sleep. His outfit seemed a sort of protest, a fuck-you to the prettiness of this place. I know what you hide beneath all of this, it said. I know what you are, and I won't let you forget it. Even for a moment, even on the Sabbath. 'Specially on the Sabbath.

The men and women and children who filled the first few rows were dressed not just in suits and dresses but clothes worthy of chiefs, in outfits like I'd never seen before, in clothes that would humble even the stain-glassed king who watched over this place. It looked a literal heaven populated by the literal children of God. If not for Tea, I would've turned and run. Better the dangers of the city than the judgement of these types. I could outrun the former. I couldn't hide from them.

Tea looked more a ghoul here than a man. The tiny hole in the neck of his shirt was suddenly a gaping gorge, the modest speck on the leg of his pants a stain, and the skin-coloured mole on the lobe of his ear a wart.

I must've looked the same. Out of place. Fugly.

A wee girl greeted me with a bow of her head. I nodded as I passed her by, careful to match her courtesy, and I followed Tea to the farthest edge of the fifth row of pews. He seized his yellowed fingers as a tremor shook his hands; he didn't speak nor shift his eyes from the back of the seating in front of us. I let my own wander. If only the kid could see this place, I thought. Would blow his mind.

Two burly men wearing white robes appeared from nowhere, and walked the church from front to back. When they reached the entrance, they pulled the wooden gates closed and the room filled with even more of the stained glass's light. Tea bowed his head, and I knew whatever I was to find in this place I would have to find alone. The men returned through the middle aisle and went their separate ways, each finding a place at the far ends of the church. As they took their seats, silence fell over the room, and jack could be heard but Tea's breath. Then, as if rehearsed, the crowd rose to their feet. I copied them, and Tea didn't.

The silence continued.

A frail man emerged from the left of the stage. Step by step he filled the room with the song of his feet. Each step and its echo grew louder and louder. I rose on my toes and tried to gain a better view; I could barely make him out between the rows of suits and dresses; I saw only enough to feel sorry for the frail man. His body was hunched, and his hair white, and his movements seemed painful. He went on 'til he took a place at the podium. Thereafter, the room fell silent again, Tea's breath included.

———

Mum used to speak a little of the church here and there. Said it was equal parts good, bad and out of touch with the communities it reckoned it served. Talked a whole lot about serving, she said, but took with both hands. Said it'd always been like this 'round here. From the very beginning. 'Would make you sick how much land the mihingare owned. How they conspired with the Crown against tikanga. Against our tūpuna.'

'Don't get me wrong,' she added when she'd calmed down, 'there were angels among them. True-blue charitable types. But still, the church has a lot to answer for. Then and now. To us and to God.'

———

The frail man spoke, and his soft voice carried over the pews. I could hardly hear him; his words little more than a whisper. His message must've been beautiful, though. It must've been. No voice so soft, so full of warmth could speak anything but goodness. The frail man finished, and the men, women and children replied, 'Āmene.' Their echo roared on while they returned to their seats, and I saw the frail man in all his heavenly glory. He wore a neat white robe that danced and swayed over his sandals. His eyes were cloudy, and his hands shook, and his skin clung tight to his skull.

'E noho, e tama,' he said to me, our eyes meeting. 'We have mahi to do this Sunday morning.'

Tea woke from his trance and clutched my wrist. He pulled me down to my seat. His voice was alive with anger, his eyes piercing. 'Keep your fucken head down,' he said, careful to keep a whisper. 'That fella there's no good. Few of them are. Spent too long in here. Drowned in all this drivel.' He closed his eyes, sighed and composed himself. 'Trust me, boy. Protect. Your. Neck.'

I wanted to say something and I didn't. I shifted my eyes back to the podium and saw a younger, more handsome man had appeared. The new preacher towered above the crowd, his cheeks red hot and his voice rousing like a drum. He was a man older than myself and younger than the man beside me. While there was power in his presence, there was also a kind of softness to him.

'We, the few,' the new preacher boasted with a redness in his cheeks and a fire in his throat, 'the sons and daughters of the Heavenly Father, stand in the light that shines in the darkness. We stand in the light that shines in the filth and the sin and the . . .

debauchery.' He paused and pulled at his beard, scanning the crowd. 'You may ask yourself as many have, What has brought this place and its people so low?

'The answer, as our Father has taught us, is faithlessness. It is for this that they suffer, and through faith that we may transcend such suffering.'

'Āe,' a fervent young woman called from the first row of pews, her hand raised, head bent, fingers pointed skyward.

'It is through our faith that we endure and through our faith that we overcome. It is through our faith that we discover the light that shines. "But behold," the faithless would say, "do you, the faithful, not suffer the same as we?" And I answer, We do not. The fearful and unbelieving suffer without an ark, but we, the pious and devout, have three canoes by which we are saved. Three canoes which lead us to know and understand our suffering.' He crossed himself and kissed his gloved hand, letting his vision roam over the brick and the flock and the leather-bound books they nursed on their laps. 'And it is through this knowledge and understanding that we are saved.'

19

The new preacher was a chorus in and of himself, a human instrument, the music of his voice pairing with the acoustics of the room. I gave to him my everything, in hopes of some great change, letting his words penetrate my guard, praying for a break from it all. And it did not come.

As the eye adjusts to the first light of the morning, mine adjusted to the church. All that was bright and overwhelming, dulled. Fell short of its first impression. How could this place live up to such an image anyway? What words could a man speak that would convey the same power as the picture of the stained-glass king? What man in stained glass could stand in the presence of such bullshit and not grow less regal? How little history would a man have to know to buy this fuckery?

The preacher went on, and the crowd went on with him, the man at the podium singing songs of reverence, wonder and respect.

In them was something absolute. I just couldn't connect. There was something off. In the sermon spoken, the stories told. Everything.

The preacher lifted his head and raised his leather-bound book skyward and smiled at the crowd. From opposite sides of the church, the burly men reappeared and roamed each row and aisle with a silver plate. The flock bowed their heads and showered them with blue, green and purple notes, with coins of gold and silver. When they approached Tea, he granted them only a sober look, crossing his hands over his chest.

The preacher retired and the frail man rose from the pae and the crowd raised their heads. 'Eight hundred years here,' Tea said. 'Eight hundred long fucken years without that Good Book. And they reckon all that's gone wrong is 'cause we don't believe enough. He aha hoki. All these fancy gears and all these rituals and they still don't have a goddamn clue.'

The frail man raised his palms up and outward. The crowd rose, and he spoke, his voice weak and low, broken by a shaky breath. 'Now go forth my children, and rest, for this is the day of the Sabbath. But keep your mind and remember the faithless, those who are damned to roam the street.'

The wooden gates opened and the room flooded with white light. Tea and I waited while the crowd gapped it. We shifted our eyes to the front of this place only as the burly men followed them outside, Tea leading me down the far corner aisle.

The church pews were unforgiving, carved from native wood, without cushions, bending a man into shape well before he could return the favour. They forced a proper posture, a straight back and a proud chest. They were a humble brown, without design or decoration. No sign of the tree they were carved from. Not a knot, not a nothing. Made custom.

A grey carpet running the length of the centre aisle aside, the floor was shaped in the same way. Native wood. Unforgiving. My footsteps echoed through my body. Every strike of my heel jolting my knees and carrying upward, making me feel every movement of my body. All of it felt a judgement. Your posture is weak, the pews said. Your body is fragile, the hardwood floor said. There's something off about you, the stained-glass giant said.

We met the frail man as he left the podium. At its base, etched into its bottom panel, was an alien language. Not Māori. The old lady had an old book on the Māori gods that had the reo written in it. (Pretty much looked like English.) This was something else.

'Aaron.' The preacher looked Tea in his eyes and spoke his name as if it strangled him. ('Course he wasn't born Tears, I thought, shaking my head at myself.) 'It is a wonder to see you here again in the hallowed light.' He paused, trying to gauge Tea's intent, the preacher blinking and scowling and trying – failing – to conceal the anxiety rising inside him. 'But you've not returned for any just reason, have you, e tama? No, I can see the hellfire is still in your eyes.'

'And what does it say, old man?'

'That you have given yourself to sin. That you have let it in, and it has wreaked havoc upon you. Please remember, it's not too late. You may yet be—'

'Redeemed,' Tea interrupted. His voice strained and his fists clenched and his eyes burned with hate. 'Still full of it, aye. Saying the same ol' shit you've always said.' He filled his lungs with air; he tried to settle the fire in his hands. 'Let me be straight, old man, the only redemption I know is our ancestors'. Utu.'

Tea met my eyes and I believed him, and then he left, his face tired and angry. The frail man shook as he watched Tea go. He looked to love him, to hate him. A feeling I knew well.

The preacher composed himself, adjusting his robe and the silver chain caught in his collar. He then set his cloudy gaze on me, his eyes scrutinising. I stayed quiet as he looked me in my face. Suddenly, something struck him. 'What a thing I have become,' he said, cupping my shoulder. 'Has blindness so taken me I cannot even recognise my moko?'

I stood back and shook his hand from me.

'You don't know? No, of course you don't. Mō taku hē. Forgive an old fool for his ignorance. Please, e tama, let me introduce myself.' Time froze and I knew what he was to say. 'Ko au tō koro. There's no doubt about it, my boy. I'm your koro.'

His hair was thick, curling at its ends, its loss of colour paired with no loss in thickness. His jaw was soft, his face round. And his eyes were large, amplifying his every expression, making no mistake of his feelings. He was a beautiful man, and I could see Mum in him.

I felt no great shock at his reveal, I was too shaken by his words with Tea and the regret expressed shortly after. Upon the podium, he was a mighty man, a prophet, but now, on even ground, he was a different thing altogether. Still, Tea had made him a villain and so, despite our whakapapa, I kept a healthy distance between us.

He began again to speak but was interrupted, the second preacher calling for him with a panic from across the room. The frail man turned, and his face became serious. 'I must go now, my boy,' he said with a sense of duty, offering me the leatherbound book in his hands. 'Same as the one your mother had.' He leaned in towards me, clutching my shoulders, scrunching his face and pressing his nose to my own, resting his forehead against me. (I can't say why I didn't step back, why I allowed him to get so close.) The preacher closed his eyes and I closed mine and he drew a breath deeply through his nose, filling his lungs with my air. 'Mauri ora.'

And that was it. Hoki atu. I watched him leave and thought long and hard about the path my life had taken. Losing the old man and gaining a koro. I turned and walked the middle aisle, joining Tea outside the wooden gates. He greeted me with a grief-stricken smile, and I could tell he'd heard us speak.

'Kia tere,' he said.

20

Most of the crowd drifted into the distance, shrinking beneath the grizzled steel of the city. The few that remained walked the concrete paths to the concrete steps to the white six-panel doors that marked every house here with a cross. When their doors closed, their houses exploded with bright lights and the hustle and bustle of conversation. I saw children playing with race cars, husbands and wives snuggling in front of TVs and a woman sitting alone with a book in her hands.

The whole of it blew me away. Who were these people and how did they get such riches? Tea walked and I walked with him, wishing to ask the question and fearing to know the answer. Their ancestors left them these like yours left you that body hanging gaunt across his couch.

A faraway voice called us to a standstill. 'Aaron,' its sound carried in the wind.

We checked our shoulders and saw the younger preacher chasing after us. 'I'm stoked to have caught you,' he said, winded. 'Koro David said . . . He told me you had come 'round.' I was struck by the difference between his speaking and his preaching. On the sidewalk, he spoke like he was two drinks in: straight out of the pub.

Tea replied with caution. 'Streets reckon you own this place, Bent, soon as the old man folds.'

'That's what he wants, aye.' He paused, thinking and catching his breath. 'In all honesty, though, got no idea what I'll do. We're not the same, though, David and me. He's firm in his faith, but I feel still a member of the flock.' There it was again, the Good Book in his voice.

'Your mahi here is what then – you compensating?'

'Just following Koro's example.'

Tea pierced his eyes, his face twisting into a scowl. 'And what if he's wrong?' he said, emphasising his last word. 'If they don't need all this paternalistic crap? Need someone in the struggle with 'em. A Parihaka kind of approach, yah know. Less pretending like you know it all.'

There was a pause and Tea turned to check I was good, while Bent wrapped one hand around his body and the other around his jaw, looking straight at me.

'The lad's not—' the preacher paused.

'Sarah's?'

'Yeah.'

'Yeah.' Tea slapped my back. 'Old man passed a few days back. Now the kid is chief.'

I didn't react; my body was frozen in its place. From my puku, this feeling radiated outward, a tremor building in my hands.

The preacher packed a sad. 'She's gone?'

'Gone gone.'

'It can't be.'

''Course it can. No different for her than everyone else 'round here.'

The preacher seemed to waver, he turned away from me.

I was a statue, trying as best I could to intuit what wasn't being said. That which caused such a rapid change of emotion. In this place – this taniwha – my story must've been shared by many. Those without mothers and many more without fathers. What I'd been through was no special thing.

Tea stood impassive in the face of Bent's emotion. 'You all good?' he asked. The preacher didn't respond, and Tea's confusion became concern. He rested one hand on the teary-eyed man and asked again. 'Got to tell me, Bent. The fuck is going on?'

He shook Tea's hand off. 'You know what she meant to me. I just . . . need a minute?'

'We're all gutted. But you're acting sorta shady.' He combed his fingers through his beard. 'Haven't asked what went down. What's the go. Anything.'

Bent's eyes grew wide and hateful and his voice broke with sudden violence. 'Make no judgement of me,' he snapped. 'You who are wretched and sinful.'

As quickly as his words left his mouth, he tucked his chin – for good reason. Tea loaded a misshapen fist behind his shoulder and slammed it forward, striking the preacher hard across his cheek. Smoking him. Sending him backwards into the street. His face reddened. Swelled. Pooled with blood. And Tea stood over him and spoke with a whisper. 'I ain't the one.'

Bent's eyes watered. (Maybe that's how Aaron got the name Tears – 'cause he summons them like the tohunga summons whales.) Bent touched his cheek with two fingers and checked them; they were covered with blood. Shitting bricks, I looked around to see if anyone had seen Tea throw that punch: the widow watched us through her living-room window, a landline in her hand. No doubt calling the cops.

Trying to put space between him and the pisshead, Bent crawled backward then turned and gunned it, disappearing into the church. Tea ran his hands through his hair, breathing a long breath. 'For fuck's sake,' he whispered. 'Fella snaps at me and expects what – not to get dropped? Dickhead should've known he would get it.' He checked his knuckles (grazed) and kicked at a stone on the sidewalk and put his eyes back to the grand brick building. 'Should've known.'

'Hoki atu ki te kāinga,' he said, turning to me and raising his voice. ''Fore the cops come. We'll catch up at yours. I just got some shit to sort first.'

21

The day still early and the city still quiet, I allowed myself to roam, to take the long way home. I needed to clear my head. Calm my nerves. There was no rush to get back to the kid anyway, I assured myself. What's another half-hour with the taniwha? I walked and searched for splashes of the olden days. Things like the pub and the small woman's store. Tea had mentioned an eight-hundred-year history, and I wanted to check it out.

Though I looked and looked, I found little. Boarded-up stores and boarded-up apartments and a heritage building from the 1800s. An old hotel turned TAB.

What about the seven hundred years prior? How did they live, love, provide for their families? Mourn their deaths, pass the time, shelter from the wind and the rain, pray to their gods, win their favour? How did they eat and sleep and explain the world?

By chance, I stumbled upon the empty street where the stones shone like pāua in the concrete. The two framed windows. And finally, the small woman working beneath a lopsided banner. With a stained rag and a steel bucket, she mahi'd over the panelled glass. The small woman circled and circled and circled the glass, running her rag and the window dry. I got her attention only when she turned to her soapy bucket to kick off anew.

'E tama,' she said, never looking up. 'I'll meet you at the till.' I nodded and did as I was told.

The hum of the lights carried at a constant volume across the rows and the aisles revealing every detail of every carton of eggs and bottle of milk and paper bag filled with flour, of every jar of jam and tray of kūmara and carboard box filled with colourless cereal. I browsed each aisle, keeping an eye on the small woman working away outside. A long minute passed, and she joined me in the store.

'Kui,' I said. She laughed, too polite to growl at me for implying she was old. 'I don't reckon I need anything at the moment. To be honest, I was just kind of roaming; didn't even mean to come here.'

'That's life, e tama. Ko te whai ao ko te ao mārama. Few things are built like buildings are.'

'While I'm here. I should probably say thanks.'

She stopped me with a stern voice. 'I plant seeds,' she said. 'That's what I do. What fruits are born I pay little mind to. Waiho tō mihi. If you should feel any reason to thank someone, thank the seeds and the soil and the sun. Te taiao. That's who does the work.'

Confused, I screwed up my face.

She laughed and said, 'I plant seeds, e tama. Sometimes, I figure, that's all we can do.' Her face became serious, filled with darkness. 'When I was young, before this city grew old and cynical, we held church in a makeshift marae. An old town hall dressed in toi Māori. The first Sunday of every month, the local Māoris – men and women from every corner of the maunga – would catch up and our tūpuna would tell us stories. Kōrero tuku ihos and parables from the Good Book.' She gestured to the leather-bound thing in my hand. 'Then we'd eat and while we cleaned, the real kuis – women much older than me, thank you very much – would answer our questions. That's when my nanny told me what I'm trying to tell you now, e tama. There's no tukutuku without flax and no flax without seeds.

'It was a wonderful time,' she continued. 'But they've passed now. Moved on again. Their marae sold. Their gardens dug up.' She took two muffins from behind a glass cabinet, placed them in a brown paper bag and taped it down with a strip of sellotape.

'Lucky, we still have our seeds, aye.' She laughed and resumed a cheerful voice and handed me the paper bag, winking.

22

A car passed me on the way home, going the opposite direction. A white hatchback. Brand new except a splash of dirt kicked up by its tyres. The men inside didn't turn their heads as they rolled on by. Between this and the state of their whip, I knew they weren't from 'round here.

I walked a little while, wondered who the men in the hatchback were and, as a thought came upon me, I boosted it, running as fast as I could home. Those fellas were probably CYPS – all the way out here hunting down the kid. I pumped my legs and searched my head for any memory of a little passenger in the back seat but couldn't be sure.

If CYPS found him, they would've taken him. No doubt in my mind. Those motherfuckers played no games. Would soon as uplift a kid as see him, barefoot, tracking through the grass and the gorse, playing by himself outside.

Sweat dripped down my face and in my eyes, blinding me, and the book tossed backwards and forwards in one hand and the paper bag in the other, the kai inside being smashed to shit. I cussed out CYPS for being CYPS and Tears for dragging me back into the city and the old man for leaving us alone and myself most of all for fucking up again. How could I have left the kid on his lonesome? What the fuck did I think was gonna happen?

I turned down the track, almost wiping myself out as I took the corner, and slowed to a jog, scared out of my mind to see if Black was gone. Poor thing would drown in the system. Be eaten alive. The kids in there, those children of the state, their hearts have been made hard from constant wanting and their bodies have been made tough from every flavour of violence they'd suffered. And survived.

A hundred metres from the porch, I slowed to a walk, my eyes wide and my breath heavy and my legs weak. The door swung open but, blind from the sweat in my eyes, I couldn't see inside. A shadow limped through the doorway. I stopped where I stood, clearing my vision with the sleeve of my shirt, and the shadow limped on, stepping down from the porch. I asked myself if he were real or a vision of the old man here to haunt me and the shadow answered – my vision clearing – it was little ol' Black.

I had only a second's worth of relief before I saw Black's foot was munted. His face twisted with pain.

My heart broke. And I wondered if the old man had ever felt ashamed. The kid stumbled forward and I went to hug him and he shook his head at me. His eyes were red with anger and he was looking at me as I'd so often looked at Dad. 'You said you wouldn't leave again, Kauri.' His voice was hoarse.

I passed the paper bag and he caught it and I hid the book behind my back.

'Could've woken me,' he said. 'Taken me with you.'

I nodded and continued towards the porch, stepping and skipping ditch and puddle, the damp soil mushing beneath my feet.

'You piss me off sometimes, Kau.'

'Language.'

'Piss isn't a swear word.'

'It is to me.'

'Whatever.'

I looked the kid up and down, shaking my head at him and he did the same in turn.

'What's up with your foot anyway?'

'Don't change the subject.'

'I'm not.'

'Yes, you are.'

'Bro, you gonna tell me or what?'

'It's nothing.'

'Nothing, my ass.'

'I just hurt it.'

'Again – or the same cut from the glass?'

'Well, you went to the city without me so . . . I went to the river without you.'

'It just fucken rained,' I growled, the blood boiling in my throat.

I tasted the old man's anger on my tongue and wondered if this is how it was with him too. If his blowing up started in some sick way with him trying to keep us safe – both me and the old lady.

'What else was I gonna do – sit in the house all day by myself?'

I ran my hands down my face, calming myself down – knowing my blowing up would hurt more than it helped.

'When I got back, it just started hurting.'

'You get mud in it?' That's what Mum would've asked.

'Nah. I think it's just from all the jumping.'

'You sure?'

'It doesn't matter anyway. You broke the rules first. You went to the corner dairy without me.'

Mum taught us never to go in the water after it rained. It carries all kinds of crap – literal crap and fertiliser and effluent – from the farms and dumps it in the tide. Swallow enough of that stuff and you're as good as gone. No clue what happens when it gets in cuts. I guess we were about to find out.

Truth was, though, Black was right. It was all my fault. I abandoned him again. What was he supposed to do but pass the time as best he could? Bloody toe-rag. It was like the old lady said: It's the mahi of children to break the vase. It's why she made us play outside. Why she made me go with the kid whenever he left our paddock. Only so much mischief the young can get up to with an older brother on them.

Maybe the cop really was right. Black and I needed a tribe. I was wrong to leave him, I knew. Still, I couldn't live the rest of my life stalking the kid, could I? There was always Tea, I s'pose.

Fat load of good I figured he'd do, though. The city's hooks were deeper in him than they were in me.

'Why'd you take so long anyway?'

'Got stopped on the way,' I said.

'From the dairy?'

'Kāo-re.' The word was disfigured, mispronounced. 'Just happened on it after.'

'Why'd you go then?'

Figuring I'd kept enough from the kid, I reckoned it was best to be straight with him. 'Our koro, Black.'

The kid's walk slowed and I slowed too.

'And that ain't even half of it. Remember that fella I told you about – the pisshead who knew Mum and Dad?'

'Yeah.'

'Reckons he's gonna visit us soon.'

'When?' he asked, failing to mask his interest.

'Not sure to be honest. But soon.'

'Really?'

'Really.'

'Promise?'

Already I began to regret my telling him. 'Promise.'

I koha'd the kid a glass of water from the low-pressure pipes in the kitchen, the faucet dripping only when its handle was turned all the way to the right. He drank from his cup and pulled apart the brown paper bag and offered me a muffin (surprisingly still intact after my sprint home). I shook my head and he served himself and I lay the old lady's leather-bound book on her bedside table; then, having collected the two buckets from beneath the leaky ceiling, began towards the river.

The earth was soft and the grass patchy and strips of corduroy floated in discoloured pools of rainwater. The dirt track was a mud track and the porch railing leaned and the hills appeared to have shrunk. The dandelions were missing and the gorse had fallen over and the old man's resting place caved in its middle; it looked as if the earth had tried to swallow him. I emptied both buckets on the lawn and refilled one half-bucket with soil and made the patch flat that marked the old man's grave. I wished him peace and, more than that, health for the seeds that would become his memory. 'Specially now, knowing the small woman's wisdom.

Thinking long and hard, I made my way to the river, mulling over mixed thoughts of the old man. Every day I felt something new towards him. Some days, it was the twisting of something small, on others, stuff more serious.

The rain had returned the stream to full strength, its current climbing the bank and wearing it down to a smooth surface. Though the grass was dense, it was taken by the tide, some of it broken up and carried, the remainder pulled right from its root.

I sat atop the bank, rinsing and cleaning the buckets, two and three times over, then filling them with water. As the sky darkened, I made my way home, trying as best I could to keep the water in the buckets. Though my bad shoulder rang with the weight – the buckets only half full – I endured. I'd learned the art of endurance in the violence of the old man. All you had to do was hold your breath and tense from top to toe.

Black watched me from the porch with a pair of cups in his hands, and a couple of small plates and the brown paper bag at his side. I knew what he meant to do, and I loved him for it.

'Saved you some.'

I shook my head.

'We can share,' he said, opening the bag to reveal the last muffin sliced neatly down their middle.

We sat on the porch and pulled the smashed-up muffin even further apart, going for the next piece as the last melted in our mouths. I finished and stretched my arms and watched the track, barely making out a set of boot prints too big to be mine and too small to be the old man's. When the kid finished cleaning the cutlery, I asked him whose they were.

'Oh yeah,' he said. 'A couple of men visited while you were gone.'

'They come in a white hatchback?' I asked, letting a few seconds go by, not wanting to come across too interested. This was the kind of shit Black was best not knowing.

'What's a hatchback?'

'Never mind.'

'Okay.'

'What did they want?'

'They were looking for Dad.'

'Police?'

'Nah, not police. Fancy men in dress shoes.'

So it was them. CYPS. Fucken bastards were gonna try their luck again. Take the kid away. I wonder if they'd heard the power was cut off. Or someone in the city had got wind the old man had kicked it and they were following a lead.

'What did you tell them?'

'That he was gone.'

Gone gone or gone?'

'Just gone.'

'And they were all good with that?'

'Well, then they asked when he was coming back and I didn't know what to say. I just kinda did this.' He shrugged his shoulders and screwed up his face. 'They said they're gonna come back and to tell Dad he better be home.'

They weren't mucking 'round anymore. No doubt about it. And with the kid clueless about when his own father would return from wherever he was, they had more than enough reason to push things. To come back and kick the door in. Drag things into the courts or just take the kid, straight up.

I faked a smile. 'Shot, bro.'

———

The day grew a little older and the kid limped 'round the paddock and I stayed glued to the porch, thinking through what I could do about the CYPS. I was gonna have to pull something slick. Trick them somehow. Do whatever I had to do, 'til I could find a fix for this mess.

'I've been thinking,' the kid said, interrupting me mid-thought.

'Yeah?'

'We have to wait until Tea visits, right?'

'Right.'

'So why don't we do something in the meantime?'

'Like what?'

'Why don't we fix the house,' he said. 'Make it like it was when Mum was around?'

The kid continued, speaking about our whare as if it were once a palace, his memory distorted by nostalgia. His voice was hoarse, probably the kid was coming down with something. I asked if he was feeling all good and he said yeah and I said as long as he was all good, I'd help him. It was the first step, I figured, in making a fool of CYPS. Without a clean house, we were screwed. No trick of the tongue could make this shithole look habitable. We would have to put the work in. I decided I'd labour on the earth and the kid reckoned he should work inside. He would start by ridding the walls of the mould that built up in the rain.

Mum always stayed well on top of that stuff. Since she'd been gone, it'd been left to spread. The kid would have to scrub the walls raw to rid them of their gunk. I tried to get him to put his foot up for a bit, but he wouldn't have it. 'Real warriors don't rest,' he said.

We used to have sprays here, chemical sprays that would make the clean easier. The old lady kept heaps locked in a high cupboard. They weren't there anymore; the old man had long gotten rid of them. No doubt all that shit reminded him of the old lady, that woman always cleaning. The week after the old lady left, I spied that hulking, drinking, fighting man return from the city in the early hours and tear the kitchen shelving from the wall.

He used only his hands. Hooking his fingers anywhere he could get a grip and pulling with the might of his back. The veins in his neck bulging. The cupboards resisting only a moment before, like the thrown plate, they flew across the room. When morning came, I found their wooden remains on the lawn, a different kind of tekoteko, the dishwashing liquid and the fridge door and the bleach and the glass and surface spray lying beside them.

The insides of the cleaners were toxic to the grass, every blade bending over, turning darker shades of black. That was the same month the karaka stopped bearing fruit. I reckon the chemical did that too. From then until now, what remained of the kitchen cupboards stayed empty. In their stead, we cleaned the house with nothing but soap and water.

I tousled the kid's hair and he reminded me the top of the head is sacred. I smiled and apologised and mihi'd to him. 'Not a bad idea, bro. Old lady would be proud.'

'Of both of us, aye?' he asked.

I nodded but I wasn't so sure.

23

The colour of the house chipped and peeled all 'round the outside, and everywhere it didn't chip and peel, it faded, except where the roof provided shade and where the earth crept up on it at the bottom. It was built from long lengths of timber; each piece a different age, a different width and a different tree; every length of timber more a cousin than a brother. They were tall and short, stiff and loose, smooth and rugged, and year by year Mum and Dad replaced the worst of the rotted timber with whatever they could get their hands on, one plank at a time. A person couldn't find a more eclectic mix of wood in the woods.

The porch ran plane on one side and dipped into the dirt in the other. The windowsills were dry-rotting and barely kept out the rain, and the flesh of the wood exposed was weak and hollow. The bathroom window was boarded shut with eight nails and a sheet of plywood; it'd been that way since we first moved in, no glass ever decorating its grimy frame. The remaining windows were unremarkable bar a small chip in the one in the bedroom the kid and I shared. An ancient mistake I've lied so long about I cannot even remember what happened; I remember only playing, then panicking, then fibbing to the old lady, who was more concerned with my tears than the chip. The growling came eventually.

The roof was tiled, and the tiles were made from clay, and they made the roof a crooked hump, like the one on the broken bartender. Each piece looked as if picked and placed by a different person, their colours clashing, a wild array of red and orange, sitting crooked against their neighbour.

When the old lady was around, she spoke all the time about restoring the house, making it whole again. With her, we could've done it. I reckoned we couldn't really do it now. Maybe, though, just maybe, we could do enough to keep CYPS at bay.

So Black cleaned the walls and I fixed the track. I began by making a drain, labouring with the old man's tools, kneeling on one knee and ripping the earth with the sharp edge of his spade and removing what was broken up with the shovel, evoking all the might of my legs and the same from my body above. With every movement, blots of mud and sweat caked me. An hour passed and my muscles grew weak. Numb and unfeeling. And I went on, kneeling and ripping and removing and pausing to catch my breath, and kneeling and ripping and removing again.

The twin peaks of the maunga stood proud, his head of snow falling down over his shoulders, the rest of him dressed in a cloak of clouds. Once upon a time, he was a priest. Like Koro. Then one day he hit on another maunga's missus and got the bash. I can't even imagine how two maunga fight. Maybe they had hands back in the day and threw punches like men threw punches or maybe they shot lava through their heads and that's why their tips were tapu. Either way, our maunga got sent to the coast, made mates with the ranges and settled in, still lusting after the other maunga's missus. The stones in these parts are said to be his tears. Poor fella must've cried for ages.

Ka aroha. What you get for playing up. That's what Mum said once she checked I was good after chipping that window. She was a loving lady. Just didn't play silly buggers.

———

A gruff voice interrupted my mahi, carrying over the sounds of my huffing and puffing. 'Ko koe ngā waewae o Tāne,' it said, and I turned to see Tea standing over me. My surprise turned quickly to shock. He'd dressed up nice and looked all the worse for it. His eyes were yellow and pale and sick.

Tea was all I said, all I could say, propping myself up on my spade and trying with shaky arms to stand up straight.

'This your place, boy? Pae kare. Didn't fare too well in the rain, aye.'

I held on to my silence. By the look of Tea, I could tell he brought no good news.

'S'pose I should explain myself, ne. My leaving you, I mean. Needed to catch up with Koro.' He spoke about him with contempt, forcing the words through closed teeth. 'Needed to catch up with him ASAP. Real urgent, yah know.'

'I get it.'

''Course you do.'

'How is he?'

'Still a know-it-all.'

'And the other one – Bent?'

He breathed a half-breath. 'He'll be all good. Last time I was there didn't go too well neither. And it'd been a while. Was always going to be some beef.'

'Beef?'

'Ā tōna wā. Let's catch up inside, aye.'

We weren't far from the house; I had carved only 30 metres down one side of the track.

Tea scanned the whole of our basin. His eyes stayed mostly on the house, though he did his best to acknowledge my mahi. 'Right to wait for the rain,' he said. 'Water does well to soften the ground. Old trick of Rehua. Where would we be without his kete, aye?' He moved as if to laugh but remembering something, kept a serious expression. 'Won't stay soft, though. Weather will clear and the earth will up and harden again. After that, you're pretty much stuffed.'

I nodded, though I remembered all I did for the old man. Tea might not believe it, but I could carve the track even in the driest of conditions. The old man did it. I could do it too.

'Hei aha. I can help you while I'm around. Would be doing me a favour. Used to love a bit of gardening. Don't find it in the city like you find it out here.'

He leaned one arm on the storm-bent railing, lifting one knee then crashing his boot down on the timber. The pisshead then did the same on the other side.

'Life in the city has made these bones soft,' he said.

'I reckon,' he continued as if unable to stop, 'if it weren't for your happening there, boy, I would've let that place kill me.' He drew his thumb across his neck. 'Happens to everyone there eventually. Except that goddamn barman – he will live forever.' He laughed. 'Poor bastard. Hoi anō: Never even thought about leaving the pub until the night we met.' He filled his lungs with air. 'Men like me aren't meant for long lives.'

His eyes watched a faraway world and his shoulders rose into his neck. His jaw clenched.

'You get me, boy?'

I shook my head in the hopes that he might speak more straight, lay bare all he meant to say.

'Hei aha. Probably for the best.'

The setting sun coloured the earth with a red glow, its shine illuminating the house and the pisshead. Their shadows blurred into the beginning of the night. Tea stretched a shaky hand to the front door and gripped its handle tight, breathing in a broken rhythm. He opened the door, revealing the kid soaked in soap and water.

Black froze and looked the stranger in his eyes. They stood in silence, their lips parting and their mouths closing and the sides of their jaws bulging and their throats convulsing as they swallowed the unease that built up.

Tea, trying to break the tension, greeted the kid with a feigned softness. 'E tama, tēnā koe.' He smiled a strained smile, the best he could muster.

The kid caught sight of me and ran to my side.

'This is him, bro. The one I said would come.'

The kid distanced himself from the stranger, ready to boost it. Tea paused and pierced his eyes. He seemed to be searching for something. What it was, I couldn't see. He combed his hair, double blinked his eyes and resumed a friendly expression. 'Should probably get back to whatever you were doing, aye,' he said. 'Nothing like a bit of mahi to make the body strong.'

The kid checked my expression, nodded and said jack, limping off into Mum's room.

'He okay?' Tea asked.

'Just cut his foot,' I replied and led him to the table.

Tea sat heavy on his chair and set his eyes on me. He opened his mouth to speak, but closed it again as the hurt in his eyes seemed to increase. What could cause a man so full of words to lose his voice?

My body shook in anticipation; my throat seized as quiet settled over the room. The whole house felt like it was about to cave in upon me. A part of me wished it would. The only relief was a single stream of silver moonlight shining through a tear in the blinds. It marked the beginning of what was sure to be a long night.

Tea edged towards me and stood and rested his hands on the kitchen table, staring at the strip of silver light. He parted his lips and said jack, his eyes darkening, his face twisting. His thumbs rolled against his fingers. Then, with a heavy sigh, he killed the silence.

'After all that crap with Bent,' he said, 'I met Koro at his place. Was something suspect going on, yah know. Had to sort it out. Figured David would know what's up. Fucken know-it-all.

'You've got to understand, boy, that man made it his business to know the city inside and out. He was connected that way. Had all sorts of strangers sit in those pews and gossip and share their life's story. Just the way he was. The real deal, yah know. Heartie. Hoi anō: Went to see him. Kanohi ki te kanohi. Knew if anyone knew anything it was gonna be him.

'And so, what's next won't be easy. But I heard it from the minister himself.' Tea breathed a broken breath and set his eyes on me, his face shining silver. 'Ratshit as the truth is. You deserve to know.'

'The kid ain't your brother. Was born to a different man. Your old lady cheated, boy. With Bent.'

24

Tea recalled his conversation with Koro David, speaking a solid hour of I-saids and he-saids, recounting even the most mundane of details.

'It was fucked, aye. The dickhead just went on and on, walking backwards and forwards and backwards and forwards, looking to the sky like his Lord was looking right back at him.'

He licked his lips and chugged an invisible drink and took on the air of the minister, his body contorting, stooping at the shoulders, and his voice trembling, his eyes full of energy. I sat in silence, clenching and relaxing my jaw, following Tea with my eyes, but inside me, seeing it all. Koro telling Tea how he stumbled on Bent and the old lady going at it. The more he told, the more I lost myself, a river of emotion swallowing me.

'David reckoned he'd seen something was up with Bent,' Tea said. 'Said he was acting all sorts of strange. Showing up late, leaving early, that sort of thing. Made him worried, yah know. Ain't too much that shakes a young man and ain't none of it good. Good as the Good Book says so anyway. A few days go by apparently and the out-of-it stuff goes on and David makes an effort to keep an eye on him. Popping 'round his whare without notice and walking in on him while he did his studies out the back at church.'

Tea's face flared with anger. 'Can you believe that shit? Calls himself a goddamn Christian and does his own prospect like the police.'

So it went that David kept on keeping on and eventually, Bent as bad a sneak as he is a Christian, he snapped that fella with the old lady. No-one but Bent knows exactly what happened. But they fucked up. And David caught the old lady 'round Bent's pad, the old lady sneaking out in the wee hours of the morning. Fella reckoned she spotted him spotting her and that was that. The affair officially over. Mum gapped it that same week, moving with Dad and a younger me to the wops.

When David asked Bent about it, years later, he claimed they just got caught up. The first time was a mistake and the rest was straight up sin. Bent knew the old lady was pregnant and the baby his. Mum made clear she hadn't slept with the old man in ages – years. Reckoned he had no idea what to do about it, though. The old lady was never gonna leave the old man, fuck knows why, and the old man s'posedly asked no questions. Went along with it all.

'The whole thing was a trip,' Tea said. 'I've never heard anything like it. David didn't skip a fucken detail. I know real-deal court cases that didn't dive as deep as he did.'

It all started after Tea left, the old lady and Bent spending every Saturday together, mopping and sweeping and decorating the place. They joked and teased and fell in love with each other, just the way it happens with young people, with a too-long look and a protesting-too-much and so many sleepless nights.

'Whatever their feelings were, they never matured, yah know. I left that church and a few months later so did your old lady. David reckoned it wasn't related but who knows? I like to think your old lady saw the same shit I saw and gapped it. The hypocrisy. Unlike me, she returned, though. Was older then, a wife and a mother. Was pissed at the way her life turned out. You ever felt that way, boy?' He paused. 'Hoi anō: Running after nostalgia – that young ihi, yah know, passion – she lost herself. And that was that. They fucked each other.'

In a weird way, it all made sense to me. She ran away and grew old and found a man who was the opposite of her father, a man she thought she could love, her favourite thing about him probably how different he was to anything she'd ever known. Then she bore his child and loved the man all the more for it. But as the child grew (as I grew), they grew apart, the man fucked up by the stress of it all.

Eventually, she must've had enough – taken one beating too many – leaving home to look for all that she'd left behind. She thought she'd found love again but, much like the first time around, it was fuck-all but shame and regret. And so she returned to the old man and left the city, putting as much distance as she could between her and the man she cheated with. Misery following her like a fly follows shit – there and back again.

25

Tea struggled to get the words out, his voice trembling and breaking and shaking and pausing on occasion, a moment for composure, breathing long and heavy breaths and leaning his head back to stare into the ceiling. I held my tongue and listened, my own emotion raging like the rain so many days gone by.

He went on and my mind drifted and I turned to see the hole the old man had made in the wall with a thrown plate. For a decade, I'd thought it was him just being a dickhead like always. Figured Mum's morning sickness had primed his violence. Now I knew the truth. Fella was throwing a fit. He was heartbroken. Betrayed. Still, somewhere deep down, he must've known he'd driven Mum to this. How many times can you put your hands on a woman before she takes her own kind of utu?

He must've known that eventually the old lady would grow so sick of his shit she'd steal back all she gave him. Her love.

Her loyalty. Probably that's why he never threw it in her face. Her cheating. Black was surely a living reminder of his fuck-up. Would explain why he never struck the kid. Was scared of him. Watched him instead like a curse. Mākutu.

Watching Black long enough did change him in the end. He stopped raising his fists at the old lady. Perhaps there was a lesson he learned from the kid. If so, that kid really was magic.

———

I heard something hit the floor and Tea stopped his story and I turned to see Black's face twisted with anger, the floor beneath him soaked in soapy water. The poor thing had heard all he needed to hear. Before I rushed to help the bro, I mouthed the words 'how long?' at Tea and he shook his head. Fella was so lost in our conversation he didn't even notice Black walk right on in. Eavesdropping. Probably wondering why we were taking so long or was feeling brave now and just wanted say tēnā kōrua.

'All good, bro?' I asked, playing it down.

He didn't reply; he stared at me.

Reading the room, Tea fixed his clothes and gapped it, tousling the kid's hair as he passed him by, ducking outside and onto the porch.

'How's the room looking?'

Again I tried to play it off, and again he didn't reply; he just kept staring.

Buying time, I lit a couple of candles to illuminate the room and made him a feed, three slices of rēwena and a small bowl of beans from the kitchen cupboard, placing the plate and the bowl on the table in front of him.

'All yours, bro.'

He shook his head, and I felt the anger rise inside me.

'I get it, Black, but you need to fucken eat, okay? We gotta talk, but we'll do it afterwards. I ain't saying shit to a kid in your condition.'

It was late. He was tired. It'd been a long day. His foot was still hurting from the river. Black wasn't his best self right now. Neither of us were. The least I could do was feed him before explaining how Dad was not his dad and we weren't fully related. Just another whānau of half-castes and half-brothers.

The kid stayed where he was, staring me right in my eyes and the anger burned in my throat. I breathed deep and tried to swallow the anger down, knowing the kid had every reason to be a dickhead right now.

I took the plate to the kid. 'Just have a bite, 'kay?'

He kept on staring, his face screwed up.

'We'll talk after, okay? Promise.'

I nudged him with the plate and he knocked it out of my hands. The plate smashing and the bread soaking up the soap and water.

'The fuck are you on?' I snapped, getting in his face. 'First, you storm in here making Tea feel unwelcome. Great fucken host you are. Then you come at me like I've taken something from you. Like I don't get enough of that from every other ballhead in the wops. Now you wanna waste kai and make even more mahi for us. You sick in the head, Black? Acting like we ain't going through the same shit – like we didn't just both find out our mum's a fucken two-timer.'

'Get stuffed.'

'Say it again. I dare you.'

'Get. Stuffed.'

I grabbed the kid by the scruff of his shirt and he launched himself at me, punching me square in the jaw. Caught off guard, I checked my face with my hands. The kid bent down at his hips and tackled me, the bro too small to get me to the ground. Instead, he drove me into the kitchen cupboards, pinning me and kneeing me over and again in the legs. Coming back to myself, I felt the fire in my hands and grabbed the kid by the back of his head and tore him off me.

Black charged straight back at me, throwing punches in bunches, to my face, to my chest, to my puku. He was small enough that it didn't rock me; still, he'd pissed me off. And so, I shoved the kid. Right to the floor. Not hard enough to hurt him, but enough to make my point: I ain't the one.

The kid shook it off and rushed me again. Ready this time, I got him before he could get me, shoving him again, sending him into the lounge. Tea walked in from the porch and paused at the doorway, probably guessing at what was going on. How else were two boys out in the wops expected to take this news?

One last time, the kid rushed me and, one last time, I sent him backwards. Changing strategy, he backed up, putting space between us, his teeth clenched, loading both his hands with books from the old lady's library, throwing one by one with all the strength he could muster. I shelled up and they rained on me, a hardback book on history smoking me in the nose, the blood running into my mouth.

When at last he was out of ammo, I wiped my face with my arm and walked him down, ready to slap the shit out of him – one good one across the cheek to make my point. How fucken dare he pull this shit. Kid or nah, bad news or nah, you wanna act like a man, you're gonna get treated like one.

———

Before I could make good on my anger, Tea threw himself like a korowai over the kid. He didn't say anything; he didn't need to. I stayed where I was and Black tried to wrestle away the stranger. He couldn't. The whole time, Tea repeated the same five words. You need to breathe, kiddo. The kid screamed to be let go and Tea held on. Speaking the same words. In the same tone.

It went on like this a while longer, Black's voice growing softer. His screaming becoming pleading becoming a whisper. All the while, I paced backwards and forwards, unclenching my fists, pinching my nose and tilting my head back to stop the bleeding. When at last the kid calmed down, Tea let him go, turning to look at me, checking that I had chilled out myself. That I was seeing what he was seeing.

The kid's body was folded over. His face stuck in a permanent wince. His lungs breathed half-breaths. His everything rested against the wall. His legs shook. And he cried, soundlessly, soaking his cheeks and his hands and the carpet with the salt of his tears.

'My bad, Black,' I said, sympathy overcoming me as quickly as the anger did, getting down beside him, Tea resting a hand on the kid's shoulder.

'Is. It. Real?' he said, struggling to speak through his tears.

'Mum cheating?'

'Not that.'

'What then?'

'You. Not being. My bro.'

Before I could answer, the kid buried himself in his hands and cried. He cried harder than I'd ever seen him cry before. Than I'd ever seen anyone cry before. His body convulsed, the whole of him heaving with every breath forced through his tears. And so it went, until he cried himself to sleep, Tea rubbing his back and me just watching. The kid wrapped himself around himself. Became more a koru than a boy.

Like the old lady's necklace, Black's skin turned whalebone white. The candles flickered and the room grew dark and I rolled him into my arms. Tea patted his pockets, searching for a packet of ciggies, then finding none, took the kid's place against the wall. I let the pisshead be; I carried the kid into our bedroom. I lay him down and checked his foot. There was no doubt, the fucken thing was infected. A problem for another day, I reckoned. And I tucked him in. Wiped his tears with the front of my shirt. Left and closed the door. It coasted open as I walked away. And so, I went to close it a second time, looking in on the boy before pulling it shut tight.

There he lay alive and lifeless in the centre of the bed – lost in a sort of purgatory.

Part Three

26

'Fucked that one up,' he said, still resting against the wall.

'Not your fault, Tea. Neither of us knew he could hear us.'

'How much you think he heard?'

'Enough.'

'If it helps, I reckon it's probably for the best anyway. If we got to suffer, might as well suffer the truth.'

I folded my arms across my chest; I whispered my reply. 'I hope so.'

'It'll be okay, boy. Give it time.' His voice shook with doubt. 'Rest for now. Nothing more to do. And I'll catch you tomorrow. We'll figure something out.'

'Tea.' I swallowed the choke in my throat and considered what I was about to say, knowing he'd resist. 'Don't go.' I could hear the kid in my voice. I didn't wanna be left alone. Not tonight. 'Stay with us. We've got a bed, kai. Everything you need.'

He walked to the front door and looked as far into the night as he could look. 'Don't know, aye.'

'What're you gonna do there anyway?' My voice stayed low, the anger in me exhausted. 'Drink, smoke and fall asleep who the fuck knows where?'

'You for real right now?' he snapped, staring through me, his fists clenched at his side.

I stayed where I was, unflinching, channelling the old lady. 'I'm tired, Tea. If you're gonna blow up then just fucken do it.'

A few seconds of tense silence passed and he relaxed his hands. 'My bad, boy.'

'I get it.'

'Sometimes my instincts get the better of me, yah know.'

'I know.'

'I still gotta go, though.'

'You really don't.'

He screwed up his face.

'You remember what you said when you first came here? You wanted to mahi. Well, here it is. Not the track but the kid.'

He combed his hair backward with both his hands, eyes closed, breathing deep breaths and I went on.

'Take the old lady's bed,' I continued.

Tea turned away from me and walked outside and sat on the porch, and I walked to him and lay a hand on his shoulder. The muscle was dense; the man made of concrete. He told me he'd stay, and we spoke a while on the porch, and he asked about that flat patch of earth, and I told him the old man was buried there, and the conversation stopped.

Our paddock stretched into the night. The ruru was out again. The pūkeko too. They each took turns calling to te pō. Tūī aside, there's no birdsong as beautiful as the ruru's. A native sort of lullaby.

Ru-ru. Ru-ru.

I remember walking to the river with the old lady once. Somewhere along the way, we caught two tūī going back and forth on the branch of the harakeke. Was like poetry, trading line for line with each other. We watched them for ages, Mum and I. Their bodies jumped with every call, their chests and throats filling then emptying then filling again, their heads whipping all over the place, looking each other up and down and the wops beyond them, their beaks parting to reveal the pink roofs of their mouths, their korowai fluttering like the wiri of our tūpuna. Mum was overwhelmed by it all. Even cried, her big eyes filled with emotion. Almost cried myself.

When the night grew late, I felt the skin on my arms rise and a film of water coat my eyes. It wasn't sadness, but the last of the sun abandoning us. Tea showed no notice of this change in temperature. I s'pose he'd spent too much of his life enjoying the cold and lightlessness of the night. Soon enough, I coached him to his feet and led him to the old lady's room. We said laters, and the house rung again with silence.

I woke against my bed. Not on it but against it. I had dreamt of something I couldn't recall, its memory escaping me. A new sun kissed the white lips of the windowsill, barely lighting its surface, and the shadows retreated into the corners of the room and the house swayed with the sounds of Tea's sleep.

Black lay in the centre of his unmade bed, packed in a mound of fabric. He looked no better, and he looked no worse. His head leaned off to one side; he hadn't moved in the night. A feeling of fear and familiarity swelled inside me, and yet I reckoned he'd get up soon. I'd always stirred early; he'd always slept late.

I rose with the birds and woke with a splash of water from the rusted bucket we kept in the kitchen, and I went straight back to business, fetching the spade and shovel and working on the track. The mahi was hard today; my arms were knackered, and my back wouldn't pull. Still, I didn't quit; I went on, hacking at the earth and carving out the gutter. I imagined I was Māui's tuakana hacking at his great fish.

Ka aroha. What you get for leaving your catch behind.

In the distance, a man on his quad sailed across the hills, stopping at every gate, dismounting to open it, only to remount, drive, dismount and close each steel thing behind him.

He wore a pair of Stubbies and a singlet, his arms strong and his gut huge and his body dressed in layers of dark hair. Even from this distance, it couldn't be denied. As he drove, his hair blew in the wind, the curly locks on the back of his head like the flax of the piupiu. The other farmers were older. Less built. More hair on their bodies and less hair on their heads. Perhaps he was some kind of contractor. Every now and again they came 'round. Surveyors or fencers. Neither well liked by our tūpuna. This one looked like the former. They came in only two shapes. Young and built like a boar. Or old, leathered from the sun and carved from obsidian. The latter were a special breed. Men as small as me and unstoppable. Old-man strength I heard it called. Raised on the farm well before new tech had made it a rich man's game.

They're how I imagined my tūpuna. Physical marvels. Like the small woman.

An hour passed and my legs grew tired. Though I made little progress on the earth, I was all good. It was enough for now. With a clear head and sore legs, I returned to the house and nodded what's up to Tea. He sat upon the old man's leg rest, shifting and muttering to himself as he moved. Far away in a daydream, he didn't notice me.

'Looking good, old fella,' I said, careful not to jolt him.

He looked at me, but he didn't reply straight away. 'Too good,' he said, at last, speaking with the rhythm of a man new to the tongue. 'Ana. Too good. Ain't slept that well in fucken ages. Not since I was a boy myself.' He blinked and rubbed his eyes. 'My kind don't ever sleep too well, yah know. All kinds of evil visits us in the night. Still,' he shook his head and resumed an easy tone, 'should probably mihi to you. Without you, would still be slumming it in the streets.' A flash of shame fell over him. 'He pātai nei māku: Do I look a little less old today? Feel a little less old. Couldn't find a mirror, though.'

'Yeah, definitely,' I said, and I wasn't lying.

He went on, his talk trivial and troubled, a subtle war taking place within him. Despite his trying, he couldn't keep it from leaking into his speech. It hinted at the absence of something. Something unloved but missed. 'Nei rā te mihi atu,' he repeated, speaking a phrase he had spoken two times already. 'How's the bro anyway? Been meaning to check him, yah know, after everything that went down.'

'He's okay. Still sleeping. The kid's young, growing. Needs it more than us.'

'And his foot?'

I shrugged my shoulders. 'Infected maybe. I can't tell for sure.'

'Kid needs some strong spirits: one hundred proof. Shit kills bugs faster than it kills men.'

27

The kid slept on and I rewrapped his wound, cleaning it with a
one-two combo of soapy water and spit, rewrapping it with a new
tea towel. Wop-wop medicine. He winced and opened his eyes a
moment, pulling his feet away from me, mumbling. I told him
to go back to sleep and he did. The rest of my morning, I spent
passing the time. I had a good wash, 'specially my hands after
touching the kid's cut, and changed my clothes and tried to read
that book on the old lady's bedside table. The whole time, the call
of the city grew stronger. It was as if Tea's craving was contagious.
There were moments when I would've sworn I felt its literal pull.

I had an early lunch on the porch. A half loaf of takakau and
a cup of water to make the going down easier. Stuff was reka but
goddamn was it dry.

The paddocks were empty, no more cows and no more men
on quads sailing across the top of their hills. Their odours still

165

hung in the air, fuel and fertiliser, gas and piss and manure. Their smell would stay days after the animals themselves had left. The manu filling their lungs with that vile stuff and the plants forced to carve their way through it. Not to mention those of us who have to look at those paddocks every day, knowing whose bones lied beneath all that mess. Haere, haere, haere atu rā.

Tea joined me once I'd finished eating. He didn't say anything – he didn't need to – he simply sat beside me on the porch. We watched the earth roll into the horizon and listened to the place beyond call to us. Tears. Kauri. The pisshead. The half-brother. We were each captured by its mākutu. The street, the drink, the smoke.

He seemed to grow old in my periphery, gradually becoming again the man I first saw in the pub. It was not his face that changed, it was his being. His mauri. He shrank before me, his spine folding and his neck rolling and his chin jutting forward. The silver in his beard turned grey and the circles under his eyes cast a darker shadow. He curled and uncurled his fingers, sucked his lips, blinked his eyes, tapped his legs, combed his hair, held his breath and sighed. He jittered and twitched.

I watched him, knowing his will wouldn't last. And I began to justify my going to the city with him. Not going for myself, I'd say. Going for Tea. To keep him out of trouble. His life on track. Shit, maybe I'd even find some 100 proof for the kid's foot.

A family of clouds passed by the sun and a chill fell over us, their shadows rolling across the earth like a waka in the ocean, rising and diving with the surface of Papa's chest. They sailed over the house as if it were nothing, their shape changing as they scaled its walls, swam across its broken-tile top. Then into the distance the shadows moved, the family of clouds farewelling the sun. They would come together at the maunga's peak, meet where our tūpuna meet the newly departed to take them back home. To a land that cannot be confiscated.

The city continued to pull, evoking in me something more than desire. Something more intense. Desperate. My will died away, and I found myself weak against my cravings.

I wondered if the tūpuna called the same way the city did. Encouraged the newly departed from their bodies and onto the road the same way the pub encouraged the punters, with their hands outstretched, too ready to return these chiefs to their rightful pā. Of all the tūpuna, I wondered who would do the actual calling. What words would they say to those they welcomed? What looks would they give? Knowing all we've done, could they possibly still love us? (If it's Mum who calls me one day, would I be brave enough to face her?)

I rose from the porch and felt Tea's eyes on me, and I began down the dirt track. Who the fuck is the old lady to judge anyway? It wasn't like she'd never done someone dirty. Dad threw his hands when shit got hard and Mum two-timed and I take off to the city. Might not have done the old man too good but it solved the old lady's troubles. Fixed her marriage. And it wasn't like the kid was going anywhere anyway. The bro was out cold.

———

Tea walked and walked on, saying jack, his eyes glued to the sidewalk. I didn't know where we were going; couldn't even tell which one of us was leading. We walked, each using the other as an excuse. Trying not to remember the sick kid lying in Mum's bed. He wasn't going anywhere, but his sickness wasn't the only problem. Any moment CYPS could come knocking down doors with a warrant to uplift.

A few blocks later, Tea's head lifted. It was a strange lifting, as though against his will. I watched his eyes roam and wondered what evoked this change in him. The buildings were made from brick and timber and painted neutral colours. Windows were smashed and floors were burnt out and the emergency exit stairs bolted to their sides were rusted through. Doors were kicked in and the gutter was dotted with glass and an aroma hung in the air like piss on concrete.

'You know this place?'

'Used to worked here, aye.' He scratched at his beard. 'Helped the people here move.'

Tea dropped his eyes and breathed deep. His past weighed heavy upon him; it broke his posture, beat his body into the sidewalk. I meant to change the subject, to try to raise his spirits, but Tea went on, speaking with a gravelled voice. 'Work was slow. Barely made enough to get by . . . Few but the heartbroken move 'round here. And none move far.

168

'We mostly ended up working for the kutukutu. That's what our tūpuna called 'em. Maggots, yah know. The kind to see people hurting and think opportunity. Heaps of them 'round here. Hoi anō: Was all a poai like me could do to keep from starving. Was what, sixteen, seventeen. Clashed bad with David the year before – couldn't stand the way they treated every sorry sack of shit 'round here who didn't pray the same way they did – and gapped it from the church. After I was cut off, that was the only work I could find.

'Didn't keep the job for long. Came and went away pretty fast, aye. Probably shouldn't tell you why.' He paused. 'But I reckon I will anyway. Got to tell someone sooner or later.' He combed his hair hard, separating its locks with the nails of his hand. 'So, this ballhead hired me to help him move. One of the kutukutu. The kind who got rich on false promises. "What you give to me," he used to preach, "the Heavenly Father will give thrice to you." That brand of man, yah know. Fella sold salvation as if it could be bought. 'Course they gave and gave and gave. 'Else are the desperate s'posed to do? And 'course nothing changed. The poor stayed poor. Were made poorer.

'Eventually, I just couldn't handle it, aye. Stand by. Watch this ballhead get away with it. So the day of the move comes. Me and another fella loaded then unloaded this preacher man's gears at his new whare, each keeping two pockets full of jewellery and a bottle of piss for ourselves. Barely a dent in the fella's pockets, but it was the precedent of the thing. Boss couldn't prove nothing but fired us anyway. We kicked up a fuss for appearances then let some time

pass 'fore we rolled back through the hood and sold that shit cheap
to one of the chapters, if yah know what I mean. We both done
our time with that lot – my partner more than me. Some of that
cash we shared with those we knew were having a rough go, big
families in small houses and that kind of thing. Helped ease the
guilt. The rest, like the piss, we kept for ourselves.

'Was a righteous act, we reckoned. Told ourselves we'd done it
for our tūpuna. They'd fought and died for such an opportunity.
To return a fraction of what was stolen.

'Wasn't just the two of us alone in it either. Kāo. Were revered by
those few we helped, yah know. "The poor man's saints," they called
us. And we gapped it anyway. Figured it was only a matter of time
'fore somebody came knocking. The kutukutu or someone else.' He
scratched at his beard. 'Anyway, a little time goes by and we found
ourselves just like the ones we'd tried to help. Poor and without
the gear to feed ourselves. House ourselves. Where we split, yah
know. Went our separate ways. Me falling in with the taniwha.
And your old man falling in with your old lady.'

The hair on my arms stood on their ends. Time slowed. My
throat swelled almost all the way closed. My stomach twisted. I felt
like I was gonna vomit. Cry. My every heartbeat radiated through
my body. A rush of heat flushed my face. My legs went weak. My
vision closed like a fist. Tea's voice played again in my head.
I double blinked my eyes. And shook my head. And fought back
my closing vision, turning to him and fighting to reply.

'For real?'

'That's where we met, aye. Me and your old man. Me black as night and your pa pale as the moon, both working that job for the kutukutu. Spent a good year getting to know each other 'fore we went our separate ways. Heard it happened heaps back in the day. Māori and Irish bonding over a common enemy.' I was struck dumb, and Tea continued with his story. 'Was a good man, your pa. As good a man can be, given the hell he'd been through. State care then juvie then gang shit – not that he was one for talking, let alone sharing. Without a doubt, he was a real-deal rebel. An OG. Loved Māori music. And women.' He shrugged a take-it-or-leave-it shrug. 'Fucken hated the reo, though. Was paranoid, I reckon. A part of the lifestyle. Made him worry shit was being kept from him. Hoi anō: Didn't see him again for ages after that. Met again by accident. At the pub. Meantime, I kept myself busy rolling over the rich.

'It's crazy how much expensive shit is only a smashed window away. I shared most of what I took. Kept enough to keep myself alive. As time went on, I started rolling over the little-bit-less-than-rich. And shared less, 'cause I had less to share.' He winced, like his conscience had slapped him across the face. 'Went on like that 'til I was taking from anybody and giving nothing back.

'Wasn't a good life. Trust me. Just was what it was. Took whatever I needed from whoever had it.'

He paused a long while, rubbing his eyes. 'I reckon,' he said, 'that's what haunts me more than anything. Not the crime itself . . . That I got away with it. All this sin and I was living better than ever. What fucken God would allow that?'

171

I had no way of understanding everything Tea said. If I didn't know him better, I would've sworn him heartless. In no way did the label stick. He was many things but, through them all, you could see the heart in him. It beat with desire and regret, compassion and contempt, love and its opposite, whatever the hell that is. I s'pose he shared his story as a sort of confession, an expression of vulnerability. My mahi (my departing from the porch) had made me weak and he made himself weak in turn.

And yet, there remained all he said about the old man. Had life changed him as it'd changed Tea, turning even his better instincts into vices, transforming the steelen-from-the-rich-to-give-to-the-poor man into that violent thing that loved and didn't love the old lady? Or were both these things always in him, Robin Hood and a hood upbringing?

28

A dog lay stretched out beside a frazzled old man. They lived in a kingdom of tobacco and blankets; those linen things packed up higher than the dog was tall. The frazzled man's beard was long and knotted. Brown at its ends and grey everywhere else. He sat with his legs folded, his body bent over, the piles of clothes he was wearing bunching above his knees. Three t-shirts and a sweater. A jacket and a brown feathered cloak.

A woman with a plastic bottle got down low beside him and filled his dog bowl with water, a blue ice-cream container missing its lid, stroking the dog before she went on. Both the man and the dog stayed still (wagging tail aside), resting on a thick duvet. It still had its tag.

Dry clean or gentle hand wash. Do not tumble dry.

We turned down a quiet city block and the sun rose above the city's skyline. It lit the way and left our shadows small, warmth overcoming us and blinding rays shining down. As we approached the small woman's store, another change washed over Tea. His steps became small. Fella started to drag his leg. He bowed his head and lowered his eyes, drifting further and further behind, then stopping a few metres from the glass door. I waved him on, and he stayed there. Watching me, wide-eyed and frozen.

I nodded and allowed him the moment. This place inspired in me the same awe the first time I laid my eyes on it – the store so warm and clean and different than everything else 'round here. He'd join me when he was ready, I assured myself, going on without him. When I walked through the door and looked back at Tea, I saw him peering through the pane-glass windows with a wrinkled brow, his eyes afire with guilt. They didn't see me anymore; they watched the small woman.

'E tama,' she said, wiping the remnants of flour from her well-worn apron. 'Nau mai, nau mai. How's the little one?' She stopped, noticing Tea.

He swung his head to hide his face, then took off down the street, out of sight. The small woman pierced her eyes. No doubt wondering why the pisshead was acting like such a weirdo.

'He cut his foot,' I said.

'That won't do.' She kept her eyes on the street a little longer then turned to give me her full attention. 'Rangatahis are always getting up to mischief. Koirā tāna mahi. It healing okay?'

'Might be infected, I dunno.'

'Pae kare. That's no good. Ever tell you I got two of my own,

174

e tama? My Lord, do I know the work it takes. My two were always playing up. How are you looking after him?'

'Soapy water and spit, mostly.'

'Spit?'

'Old Māori medicine.'

'Hika mā. I've never heard that one.'

'Mum said so when I was little.'

'She being honest, you think, or?'

Oh shit, I thought. The old lady was straight lying to get me to stop crying. Same way she used to get me to hold my breath.

'Hei aha tērā,' the small woman said, pausing unnaturally. 'Who do you stay with anyway?'

'Just me and the bro at the moment . . . Oh and the man outside. Tears.'

'Ko wai ia?'

'Well, he's got a few names, to be honest. Mostly we just call him Tea and Tears.' Her brow furrowed. 'Reckon I should apologise for him. He's a bit sick himself. Used to drink and smoke and spend every night in the pub.'

'Is that so?'

I nodded my head.

'You know which one?'

'Dunno but it plays Māori music.'

'Tika?'

'He doesn't drink anymore, though, doesn't smoke. Fella's really going through it.'

'Ka aroha,' she said, moving her eyes back to the street.

She narrowed her eyes, the folds of her skin creasing in their corners. Like the minister, her old age was most obvious in her pupils, their colour cloudy 'round their edge.

'My Lord,' the small woman snapped, whipping her head, 'the kid's cut. I almost forgot. Back in a minute, e tama.' She disappeared behind the counter and the door behind it.

Waiting for the small woman, I thought about the way Tea had looked at her, his panicked face making clear she was to him some kind of kēhua. An unwelcome reminder. Of what, I didn't know. Maybe she was a victim of his steelen. She would be an easy mark after all, trusting and easily taken from.

The small woman reappeared holding a brown paper bag sealed down in her usual manner, pausing along her journey to catch her breath. Her frailty made me sorry for her. 'My body doesn't always do as I ask these days.' She laughed, gifting me the brown paper bag. For the first time, I laughed with her. I couldn't help myself. Why would anyone steal from someone so generous?

At length, she spoke of the plant medicine in the brown paper bag. Rongoā from the land before this one (Hawaiki) passed on to her by her mother and to her by her mother and so it went until the waka. I listened closely, her talking about history reminding me of Mum. When she finished, she offered me another ride in her neighbour's car and I shook my head and she sent me on my way. 'Straight back to the kid now, you hear.'

I asked myself again: Why would anyone steal from someone like this?

29

The city was still. The roads were empty, the only signs of life the garbage blowing in the wind.

The rest of the walk home was lame. It was cold. The animals had settled, most too tired to look as I passed them by. They kept on doing only what they always did. Chewing the cud. Pacing. Polluting.

The sky was pink. One half of its border a trim of red and the other orange and yellow. It washed over the sky in streaks. Its colour most dense at the horizon, the rest of it spread across Rangi's coat, stretching all away across the heavens. Like a wave, it washed over the sky. Lifting, peaking, at last crashing upon the rolling fields. I walked on and I felt a growing uneasiness. This feeling settled only as I crossed from the pavement onto the track and saw the front door open and rocking in the wind. Tea had made it home. Or the kid had got up.

The soil was firm beneath my feet, the earth hardening as the last of the rain evaporated. A chill carried in the wind. An eerie cold, like the one that would follow the old man home from his playing up in the city. If I were superstitious, I would've taken it as a sign of something cruel to come.

I kept going and soon saw more than the front door open. Every door except the kid's hung from its hinges. He must've gone on sleeping. This left only a single possibility. Tea's criminal past flashed before me and I felt the chill stronger than ever and my unease returned. I feared the worst and ran inside the house and called his name. 'Tea.' The sound of my voice echoed. There came no reply. Bar the kid, the house was empty. My fear grew worse and I felt the beginnings of betrayal fill my lungs.

In my head, I saw Tea stumbling through the front door, tearing through every cupboard and room, desperately searching for anything that could be sold. I saw him in the kitchen, in the bathroom, in the old lady's room, laid out on his stomach, rummaging through the shoebox hidden beneath her bed, that cardboard bank stuffed with banknotes and plastic baggies filled with coins. I saw the thrill on his face when he found it and I heard the gasp he made as he took a quick account of his new riches. I saw him scramble and panic and close the shoebox tight, and I saw him shoot through the front door with an excited limp.

———

My fears were false. Nothing was missing. Not the shoebox nor the bread nor the tools nor the leather-bound book on the bedside table. The fucken doors must've opened themselves.

The air stayed cold, settling over the house, burning in my throat as I breathed it in, visible in the air as I breathed it out. Reminding me to stay on guard. I choked back what tears I could and wiped my face with my shirt, heading through to check the kid.

Black laid as the old lady had laid before him. I brushed the hair back from his face and opened the brown paper bag. Out tipped a silver spoon and a small glass jar. The jar was dark with a twisted lid, a gluey residue on one side of its shape. At last came a neat handwritten message, a blue-lined page with rounded corners torn clean from the spine of a notebook.

For the little one,
To be taken after the sun rises and again after it has set.
Piki te ora.

The note read with the small woman's warmth. Each syllable sounded in my head as if from the source herself. I filled the silver spoon with the plant medicine. My nostrils tensed in anticipation of a godawful smell, but the rongoā dripped and the spoon filled and I couldn't smell shit.

I edged the kid's mouth open with my thumb and forefinger and let the medicine fall upon his tongue and run down the back of his throat. Black continued his sickly sleep. I placed the bottle and the note and the silver spoon on the bedside table, and I tucked the bro back into bed, moulding the blankets around him, brushing his hair one last time, listening to him breathe.

'Half-castes are still Māori. And half-brothers are still brothers. You know that aye, bro?'

He rested in the dent his body had carved into the mattress, looking more like pounamu than flesh and blood.

30

The next day, progress on the track was slow. Three hours passed and I'd carved little more than another nine metres from the house. At this pace, it'd take half a week to dig this border and another to dig out its opposite. CYPS would be here long before I could finish.

At this point, they weren't really the reason I was doing this anyway. It was for the kid – he wanted to pretty this place up – and Tea reckoned I wasn't man enough to carve this track when it dried, and it was for myself most of all. If I could do the track better than the old man did it, maybe I could raise the kid better than Dad did too.

Frustrated by the lack of progress, I rested on the porch with bread and water. There seemed nothing I could do well. When I'd eaten all I could bear to eat, I went back to my mahi. So I went, repeating myself 'til the sun was swallowed by the hills and the new moon rose across the way. I didn't check the kid; he needed the rest.

When it got dark, I gave him his second dose of the day. He reacted the same way he did in the morning. Choking it back without a wince or a flutter of his eyelids. I tucked him back into the bed, tucking his blankets beneath him. His foot was looking better today, cleaned with soapy water (no spit) and rewrapped in a tea towel. And his skin was looking worse. Whiter than whalebone. Yesterday, he opened his eyes and I encouraged him back to sleep; today he slept right through.

The more I thought about the kid, the more I thought about the old man and the more I wished the old lady would come back to us. She'd know how to look after Black. How to make him better. She knew everything about everything. Deserved so much more than what she got, so much more than a shithole house in the wops. An unmarked grave. Tomorrow I'll look for her, I thought. I didn't know where I'd look, but I'd look anyway. I nudged the kid with my elbow – 'Right thing to do aye, bro' – then left the room and lay down on her bed.

When morning came, I didn't hesitate. I ate and washed and looked after the kid then set myself to finding Mum. The earth woke up cold, the sun shining a soft orange light. Papa welcomed my looking for the old lady. There was no better weather to unbury a body. The orange light would hide jack, the cold would keep me focused.

I started at the old man's grave. Its shape and size showed me just how the dead disturb the earth. Although the old man hadn't been buried long, his example was the best these parts could provide. The earth ever so slightly raised and the soil a lighter shade of brown. I walked to the top of the basin behind the house, half-concealed masses of stone marking the earth's skin like scars, and kicked at the dirt with my feet. The old man would've buried Mum high, anywhere else and the rain would've got her. While it didn't rain here often, Dad was a practical man. He must've buried her high. Any other place and we would've found her by accident already.

A third of the paddocks behind the house were fenced and unfarmed. Some man overseas had bought them on a map then sailed over only to find them useless. The soil wouldn't grow maize and the cattle were always breaking their legs on the stones. In a year, fed-up, he got on another ship and returned from where he came, and the land became ownerless. Seeing the state of it all, no other farmer would buy him out. Place was cursed, the rumours went. And so the stories spread like wildfire, tales of what'd been done to the locals to move them on, and what they'd done in return. Utu.

A whole tribe condemned without an honest trial to be hanged and quartered. Then shipped down south for hard labour instead. Die anyway. Be buried anonymously.

The women and children packed their stuff and left. Moved someplace different. Making sure as a parting gift that all who occupied this land would hurt as their sons and husbands and fathers and koros were made to hurt. Mum said her koroua was a kid at the time. Said he remembered leaving but didn't remember any mākutu. Only a karakia before they made their way to the city. A few sad songs along the way. Don't tell the farmers that, though, he told her. Better to leave that superstitious lot alone.

————

The sun rose higher and the light shone brighter, and I was no closer to finding the old lady than when I began. She could be anywhere. In any paddock. Wasn't like the old man gave a fuck about property rights. Her grave only needed to be higher than the earth around it, high enough to avoid the flooding of the rain. Over one last fence and through one last paddock, I returned to the house for some takakau. I washed my hands and ate and tried as best I could to remember the morning that I found her lifeless. Transformed into a tekoteko.

I recalled seeing her. I recalled watching her until the old man woke. Something held me at that moment. I couldn't move. Couldn't cry. Couldn't do anything but watch. If I felt anything, I don't remember it. If I thought anything, I don't remember it. It was like a dream.

The week that followed was more of the same. No thinking, no feeling. Whatever held me wouldn't leave.

It was worse for the kid. He didn't get to see the old lady lifeless in her bed. (I'd always stirred early; he'd always slept late.) Don't think anyone ever told him either. Not out loud. She carried him to bed one night then disappeared, vanishing into the wind. No-one even seeming to notice she was missing.

Poor thing must've been so scared of the answer, he didn't ask where she went 'til a whole day had passed us by.

'Where's Mum, Kau?'

'Gone.'

'Gone?'

'Gone gone.'

'Oh.'

31

There were times in my life when they got along, the old man and the old lady. Times when I saw the love that once was, the man the old man used to be. He would stand over her and she'd rest her head against him. He would look at her and she'd smile. I was younger then, the whole of it confused me. Fighting then loving each other then fighting again. It was only when I grew older and these moments became more rare that I came to appreciate them. Began to miss them. The loving – if it could be called loving – between the fighting faded and went away. I didn't know why. I was younger then, I didn't get it. Even now it makes no sense to me.

I chewed the last of the bread and drank the last of the water, and heard the kid stir next door, the sound of his rusted bedsprings echoing through the house. He can't have moved much, to be honest, the sound was too short. Still, he moved and that had to mean he was getting better – it had to.

The maunga was uncovered, not a cloud surrounding him. What a chief he must've been. I've heard of Māori who wore the feathers of the albatross and Māori who wore leaves of kawakawa. But I've never heard of a Māori so respected he wore a coat of snow.

Birdsongs carried in the air. The incessant chatter of magpies and the cheeping and chirping of fat little birds. Sparrows and finches. Arrows of ducks flew overhead, their quacking erupting and disappearing as their family V steered through the sky. Far off and away, a hawk circled his pā. He wouldn't dare come this way. Magpies are a ruthless bunch. Many times, I've watched them swoop on the mighty hawk, chasing him to the horizon in a wild display of grace and control, swimming through the air as the tuna through the tide. Mum told me our tūpuna learned many things from the birds. How to speak and sing. Maybe they even learned war too. She did say while some of our lot wore feathers in their hair, others wore feathers on their weapons.

The kid stirred again.

———

Black lay as he'd lain the last two days, his face thinning and caving in and around his skull.

The pale colour that streaked his skin radiated like the late rays of the sun. Soft hints of darker shades folded into the sockets of his eyes. They were closed and did not move; the yellow hue that circled them had disappeared. If this was any sign of getting better,

I didn't trust it. I'd seen yellow eyes on the living; I hadn't seen these shades of blue and green. Beads of sweat sat clean against his forehead. They shone in the light of the bedroom. A glow leaking in from outside.

I stripped the kid down to his gruts and wiped him down and wet his hair. Feels like I've spent a good fucken year doing this sort of stuff. Looking after people. The old man. The kid. Black's body was limp. If it weren't for his gentle breathing, I might've thought he was dead.

He didn't stir in my company. There was no reason for hope, and still, I felt it. One day soon, I reckoned, with the help of the small woman's medicine, he would get up and be himself. His cheeks would become chubby again. I nodded, reassuring myself, and I dried his hair, and I swapped his pillow for Mum's. Hers was not wet with sweat. I fixed his bed and combed his hair back, the heat of his head warming the tips of my fingers. Finally, I adjusted the bedsheet blinds and kept the bedroom door a little open. By dark, I would know whether it was the sun or his sickness that made him sweat.

———

My search for the old lady didn't go any better in the afternoon light.

The sun grew hot; waves of heat lifting from the mounds of rock. A quiet searing. No cluster of clouds floated across the heavens. Nothing to shield Papa from his harsh rays. She and I would have to suffer his revenge.

That's how it felt. Like the sun's utu against the man who crippled him. (You aren't Māui, boy, he must've said. But you are his kin and that's good enough.) When I looked to it, I thought I saw it look back, a blue-white face scowling behind its blinding light. I pūkana'd and tried to earn its respect with an I-belong-here-too fire burning in my eyes. Was no use. That great ball of fire saw through my trickery and did only as it always did.

I walked and walked and tried to find the old lady. I had no real way of finding her; I let the fences guide me. A minute passed, then ten, then an hour. There was no sign of her anywhere.

———

A gang of rabbits wove through a field of gorse, their tails popping in and out of a sea of green. The gorse was protection for all kinds of pests. Rabbits and weasels and stoats and possums. No hawk could get them. Neither the farmers nor their guns nor their dogs. The road does the most to cull these pests. But it cuts both ways. No special thing to see a pūkeko driven into the asphalt. No-one drives slowly through the wops.

The river 'round here is deep – the same one as our bend. Has the same mauri, that same feel on the skin. Only difference is the water here runs fast, no grass growing along its bank, all of it naked, worn down to nothing but wet-black soil and a collection of sticks and branches and river plants washed ashore. I remember visiting this place when I was younger; I thought the rush of the river would make the washing easier. One day, I brought a bedsheet from the house and washed it here instead of the stream. Fucken thing almost killed me. The moment the linen touched the water, the tide took it as its own, ripping that thing from my hands. Bastard thing almost took me too, my feet slipping down the bank, the earth catching me only an inch from the water's edge.

I should've drowned that day. That's probably why Mum didn't growl me for losing the sheet. Why Dad didn't kick my ass. My almost dying was lesson enough.

That bedsheet had tossed and turned in the tide; it wrestled with the water and lost. I'd walked beside the river the whole afternoon, hoping the linen might've snagged somewhere along the way. The further I'd walked, the higher the river rose and the more forcefully it pulled. And I learned that what the tide took would be gone forever.

Standing on the highest hill, I watched the river roar. Rushing, pulling, tearing. And I decided to follow it a while. I pictured the old man walking the neighbouring bank, Mum's body in his arms. He cradled her, keeping his love close. His eyes were dry, fixed on the horizon. He didn't dare look at the unbreathing thing he held. His boots beat the grass flat, the soil rising around them, staining their bottom brown, everything except the gorse being crushed beneath him, dandelions and other pretty things I do not know by name. Beads of sweat pooled and ran down his scars and stained the collar of his shirt grey. He was a mighty man, but even mighty men are poisoned by knackeredness. Her body bounced as he walked. She did not melt into him. Her frame was stiff. Like deadwood.

The old man would've said jack the whole way. They only spoke when necessary. When it couldn't be avoided. Their last walk would've been silent. Beginning to end.

I saw it all. As real as the hills and the river, it played before me. He in his military boots, black trousers and brown coat, reeking with the scent of smoke and reeling from the night before. She in her track pants and a tee, her whalebone koru hanging from her neck, dancing one last time in her lover's arms. The last of it began with a too-far stare and a too-short pause, the old man coming to a halt. He reached his arms straight and let the old lady fall, the deadwood woman's arms barely lifting as she fell through the air and into the earth. Like rain, she settled into the soil. No monument to set her place but a patch of disturbed dirt.

The old man stood there a little while longer. His hands were empty, his eyes dry and swollen. The light of the day settled and a soft breeze followed the bank and the old man's coat kissed his frame, its tail shifting to and fro. This was no mighty thing. This was a thing different than the thing who walked here. Something had changed. Dad stayed another moment. And he didn't speak. And he turned and walked away. The man who left – the man who returned – the man we buried. It only made sense, I s'pose. He'd buried the only one who really loved him after all. Her and the kid.

32

I followed the vision of the old man home. He walked with a steady gait, never once turning back. His boots sank deeper into the earth with every step, the soil colouring the legs of his trousers a dirt brown.

Fella didn't even stop when he got home. The old man went on. Joined the path he carved, not bothering to check on his kids. The one who found his old lady dead. The two who'd lost their mum. Through the lounge window, a younger me watched the old man. He didn't cry. Didn't chase him down. He watched him walk away. It was only now I knew where he was going.

The dirt track glittered with the last of the light and its border (the one I'd carved) reached for the pavement, a spade and shovel marking its end. I barely recognised this place. It bore so little semblance to its younger self. The path had warped and become corrupt, and the bone tree had gone into the smoke, and the grass was littered with the charred remains of the great fire, and the porch had edged into the earth, and its timber was dotted with the frayed corduroy remains of the old man's couch. Nothing was like it was. It'd all changed. Even the tools. They were blunt, misshapen. Marked with dirt.

The old man didn't take them with him. He'd carried the old lady with both his arms. I never asked him how he managed it. How he lay her to rest. If I were him, I would've cast her into the river. A man should lie as he lived. And maybe he did. The cuffs of his jacket were clean after all. He didn't dig with his hands.

I saw a new version in my head, her track pants and t-shirt dancing in the tide. As she fell, they clung to her, disappearing into the river's murky waters. The awa carried her and her clothes with the sticks and branches and plants from further up. It lifted them and would not put them down. It carried them into the horizon. Her clothes spun and turned, bloating, filling and rolling over her, the deadwood woman moving as one with the water. A part of me loved the idea of a river tangihanga. It would've been a powerful final performance. One last dance. A true tribute to a life half-lived.

———

I sat on the porch and watched the last of the setting sun, a darkness drawing across the east. A single star stayed bright in the west, calling its whanaunga to life. Slowly, they woke, one by one.

Then they disappeared, Rangi's coat covering them. I couldn't stand to watch it, and I couldn't look away.

After the last star was swallowed, I stood in the lounge, the ghost of the couch haunting its centre. The leg rest. Its cushion folded two times with the memory of the old man. The house rang with silence, its walls shaking with the absence of sound. I'd hoped when I got back I'd be blessed by another vision of the old man. I'd hoped I'd see him get back from the city and comatose. Neither he nor his couch showed up. The empty room and the silence reigned.

I checked the kid. He was no better and he was no worse. I sat beside him, nudged him with my elbow and told him everything I'd done today, everything I'd seen. I lifted his body onto my knees and cradled him close to my chest. Rife with sweat, his hair stuck to his forehead. I combed it back with my fingers and saw how a dead shade of grey ran from his hairline into the blues and greens of the skin around his eyes.

I cradled his head into the bend of my elbow. 'Just gonna give you some rongoā.' His mouth hung open, his lips barely moving when he breathed. I poured the small woman's medicine onto the silver spoon. 'Stuff ain't yum, I know.' I edged the spoon into his mouth and let it run down the back of his throat. 'But it's good for you.'

Black coughed and spluttered and his whole body tensed, beginning to spasm, and I held him tight. Soon after, his muscles relaxed, his head falling into the crook of my arm and his eyes staying closed. I rocked back and forth, calling for the kid to wake. 'You're all good, bro. Time to get up now.' The bed creaked and rocked with me and the headboard tapped against the wall. The whole time, I held him, rocking on, repeating the words like they were karakia.

The night stole the old lady from me. The night stole the old man. It couldn't have the bro now, the last of my whānau. Nothing great nor strong could take him away from my arms. Not CYPS to throw him in with a stranger. They'd already had Dad; there was no way in hell they'd get Black too. Nor some know-it-all doctor to tell him he was fine anyway. Motherfuckers had killed enough of us. The kid settled into my arms. And I sighed and looked to the ceiling. My eyes welled up but I refused the tears. I lay him down, fixing his bed and tucking him tight. Hugging his blankets around him. Hoping I was right to keep him in the wops.

I ran my fingers through his hair once more and left him, retreating into the lounge. My arms were weary and my breath was short. I was ready to sleep. The light behind the bedsheet blinds and its sister shadow ran around the room, each chasing but never catching their opposite. With one final look, I closed the door. At last, the shadow caught the light, swallowing the room and the kid in it.

Knackeredness overcame me, and I walked slowly across the room, stopping in front of the old man's leg rest. My eyes weighed heavy and fell shut without my asking them to. I lay down, bending my body forward, and catching myself with numb arms, rolling, falling into the floor. The cry of the floorboards echoed through the house.

I was so damn tired. The old man, the kid, the pisshead. Over and again, I found myself doing the same stuff. Not knowing what was best. Unable to separate my instincts from my anxiety. My life spiralling into sickness and death. That fern never unfurling.

33

Just as it looked like maybe this motherfucker of a day had come
to an end, Tea stood watching me inside the doorframe. He was
dressed in a fraying pair of trousers and a white collared shirt and a
tan coat. His clothes were marred in dirt and dust, a splash of red
painting the cuff of his shirt, a little bit wiped across his chest. He
reeked of piss, a third of a bottle of vodka in his hand: 100 proof.

The candlelight lit a thin layer of sweat kissing his forehead and
I rose to my feet to get a better look at him. His face was tortured,
his eyes bloodshot, the skin around them black, his cheeks sunken.
Worse were his hands, both of them trembling.

'You good, Tea?'

'We gotta talk.'

'We'll catch up outside then, aye.' I gestured to the door, fear
taking the place of my fatigue. 'Kid's still sleeping.'

He pointed the base of the bottle at me. 'For his foot.' Then lay it down inside the door and dragged himself to the porch. I followed him from a good distance and closed the door behind me, guarding Black against the cold of the night.

With restless energy, Tea pushed his hair back from his face, then pulled it forward again so it curled, dark with sweat, over his eyes. I watched the night climb across the sky, hoping Tea would speak soon, praying for an easy explanation of his gapping it and returning looking like this. The booze I wasn't fussed about; it was whatever else he might've brought with him.

The sky was empty of its usual shine, no single star decorating it. Instead hung a lonely moon, barely visible.

'I fucked up,' Tea said.

'What'd you do?'

'I said I stopped.'

'Drinking?'

'Ana.'

'You walked all the way out here to tell me you're on the piss?'

'Puku kau ana,' he barked, a flash of anger rising.

'Was just asking.' I paused and looked him up and down. He looked exhausted. 'All good, though. It's late, aye. Probably just need some rest, maybe a bit of kai.'

'There's no resting no more.'

'I mean, you drank, Tea. We all fuck up. You of all people should know that.'

'You don't get it, do you?'

'Get what?'

'What I've done.'

'The steelen or the drinking?'

'Worse.'

'Worse?'

'Way worse.'

Panicked, I rose to my feet. 'What'd you do, Tea?'

'Nothing that can be undone, I reckon.'

'Just answer me, straight up. The fuck have you done?'

———

Tea held out his hand and I pulled him to his feet, and he stumbled along the porch.

'My whole life,' he said, 'there's been a devil that follows me. I've tried to escape her. Tried to run. Tried to bury her in the piss, yah know. Just couldn't get away.'

'Couldn't get away from who?'

'The devil,' he snapped. 'Thought I could get rid of her. Bury her. But there she was. Watching. Judging.'

'What the hell is happening, Tea? Tell me straight, maybe I can help.'

'There's no helping now. E kore a muri e hokia. Just need you to listen.'

I swallowed down my confusion and let the man speak.

His beard was wiry. It flared from the bottom of his jaw, curling downward. His hair was darkest where it was shortest, around the ears, the remainder of it shades of white and grey. It receded from the front, forming a peak over his forehead, drawing more attention to the scars that decorated his face. The mataora of the street. A history told in broken skin and bones healed crooked. Two chipped teeth.

'I haven't been honest with you, boy. Me and you are cut from the same cloth,' he said. 'Share the same iwi. Same bones.' He opened his arms, revealing the palms of his hands, looking at me in my eyes. 'We're whanaunga. Your old lady and I grew up together. Shared a pew. Shared a house. A bedroom. We shared the same parents. Why I called you over in the pub. It'd been an age or two, but you never forget your whānau. Ko koe tāku irāmutu. My neph, yah know. You and the kid both.'

For all the talk of the devil, I wasn't about to take Tea at his word. And I didn't have to. It was there in my first impression of him, there in everything he knew about Mum, in his clash with Koro – his own old man. At some level, I reckon, I knew it all along. There was just something about him from the get-go. Fella always felt like family.

He lay against the border railing, leaning his weight on it, the railing shifting a moment then fixing itself in place. A cool wind settled between us, whistling as the earth fell deeper into darkness. Tea closed his eyes and breathed in through his nose.

And he went on. 'Ashamed to have kept it from you,' he said. 'Knew no good time to tell it.'

'I get it, Tea. I do. I still got no idea what you mean by the devil, though. You reckon she's real real?'

'Real and unreal, aye. Whatever she is I can't say for sure. Taken too many shapes and sizes. My sister, my mother, my . . .'

He froze, his eyes unblinking, his mouth parted, his two front teeth just barely visible. 'My father.' He closed his eyes; he shook his head. 'Every now and again, she's even come to me as myself. That aside, boy, don't think there's much more that I can say. Just see her everywhere. Always standing there watching me. Judging.'

'So you reckon she's the devil?'

'Ehara. For what I've done now, it could only be her.'

34

The night began to clear, the brightest stars of Rangi's coat penetrating the darkness. Most of the heavens still empty. Waiting for the clouds to further part.

The stars beside the maunga are said to be the seven eyes of his son. Fella was so angry at his old man being thrown into the sky he tore them out himself and threw them up there with him. Who knows why? Men do all kinds of fucked-up things when they're angry. Punch walls, throw plates. Dislocate the shoulders of their own children.

Apparently, all the stars have such a story. A whakapapa. Some of them pieces of people or tools that people used. The waka of Rangi. And others – actual men and women. Those who were born, lived a life and retired into the heavens. Sided with Rangi after the separation. Could see no good down here in the waves and the dirt.

Be lying to say I didn't get it.

35

Tea pulled at his beard, the cuff of his coat falling to reveal the red-stained shirt beneath. Its arm bundled above the bend in his elbow, Tea staring at it.

He spoke with a soft voice. 'I hit him. Hard as I fucken could.'

'Who?'

'Your koro, neph. I swung on the old man with all my strength. Dropped the bastard.'

'Is he okay?'

'Kāo.'

Tea parted from the railing and buttoned his cuffs and turned and walked towards the house. He opened the front door and walked in the flickering light of the lounge. I breathed in the night and followed him inside, Tea pacing, quiet so as not to wake the kid.

'Where is he now, Tea?'

'Gone.'

'Gone gone?'

'After I left you, I went straight to the pub. Wanted to do good, yah know, fetch the spirits for the kid's foot. But I couldn't handle it. Was tempted. First off, I just had one to settle my nerves. Then it was off to the races. Come night, I was wasted and angry and started to stress David was gonna do some stupid shit. Fella was gonna do what he had to do to protect Bent. Protect his rep. Was just the way he was. Hoi anō: I boost it to his whare and no-one was home, so I broke the latch on one of his windows, old trick of the trade, jumped through and looked 'round his place. Looked and looked and found nothing.

'Fella turned up as I was gonna gap it. Must've thought I was robbing him. Came at me with that biblical bullshit. "You'll burn in hell for this treachery. Stealing from your own flesh and blood." Te me, te me, te me. Anyway, I tell him to get fucked and pushed right past him. What's a frail thing like him gonna do to stop me? Then he crossed a line, neph. He put the wrong name in his mouth.'

'Whose?'

'Your old lady's. Fucken asshole said I had hands like she had a heart. Wicked and covetous. I couldn't handle it, aye. Couldn't brush it off. I turned around and smacked him. Closed fist and everything. Knew straight away I'd fucked up. Could tell by the sound his head made hitting the floor.'

The whole of it played in my head. The pisshead, drunk and angry, climbing through the window he'd jimmied, the neighbours no doubt wondering what the heck was going on. Koro arriving home from who knows where to find his only son creeping through his house. What else was he gonna do but preach at him, call the pisshead every slur the Bible would allow him? And what else was the pisshead gonna do but sock him as hard as he could?

'You check him?'

'How I got covered in all this mess.' He pointed with his eyes at the splash of red on his sleeve and chest.

'And he was dead?'

'I couldn't tell.'

'But you called an ambulance?'

He shook his head.

'He might still be okay then, Tea. We could still call one.'

'Too late now,' he said.

His nose was not straight. Its bridge was bent to the left. His nostrils leaned to the right. The largest scar on him rose from the top of his lip, a half a finger long and a half a finger wide. It stretched towards his eye. Ran down his face like the river runs down the maunga. Like the streets run through the city.

'Trust me, neph – he's gone.'

'You sure?'

He nodded.

'You sure sure?'

'I killed him, boy.' His fists clenched, his nose flared and his eyes dropped and Tea bowed his head. 'No doubt in my mind. I wish I didn't. Wish I could take it back. But what's done is done.'

I buried my face in my hands, my heart hot in my chest, my body cold. I didn't know what to do, didn't know how to react. Tea was a loose cannon, for sure, but I would've never guessed he would go this far. And for what, some shit he already knew? When I looked him in his eyes, he was calm, like he'd accepted his fate. A look I'd seen on the old man as he drunk himself to death. Maybe it was always going to be like this. From te kore must come te pō. And from te pō the consequences of our actions. One son wanting to throw you into the sky. Another wanting to waste you. This time it seemed Tū had got his way.

'What're you gonna do now?'

'Moe.'

'Here?'

'Just one night, neph. If it's good with you?'

'Then what?'

'I got a plan.'

'You think you can outrun this shit?'

'With the devil following me – nah.'

'So what're you gonna do?'

'No more questions tonight,' he said. 'Just trust me, okay?'

Tea walked across the room and lay a hand on my shoulder and pressed his nose to my own. Mauri ora. His eyes were closed. His breathing deep. And I moved to wrap my arms around him, and he turned from me, walking a crooked line to the old lady's room. He paused and bowed his head, and I tried to speak, and I couldn't summon my voice. And so he left. Disappearing into the darkness next door.

36

I lit another candle in the kitchen and watched the door 'til it
burnt itself out, hoping Tea might re-emerge. He didn't. The door
stayed closed and the house cold.

The darkness swallowed the room and me with it and I
wondered if that was what death was like. A turning off of the
lights, a blowing out of the candle. That's how it felt to me with
Mum and Dad – and now Koro. They were there and they were
doing their thing and there was light and then they weren't and
then there wasn't. At least I got to know a little about the old man
and the old lady; with Koro I knew hardly nothing. Fella was like
thunder and lightning. Showed up with a hiss and a roar. Then
gone like a ghost. Stolen from me by my own fucken uncle.

Pissed as I was, I got it. Fella did his dad like I'd always wanted
to do mine. Hit that piece of shit with all my strength. Maybe
that kind of thing was just in our blood. Some families sell fish

207

and chips and others farm farms and mine blow up and rain fire and fury on those dumb enough to get close to us.

I took my place at the foot of the kid's bed and looked the boy over. Was I raining hellfire on him too? Was that why he was like this? I sat beside him and hugged my knees with the ridge of one hand and lay the other across his body. He breathed in a steady rhythm and my arms lifted with his breath, rising and falling with his chest. When morning comes, I told myself, I'll make a decision. I set my eyes on him and lost myself. Breath by breath by gentle breath, his sleep washed over me and carried me away to sleep. My last thought about Tea.

If we had to suffer, might as well suffer the truth. At last, it seemed he'd suffered his. My tired eyes fell shut.

———

When they opened again, the bed was empty, the kid nowhere to be seen. I shot up to my feet, panic taking me, gunned it to the living room saw nothing and gunned it again to the porch.

The basin was a dull grey in the early morning, a fog hanging over it, the whole of the outside world behind a blanket of grey. Shit was so thick even the sun couldn't penetrate it. Nor the morning songs of the insects nor the manu nor the mischief of the rāpeti this time of year. It was grey and it was quiet and it was only me, standing on the porch, scanning the whole of this place for the slightest sign of Black.

I tried to call for him and though my mouth would open, the fog wouldn't carry my voice. Over and again, I called for the kid, still the fog refused me and I cursed the fucken thing and my own throat for its weakness and the rest of me for letting the kid get out of bed without my notice. Poor thing was probably so restless after sleeping so long he couldn't help but race off on another adventure.

If Black would go anywhere without me, I thought, it had to be the river bend. Fuck the river rules, he would've said. I'm a big boy now. What's a promise to an always-lying always-leaving always-abandoning-me stupid idiot half-brother anyway?

I saw the gorse rustle and guessed I wasn't too far behind him and went off on my way, running after the kid. Half a minute went by and I waited for the pain to shoot down my bad shoulder and it didn't. I got my hopes up that the broken thing had finally healed – the sun really could get well and dash across the sky again.

No hoodie to cover my head or pockets to cover my hands, I crept through the gorse as best I could, getting low and turning my body sideways. The gaps were tighter than usual, closing in on me, but the thorns were dull. I saw them touch my skin and they did not cut me and I counted my blessings and crept onwards, knowing the kid could not be too far ahead.

On the other side I saw him, hoodie on, walking through the ballhead's paddock. He didn't walk towards the river bend but up towards the broken trough, the territory of the magpies where the cliff had not yet collapsed. I called again to him and the fog refused me and I threw myself over the fence, tripping over myself as I hit the ground and throwing my shoulder out again.

I called and could not call, I ran and could not run, and I held my bad arm in my other one and marched the kid down, not a damn clue about where he was off to. So it went, the kid walking on, hoodie over his head, and me chasing after him until at last I'd made it to the trough, the magpies letting me be, and the kid had made it to the fenceline.

Black slunk through the wire and peered over the cliff's edge. Fucken thing must've been twenty metres tall, the ground so far beneath it, it starts to call for you when you get too close. Starts to pull on you in a weird way, the whole of you just wanting to leap. I called for the kid, and for the first time my voice carried and the kid turned to face me.

'All good, bro?' I asked, marching on towards him, getting close enough now I didn't have to yell.

He didn't respond; he stayed staring at me.

'Bit sick still or nah?'

Nothing.

'You still upset, bro . . . about all the stuff with Mum?'

He shook his head.

'What's up then?'

He pointed at me with his eyes.

And I snapped: 'The fuck did I do?'

He stepped backwards, his heel resting on the edge of the cliff.

'My bad, Black. My bad. Was looking for you for ages. Didn't know where you had gone off to.' I rested my hands on the fence, less than a metre from the kid. 'Didn't mean to snap at you, bro. I'm just stressed, yah know. Scared.'

'Guess now you know how I feel, huh, Kau? He rite tonu.'

Struck by his reo, I stood back from the fence, dashing forward only after I saw him lean backwards. I stretched my arm to save him. To grab him by the chest of his hoodie. And I missed. And the kid looked me in the eyes. And he fell backwards into the fog. And I watched him disappear. Down into the rocks below. And I crumbled. And I wept.

A pain in my chest shook me out of sleep and I exploded awake. My legs rang with static, my throat was tight, my eyes ached and searched the darkness for even an idea of where I was. Soon enough, the fogginess of sleep retreated and I found myself in my bedroom, sitting and sleeping upright against my own headboard, the kid beside me.

I patted the bed until I could find the whole of him and placed my hand on his chest, feeling for his breathing, fearing the dream had come to warn me he was gone. My hand felt nothing and I prayed it was only 'cause the fucken thing was still numb with sleep. I put my fingers on his neck and felt for his pulse. My fingers couldn't feel his blood pump and I prayed they too were still numb. I waited a full minute in the dark, readying myself for the worst, my eyes full with tears though none yet running down my face, and placed my ear to his mouth, listening for his breathing.

Mauri Ora. That's what Tāne said when he pressed his nose to the first woman, the thing sowed in soil. The old lady reckoned he travelled ages to get everything he needed for her. Water from

Tangaroa, warmth from Tū, and all the other stuff a person needs to be. He finished with wind, taking it from his final brother and storing it in his lungs, gifting it to this thing of soil by pressing his nose to hers. Then she sneezed – tihei – stepping into the world of light and he said those magic kupu, Mauri Ora, and they both lived.

And so, I did the same, pressing my nose to the kid's and repeating those words over and again. Mauri Ora. Mauri Ora. Mauri Ora. If I had the legs of Tāne, maybe I had his magic kupu too: the power to call the unliving to life. At last, the kid breathed. It was no tihei but it was enough. My body sunk into the bed and I cried and I knew I had to get the kid the help he needed. It was either that or do to him what Tea had done to his old man. What I'd done to my own old man also. Left the dickhead to die. Ratshit though they were, they didn't deserve what they got. At least, not the way they got it.

Late in the morning, I woke again and combed the kid's hair to the back of his head, tucking his blankets around him before splashing my face with water from the bucket outside. The soil was like concrete today and the grass had begun to grow over the edges of the old man's grave, hiding his urupā of one. At its head stood the remains of the bone tree. A burned-out stump as tall as my knees and just as wide. The fire had burned it all the way down, its remains a charcoal black. I didn't know yet what I'd do with it. Until now, I'd pretended it wasn't there.

Time had made it a sort of headstone, I s'pose. Had no words nor dates to remember Dad. But it did smell like him. Like smoke.

And I figured nothing that could be written would remember him as well as that bastard scent.

I got changed and ate a little from the cupboard, a couple of pieces of rēwena torn from the loaf and listened for Tea's sleep. Hearing nothing, I figured he was awake and readied to ask what he was up to today. What he was gonna do. After everything that happened last night, I knew I couldn't take him to the city again. No doubt he'd gap it. Or worse, be pulled over by the cops and locked up for the rest of his life. I wasn't gonna let that happen. If I had to give Black up to the system to save his life, I wasn't giving up Tears too.

When I opened the old lady's bedroom door, the room was empty. The bed was neat, its pillows unfolded and its linen fitted. All but her duvet was tucked tight in the part between its mattress and its wooden frame. His coat lied on the edge of the bed closest to the bedroom door. I scanned the room, searching for a sign of his stay, wanting to deny what I knew to be true. Tea had left in the night-time. He must've paced until he was sure of my sleep, folded his coat and left it as a koha, drawing back into the darkness, into the always-there arms of the taniwha. The street, the drink, the smoke.

Why do they keep leaving me?

My eyes closed, and I wrestled back my emotion, and I took to the dirt track. I didn't pause. Didn't question where I was going. I went on and the soil turned to concrete beneath my feet, the distant birdsong conquered by the chewing of cud, the roaring of engines. An air of manure.

A fog polluted the fields, shielding the maunga and his ranges. Couldn't see beyond the fences and the hedges. The cows and the sheep. The occasional horse. Monstrous things tearing at the earth with every rotation of their wheels. Looking back, I couldn't even see the house in the distance.

Eventually, like curtains, the fog parted, the city emerging like a beast from the darkness. And it swallowed me. Making invisible the world outside, doing just the same as the fog before it. No more cattle, no more roaring engines. The scent of shit dying away, replaced by the smell of spilt beer and piss on concrete, three times as thick in the air.

All of it made my eyes ache. The corners of my vision blurred, little white dots flashing in and out of frame. I felt dizzy. Like any moment I might collapse. Pass out. I breathed deep and steadied myself. Three seconds in. Three seconds out. I couldn't focus. Couldn't keep my count. Couldn't find a pou for my attention, a place to fix my vision and centre myself. The whole world felt to roll on past me like the tide. Nothing enduring except the shadow beside me. The clothes upon my back. The cement biting at my feet, their bottoms beginning to blister.

How the hell had I forgotten the old man's boots again?

Dogs howled and men huffed and bouts of manic laughter paired with the flashing on and off of streetlights; rusted cars crawled through uncontrolled intersections and empty bottles rolled over asphalt; a hollow bang rang out from far away and my throat closed and my legs grew weak and I reckoned someone had lost their life.

I walked straight to the pub, no stops nor detours. All the while, in my head, I saw Tea drinking, running his thumb over the lip of his mug, knackered as he swallowed that toxic shit down, gulping and wincing and looking no better for its magic, his body warming and his drunken eyes scanning the room, watching the punters stumble and leave or comatose right there at their table, the broken man at the bar concerned only with the health of his establishment, moving as quickly as his mangled body could carry him to extinguish their still-burning cigarettes and fetch their glass mugs before they decorated the floor.

37

A cop was putting up a cordon, DO NOT CROSS, and another two putting up a white tent. The only things inside were a tagged-up bench and a body in a black bag. The last of the police had just finished the statement of a man on a mobility scooter, a cigarette between his lips. When I tried to walk on by, the man on the mobility scooter grabbed me by the jacket.

'Yah dumb or something, lad? Place is an active scene, you can't be walking through the middle like you're a model and that's yah bloody broadway.'

I was tired of walking and I snapped. 'Get stuffed.'

The cop putting up the cordon turned his head to look me up and down, scowling, and I turned my head to dodge him, and the man on the mobility scooter barked at me. 'Feeling brave, lad? Well go on, say it again. Watch the six o'clock news report two dead tonight.'

My heart sank, more death, and the cop ignored his threat and the man on the mobility scooter dragged on his cigarette, his eyes locked on mine until his lungs were full, turning to look again towards the scene only to let the smoke out.

'Not from 'round here, are yah?' Half the man was wrapped in a blanket, the rest of him kept warm by a thick brown cardigan and a caddy cap, more hair in his ears and on his neck than peeking out from beneath his hat. 'I don't reckon he was either. Didn't recognise him. And I've been here so long I know most residents by the sound of their footsteps. Does me well too 'cause my eyes are no good no more.'

'That him – in the bag?'

'You a few beers short of a box, lad? Who the fark else would it be?'

'And he's dead dead?'

'As a goddamn doornail.'

I bowed my head.

He chuckled. 'Keep your chin up, Charlie. This one ain't the first and sure as hell won't be the last.'

'Was he old?

'The dead man?'

'Yeah.'

'Old enough that it ain't no tragedy. Was a Maari too. That lot die even sooner than the rest of us. Seemed a good bloke, though. I asked him for a fag as I cruised on by and he spotted me the rest of his pack of greens.'

There was only one man I knew who smoked that colour.

I stumbled backward; I felt like my chest had been punched in; and I folded over, ready to be sick all over the asphalt, to fold over and die right there with him. The cop still putting up the cordon paused to look me up and down a second time, the alarm bells inside him looking like they were beginning to ring and I straightened up and pretended I was all good. Shit as this situation already was, I knew a kōrero with that fella would only make it worse.

'Takes a lot to surprise an old man like me,' the man in the mobility scooter continued, uninterrupted. 'But that did it. 'Least 'til he went and off'd himself. Then it all made sense. He musta reckoned he couldn't take 'em where he was going.'

'He . . . he say his name?' I had to be sure it was him – my uncle. Tea.

'Nah. We just talked about family. I told 'im mine were a bunch of ungrateful gits. You spend your whole life caring for 'em and soon as they grow, they turn on yah. He musta thought I was fucken around, laughing at me, drunk as a skunk on New Year's Day. He said his own were God-fearing folk.'

My breathing became fast, grew shallow. My knees stayed weak, trembling beneath me. 'What was he wearing? Pants? A red-stained shirt?'

'Church clothes, for sure. Fella musta thought the Almighty had a dress code.' He chuckled. 'Not sure it was stained, though. These eyes ain't good on detail no more. Why do you ask anyway – you reckon you know 'im?'

'I dunno.'

'Well, go on then, ask what you gotta ask to know for sure.'

'How tall was he?'

'Tall.'

'How thin was he?'

'Thin.'

I ran my hands down my face, doing all I could not to fold over again and guarantee the attention of the cop. 'He have a long beard and combed hair and a big scar on his face?'

'Definitely the first two. Blind men could see that thing that hung from his chin. About the last one I can only say . . . if he didn't before, he does now.' He chuckled. 'You get it? 'Cause the Maari fulla did himself with a gun.' The man dragged again from his cigarette and pushed the two fingers holding that smoking thing into his eye socket. 'Blam!' He released the smoke into the air, crumbling into a short-lived fit of laughter, choking on the smoke still in the lungs.

My fists closed. My heart grew hot. And I said the only thing I could muster up. 'The hell is wrong with you?'

'Fuck yah,' the man growled. 'You think he's the only man to blow his brains out? He's not even the first one on this block this year. Shit, when I saw the gun, I had half a mind to spill my own brains on the sidewalk.' He scowled. 'You wanna guess what I did instead?' He waited for me to answer and I didn't, his scowl growing fiercer. 'I took the bloke's lighter, cleaned it on this here blanket and sparked up a new fag, waiting for the cops to come and take my statement. And I gave it. Told 'em about the lighter too. You wanna guess what they did?'

The heat in my heart disappeared; replaced by grief.

'They laughed. Told me it was the best farken thing they heard in ages.'

The man in the mobility scooter put his ciggy between his lips, his waka in reverse and took off, sticking a big fat fuck-you middle finger in the air as he drove away. I watched him 'til he disappeared then turned to see the police throw the body in the black bag on a stretcher and wheel him into one of their fancy cars. They closed the door behind him and I glanced back at the bench and saw what must have been his life force drip to the concrete below. Not a moment later, they closed the tent, probably to clean the mess he made with that beloved gun of his. Fucken dickhead.

An anger boiled inside me, swallowing the shock and grief and I wished I could see Tea one last time just to punch his fat fucken nose in. It was bad enough he gapped it in the night-time but then to do this . . . it was straight-up selfish.

Did he even think about me and the kid? Did he even care?

The cop finished his cordon and a pair of men in white jumpsuits appeared, slipping into the tent with a collection of cleaning equipment. I watched them mahi through the side of my eye, careful not to pay too much attention or to allow my true feelings to leak to the surface. I stayed there a long while, choking back my emotion until I found a small peace. If a man should lay as he lived, this is probably what the pisshead deserved. The steelen. The smoking. The poking fun at the darkest possible subjects. His last five minutes were his life incarnate, minus the piss and the punch-ups. Still, it was probably as good a death as a man like him could hope for. Maybe even better than the old man's.

'Haere, haere, haere atu rā.'

Part Four

Part Four

38

I tried to get help for the kid and I couldn't. Brought the coins and everything. Didn't realise the payphones here call 111 for free.

A lady answered and asked if I wanted Fire, Police or Ambulance. I said ambulance and she put me through to another lady who asked me where the emergency was. When I said it was at home, she asked where my home was and when I said the wops, she asked me to be more specific. Asked for an address. I had no real idea what the address was. There were no street signs. Just numbers. That's how the postie managed it. What the mail read alongside Mum and Dad's names.

After going back and forth and back and forth, we got there, the lady finding our basin on a paper map, the dirt track Dad had built with boot and spade unavailable on whatever system she was used to using. At this point, I was over it. Worked up and tired. Felt like I was wasting my time, like I was better off looking for help elsewhere. Still, I kept the phone against my ear, the lady asking next about the nature of the emergency. I told her my brother was sick. That he had a cut on his foot and he'd been out swimming and he wasn't looking too flash. She asked if the infection had been spreading and I said no and she asked if he was having trouble breathing and I said no and she asked if I had gotten a doctor to look at it and I said no and she asked me why. At last, I couldn't put up with it anymore. The call dragging on and her questions becoming sharp, more a pointed finger in the face than anything even close to helpful. I fired up, all the way pissed off, snapping.

'Are you fucking serious lady?'

'Lower your voice, please sir.'

'After everything we've been through, you're gonna come with this shit.'

'Sir—'

'I should've known this would happen.'

'You need to—'

'It's the same shit you people did to Mum.'

'Take a deep—'

'I'm not having it.'

'Sir—'

'We're not doing this again.'

'If you don't—'

'I'm not gonna let you do to him what you did her.'

'I'm gonna have to—'

'I know what I gotta do.'

'This is your last—'

'Get stuffed.'

The call was cut off. Lady on the other side slamming her receiver down. I did the same, bashing that thing against the glass 'til the glass cracked and the phone was hanging from its cable in two pieces. Screw the goddamn ambulance anyway. They were never gonna help the kid. They didn't even have our house saved on their system. Showed how much they fucken cared. I slammed my fist against the payphone and walked deeper into the city, praying there was still one person I could go to for help. 'Specially now, after Tea had changed the game.

39

Every man and woman was dressed in dark colours, suits and ties and ankle-length dresses. They spoke in whispers and walked with light feet and bowed their heads and snuffled and wiped their teary eyes with handkerchiefs too damp to do anything. Their faces were strangely familiar, though I couldn't place a name or a memory to any grieving one among them.

The smell of flowers hung about the place. Piles of them were heaped at the gate alongside a mess of postcards and candles. It was an out-of-it aroma given the circumstances, and yet, it seemed everybody had made the same decision. I wondered if there was any scent appropriate for death.

The crowd walked without direction or purpose. At any moment, a small group would decide against their current position and drift through their peers into another place, sometimes striking up a temporary conversation with their new neighbours but more often than not joining them in silence. There was an anxiousness in their grief, a compulsion that made stillness almost impossible. Group by group they drifted, chatting where it made sense then fading back to silence. They never said anything important; they swapped simple sentences. I can't believe it. He's in a better place now. If there's anything you need. Only yesterday I saw him. It was his time. You'll be in our prayers. I'm just thankful it was quick/ it was painless/he didn't suffer.

A gloved hand grabbed me from behind and the pain shot through my shoulder and I spun around, still worked up by the phone call. I expected to see a vision of the old man or Tea or the man in the mobility scooter. Instead, the man who grabbed me was alive and fully able, his arm long, his face fiery and his cheek bruised. Swollen. 'We'll be safe to talk inside,' he said, walking past me. Bent. The preacher.

He walked slowly to the corner of the church, turning before he disappeared to hurry me on with flick of his head. Kia tere. I did as he asked, hurrying after him. Fella was why I came, after all. He was Black's old man. Everything else had failed. Bent was the last thing left. The crowd ignored us, busied by the routines of mourning. Remembering the deceased, reassuring the living, trading stories through teary eyes. It wasn't all cliché.

Around the corner, an old arched door hung open, Bent nowhere to be seen. I ran my hands along the brick and walked on, the grass flattening beneath my feet, a soft breeze blowing, the sun bearing down on me. The door led to a dimly lit hallway, the walls decorated with photographs. Weddings, baptisms. They were all ceremonies of some sort, everyone dressed as well as they could dress, and the photos were preserved by a lack of natural light – there was not a single window in the long hallway. Koro was in every picture. Always in that long white robe. Today, I s'pose, would be the first photo op he'd miss.

I swallowed the grief building in my throat and continued on, travelling backwards in time. The men and women pictured grew thinner and younger, their heads filling with colour, the bags under their eyes shrinking, their suits fitting better across their shoulders and their dresses better around their puku. Koro was a handsome man in his day, his hair curling into the back of his head, a monster of a moustache creeping over his top lip. A few photos were missing at the end, the wall lighter in a few places. I wondered what memories the fella had tucked away out of sight.

The hallway ran into the body of the church, the last door on the left spitting me into the first row of the pews. It was empty but for the preacher standing on the stage, his back turned. A box rested in the place of the podium, one half of its lid lifted, the underside padded with a silky white cushion, a river of cloth spilling over its sides.

A long length of multicoloured light stretched from the entrance stopping only a moment short of the box. The glow of the king's halo in the stained-glass portrait mourning the father's final day in this place. Haere, haere, haere atu rā.

'Even looking at him, I can hardly believe it,' Bent said. 'None of the younger ones here have ever known life without him. He was there, without exception, to welcome all of us into the world.

Would come always with the same gift. A small plush lamb. Always the morning of our first sabbath.

'From that day on, his role in our lives only grew larger. He was a giant among men, Goliath, his mana not a measure of his stature but his contributions to this community. He was a father for those who had no father, a teacher for those who school had beat the desire to learn out of. He was to us everything we needed as we needed it. You can see now why I took up the cloth, can't you, chief? I wanted to be your koro. He who called us to be better. He who knew this striving would not come without missteps, mistakes and misdeeds.'

He folded his lips inside his mouth, running his hands along his jaw. Wincing as his fingers touched where Tea had struck him.

'The three Ms he called them. And ain't they the truth. Don't have to tell you that, though, do I? I see the way you look at me, chief. You know what I am.' He looked me up and down, his eyes taking me in. 'We'll talk about it. I promise you. For now, though, say goodbye. I know he was never to you what he was to his moko here, but even so, you should say it.' He crossed himself and left the minister's side. He disappeared into the room next door, closing the door behind him.

The man in the box was black. My own koro. Met him a week ago and now look at him. I stepped closer and looked over what was left of the man. His face was shaven clean and his hair gelled down. Two long lengths of ribbon ran down his front, disappearing into the box. I wondered whether he was wearing his own sandals or another person's shoes. I didn't have anything to say to the body in the box and so I said nothing. Though I did wonder who'd done this to Koro – who'd stolen his likeness and left him looking like another thing entirely?

Was it Tears, swinging on the old man with all his strength – or was it the chemicals they pump the dead full of here in the city? Same stuff they put in animal feed, that's what Mum said.

———

The preacher pulled a cardboard box out from beneath his desk and lay it out on the table, setting his eyes on me. He looked like the kid.

'He would've wanted you to have this.'

'Koro?'

He breathed in deep and crossed himself, moving as if to lift the lid from the box but finding himself unable to. 'They're photos, chief. Very old photos. Once upon a time, they hung from the walls in the corridor.' He gestured to the hallway. 'After it all went down, he couldn't stomach them anymore. They were the mark of Cain to him. The reaping of what he'd sown.'

'I don't get it.'

'They were the sign of His judgement. Your koro, as he tells it, had been stiff-necked, his heart uncircumcised. Stole those words straight from the Good Book. He said he touted the values of the church in the church but left them here when he took off. Forgot them at home. He gave his thanks only with his lips, praising the Lord on High as if his tongue was separate from his body. Speaking it, but never really living it.'

I stared at him, unsure how to make sense of what I was hearing.

Bent, reading my ignorance, apologised. 'Times like this I know I've spent too much time with the Good Book and too little with my fellow man.'

'Too fucken right,' I teased, more as a tribute to Tea than a crack at Bent. And as I said it, I felt closer to the fallen man. It was no eulogy like the old preacher would've had, but it was surely the way Tea would wanna be remembered. Ridiculing the ridiculous. Laughing at his own jokes.

Bent paid me little attention, his hand wrapped around his face, thinking how to better say what he'd already said. 'He knew he wasn't a good father. Not to his own kids. Nor his real moko, you and . . . the other one.' The preacher looked away from me. 'He knew he got what he deserved when they left him. First, Tea, then Sarah, and at last his own wife. You should know he spoke of you often. Every one of you. Even spoke to me once about giving this place up and trying to make things right. But he was prideful.' He mouthed an apology to Koro under his breath, crossed himself and kissed his fingers. 'I'd come to think, at his core, he believed himself Abram and his family Isaac. That he was not really Cain but Job.'

He pushed the box across the table. 'In all honesty, it doesn't really matter what he believed. He failed to be a father. Not a good one, but one at all.' He locked eyes with me. They were filled with tears; he wasn't just speaking about Koro. 'And worse than that, he knew it. And did nothing. Tried only to hide it. Then when that failed, justify it. And when that failed and you and Tea came charging through that door, he tried to burn it to the ground.'

Six shelves of timeworn books lined the back wall, a sprinkle of trinkets dotted among them. A ceramic plate painted with a cross, a nest of wooden rabbits praying, a small golden candle holder. A warm light shone on them, from a lamp upon a desk and the sun shining through a set of see-through blinds. The rest of the room was bare. More a cupboard than an office. How Koro managed his mahi in such a suffocating space, I had no idea. Fella would've been better off working in the pub.

'He was trying to protect me. He was trying to protect this place. Figured if the other one was taken away then nothing would change. Even if it all came to light. Aaron spilled our secret. You gotta know that's why David called them.'

'Called who?'

'The ones who took him away.'

'Tears?'

'What's happened to Aaron?'

'He off'd himself.'

He stood up from his desk. 'First Black gets taken then this?'

'What are you on? The kid ain't gone nowhere. Was with him this morning.'

'They haven't come for him yet?'

'Who hasn't?'

'Then we still have time.'

'Time to what?'

'To save him.'

'For fuck's sake, Bent – from who?

'CYPS.'

40

He warped his wrist and pumped his foot, trying to sync his rhythm with the tick and quiet roaring of the engine. It began to tremble, the shell of the car rattling, Bent's head turned sideways, his ear listening for the rumble of life. In a moment, it all came to a stop, the only remaining music the ticking. He pulled his hand from the ignition, made a fist of it and bit down on his teeth. 'Frick this fricken thing.' I laughed through a single breath at his restraint and at life continuing to conspire against me. 'Course the car don't work.

I opened the passenger door and Bent grabbed me by the arm. 'Hold on, chief. Give me one more go. I haven't had to use this thing for a while. It'll kick over. Just got to give it a bit of love.'

He clutched the key, turned his head and twisted his wrist a second time, pumping his foot over and again, every new growl of the beast a little louder than the last, the whole thing in a fit, shaking violently, Bent's face wearing a full scowl. 'Come on. Come on.' The beast growled a final growl and fell silent, the tick taking over again. This time he couldn't help himself, he slammed his fist upon the dashboard – 'Fuck' – throwing his head backward, searching the clouds for a solution.

The bonnet was almost as long as the car, the beast shaped like the head of the huia. More beak than body. It was a sun-faded blue, one headlight missing and the other fogged up, a skirt of black plastic wrapping 'round its frame, and its windscreen chipped in two places. Inside, the car was no more flash. The fabric was torn, the sun visor barely held in place by a bulk of duct tape, the side windows controlled by never-greased cranks. All except the driver's side, which turned without effort, the preacher spinning its handle 720 degrees and the glass doing nothing. Fella must've forgot it was stuffed.

'Can't muck around, Bent. I've gotta go.'

I reached for the handle and a wave of energy overcame him. 'Get out of the car and get behind it. I've got one last trick to try.' He exploded out of his seat and left the door open, locking one hand in the frame of the car and the other on the steering wheel.

'This will work, chief. Trust me. Just get behind the car.'

'What are we gonna do: push the fucken thing all the way home?'

A small smile stretched across his face.

'Trust me.'

I shook my head and did what he asked anyway, pressing my back against the beast's boot, driving my heels into the ground.

'On three. Tahi. Rua.' We summoned all the strength we could, me driving with the might of my legs and Bent pushing with his arms. The car began to edge forward. It rolled into the street. Building momentum. Bent told me to keep pushing and leapt into the car, the engine coming alive and the exhaust kicking up a cloud of smoke, decorating me in its filth.

'Time to go now, chief.'

The beast rolled on, gaining speed, the preacher making clear by the passion of his voice that he couldn't stop nor slow down. Who knows what the damn thing would do? I spun from the boot and broke into a sprint. Bent stretched across its inside, throwing the passenger side door open. I timed it as best I could, reading the building speed, knowing a misstep would leave me with a mouthful of concrete and no fast way home. I counted two steps and drove off my front leg, reaching for the grab handle. Just the touch of my hand knocked it from the car, the plastic thing falling into the street. I stumbled. And the car started to get away from me.

I closed my eyes and gunned it as fast as I could, full sprint, the blisters on my feet tearing open. I got close and counted two steps again and this time reached for the inside of the passenger seat, dragging my body with an aching arm into the comfort of the car.

'I almost ate the fucken asphalt.'

He ran a hand along his jaw. 'Least no-one punched you first.'

I shook my head, Bent looking for a reaction. Fella was made of the same stuff as Tea. Serious as the maunga was tall but always playing up.

He lived two small blocks behind the church, a state–house block in the puku of the taniwha. The street was littered with broken-down cars and abandoned bikes, the fences decorated with writing that couldn't be read and phone numbers promising a good time. His neighbour's gate read Johnny's Whore House. Knock for meth. He reckoned his neighbour had done his missus dirty and she engraved his car with her keys and left this sweet note with spray paint as her parting gift. Utu.

Each house was connected to another, joined at the hip, a thin wall blocking access to its conjoined twin and nothing more, the noise penetrating the walls as though they were no more than a bedsheet. Figured this is how Bent learned what went down next door. They certainly weren't the type to visit confession and the preacher not the type to pry. Man had enough problems, his own fuck-ups always an unwelcome visitor away.

The beast coasted past a stop sign, slowing to a jog, Bent gauging the traffic (the street empty) and hitting the gas.

'What if a car came?' I asked.

He adjusted his rear-view mirror, checking the spotting of traffic behind him. 'Not too many around this time of day, chief. And anyway, there'll be no starting again after we stop. This chariot is already overheating.'

'So what: we've got one go to get home?'

'With my skills, that's all we'll need.'

He laughed to himself and his eyes stayed locked on the road. Fella legit reckoned he was a pro. What kind of pro drives a piece of shit like this, though? I buckled myself in and hoped for the best. There was no other option. No real one anyway. Take my chances with Bent or leg it myself and almost surely arrive home to an empty house. The heavens know what CYPS will do finding a kid in his condition abandoned in a whare like ours.

———

'You poor, Bent?'

'I got enough to get by.'

'That why you live in that place?'

'I grew up there. They're my people. Life has taken us down different roads, for sure, but they'll always be my people. They're why I do what I do. Like the church saved me, I hope it might one day save them. Or some of them anyway.'

'You reckon they need saving?'

'In my younger days, I would've insisted they did. That's what David taught. But I don't know. Every now and again one gets desperate or overcome by a desire for change and walks their bare feet into the church. Not all the time they stay. Most of the time they don't. And I get why. What did you feel, chief, when you first walked through those gates?' I turned my head, looking at the church shrink in the side mirror. 'When they do stay, though, things tend to get better. Got enough wealthy benefactors among the flock to tee them up with a job or some nice clothes. Got enough people in the right places to get lives back on track. Lawyers, people in the council, that sort of thing.'

I looked at him and he anticipated what I meant to ask.

'I know. It's not all they need. But it's something. And to be honest, most I've met only needed a gentle push – like this bad boy here.' He slapped the dashboard of the beast. 'So yeah, they're my people. And I tell myself between my driving a car like this and my staying among them a few will be encouraged into the Lord's house. And I tell myself the few that are will find what they're looking for in there. I did.'

———

The beast jerked and stalled as it rolled through the city streets, the engine alternating between a roar and a whisper, the preacher's face twisted with a focus as his steed kicked its feet, his foot hard on the pedal, paying little attention to the speed limit except as he pulled through an intersection. He ignored the centreline entirely, swinging his waka left and right to avoid the chipped concrete. No wonder this damn thing was such a wreck.

An album rested on the dashboard, *THE BEST OF PRINCE TUI TEKA*, the kaiwaiata an ocean of a Māori man dressed in a Hawaiian shirt that swam down his chest, a pair of necklaces following the pull of the tide. The speaker on the passenger side was blown, its sound tinny, the prince singing on anyway. O Mum. I love you.

'Thought I'd marry her, aye.'

'Who's that?'

'Your mum,' Bent said, speaking in short sentences, his attention still fixed on the road.

'I didn't. Was certain at the time, though. Whole thing felt like fate. Couldn't imagine a future without her.'

I swallowed the piss-take building in my mouth and listened.

'Truth is, your mum wouldn't have me. Told her I loved her. She only told me she was sorry. The most polite rejection I've ever tasted.' He chuckled. 'An angel until the end. 'Course this only made me love her more.' He wrapped his hands tighter 'round the steering wheel and furrowed his brow, a bitter regret falling over him. 'If I'd looked past myself, I would've seen it as it was. My telling her I loved her not sweet nothings but fricken torture. Woman used to brood over my every attempt at winning her hand. Broke her heart to break my heart, I guess.

'Nowadays, I've come to think, my love was more about your koro. He was a holy man. The saint of the lost, the lonely and the damned. The minister of the hood.' He crossed himself and kissed his hand. 'Maybe this explains my blindness. My never seeing the pain I caused her.

'Still, he was not a kind man. Especially to his own. Expected nothing less than godliness and modesty. An impossible standard only your mother managed to come close to. That was mostly to do with your nan, I think. Towards the end, she could barely tolerate her old man. Swore she would be different. And she was. Kind to everyone except herself, I used to tell her.'

The prince's song continued: To hear your voice and to see your smile. God please do keep my mum.

41

The beast flew out of the city at full speed, almost gaining air when the road dipped. Bent thrashed the gear stick, touching the brake only to better manoeuvre the corners then climbing again through the gears until the car red-lined. Third. Fourth. Fifth. The creature peaking around 115 k, its body thrashing against the wind, feeling like at any moment the bottom might fall out or the whole thing go head over heels.

The scenery faded to a blur, the power poles whipping past us as we raced into the wops, a hawk feeding on roadkill barely clearing our bonnet as it took to the air. The car's steel body swung like the fin of a fish clearing a splash of traffic cruising through the country roads.

Prince Tui's voice jumped with the car, the CD scratched, its gentle rhythm contrasted by the quick violence of the engine firing.

The road dipped and the beast came down hard on the asphalt and the chip in the windscreen exploded into a crack, interrupting Bent's vision. He almost lost control. The beast bucking. The back end swinging wildly, Bent having to tear on the steering wheel.

The veins in his arms swelled. They pushed against the surface of his skin. His eyes tensed almost all the way closed. He held his breath. I braced myself for the worst, pushing myself into my seat, seeing in the distance a family of pūkeko drift across the road. Two adults and three chicks. Little black nuggets unaware of a world outside their little hapū.

'Fucken stop.' I shut my eyes.

The beast jerked forward as Bent slammed on the brakes. My body was thrown against the seatbelt, my arms using the dashboard as a brace. The box in the back seat flew through the air, crashing against the windscreen. Frames wrapped in newspaper dressed the floor. Time played slowly. The beast slid across the loose asphalt. It fought to come to a stop, all four tyres screaming as they tried to grab at the ground. Prince Tui's voice died into static, the radio drawing its last breaths.

'Did you hit 'em?' I kept my eyes closed.

Bent didn't answer.

'Don't play with me, dickhead. Did you hit them or nah?'

Still, Bent didn't reply.

I opened my eyes. Not a metre away, the birds dawdled across the grass. The adults not even bothered to take to the air. I melted into my seat, catching my breath, checking my chest beneath my shirt for a scratch from the seatbelt.

Waves of heat lifted from the bonnet, the only relief from the heat an iwi of clouds sweeping across the sky and a budding wind so strong it shook the trees, rocking the car though its engine had given up. If only this canoe had sails like our tūpuna's, Bent and I could ride the breeze all the way home.

A thread of blood ran down his forehead, Bent checking himself in the rear-view mirror. He touched it with his hand, wincing, and cleaning himself up with the corner of his shirt, dabbing it with the white cotton 'til he could see where exactly the blood was coming from. No wonder he didn't answer me. Fella was probably concussed. Though the wound wasn't much more than a graze, the tissue around it was red and purple and swollen.

'You good, Bent?'

He nodded.

'Should've worn your belt,' I joked, trying to lighten the mood.

He stayed serious, dabbing the wound again with his shirt. 'Car's stuffed, chief. Whole dash is lit up red.'

'For real?'

'For real.'

'So what, we're gonna have to leg it?'

'You are. Yeah.'

'You're not coming?'

He checked his forehead in the rear-view mirror. 'What, you think I'm just gonna abandon you?'

I didn't know how to respond.

'No way in heck.' The wound bled on and Bent pressed his hand against it hard. 'I'll come down soon as I get this cut cleaned up.' He watched the pūkeko cruise down a hill and into a nearby swamp, the runt of the nest falling over its own feet as it tried to catch up. 'And this bloody car off the road.'

No time to argue, I got out of the beast.

With his free hand, Bent picked three of the photo frames up off the floor, jiggling them and handing me the two that hadn't smashed. 'If you hang them, chief, might do you some good. Let them know you've got a flock behind you.'

I tucked the frames against my body, nodded goodbye to Bent and began the rest of the way home.

———

The dirt track was empty, no hatchback parked beside the house and no new tracks carved into the earth. It looked like I'd made it home in time. Although a lack of rain had made Papa's skin hard so there was no knowing for sure. I ran the rest of the track, checking my shoulder, knowing that at any moment CYPS could rock up. The kid lay in his bed. His state was unmistakable, his sickness obvious even at a glance. I'd have to do something desperate. Pull one over on the child welfare workers. Find a way to convince them he was better than he was.

Bent was around now, so I was sure things were gonnna change. Between him and the flock and the church and the small woman's medicine and my cleaning Black's foot every day with soapy water and Tea's 100 proof piss, the kid would shake it off. Hell, when Māui was born unwell his mum tied him in her topknot and sent him off into the water like a ship. That fella survived that and became a goddamn demigod; who knows what the kid would become when he survived this?

My shoulder had started to ache, the numbness overcome by a soft throbbing, a soreness radiating down my arm, pins and needles whispering in the tips of my fingers. My old blisters had torn, new blisters replacing them. My legs ached, sweat coated the collar of my t-shirt and its fabric stuck to the small of my back.

No time to waste, I got on with the mahi: I sterilised a needle with the old man's lighter, burst the blisters, soaked my feet in a rusted bucket, threw a few handfuls of water over my face and neck and changed my clothes, the whole time thinking about what I would do with the kid. No bucket bath or change of clothes would be enough.

I lay Bent's wrapped frames on the kitchen table. Figured I should do what I could to pretty the house. What did Mum used to say again? You can't trick the crayfish it's safe with a pot in your hands. Something like that anyway. Used to say it whenever me and the bro played hide and seek. I would hide and the bro would seek, always giving up fast as. Check two or three places then try to trick me out of my hiding place. Say something like: This game's dumb. Or: I'm gonna have a feed. Probably some baked beans on toast. That's your favourite, aye, Kau?

Poor thing must've thought my skull as thick as his patience was short.

42

The men knocked three times on the door, the sound only a touch louder than the wind howling. I checked my hair one last time with my hands, making sure I looked presentable, channelling the trickster god as I readied this great stunt.

'What do yous want?'

They were small, not much bigger than me, men more at home behind a desk than out here in the wops. They weren't taken aback by my attitude; they looked straight through me, scanning the inside of the house. There was no attempt to disguise their prying, no niceties to dress their mahi as anything other than it was.

'We've received a call about a child who may be in need of some support.'

'Support, aye?'

'That's right. Support.'

'And who was the nosey bastard so good to have called you, huh?'

'Unfortunately, we're not at liberty to disclose such information,' the more bookish of the two men continued, pushing his glasses off the bridge of his nose, 'but we treat all such calls for action with the utmost seriousness.'

Would've thought the man was speaking in front of a judge, his speech was so practised.

'And who's this guy then?' I looked the other man up and down. He was younger than the first one, maybe only a little older than me. He was Māori too but a fella from a world away. Rich, university educated. What's a guy like this know about living in the wops, I asked myself. Yeah, he's Māori, good on him, but that and a couple books don't give you the right to rock up on a stranger's house and tell them they ain't raising their bro right. 'Specially when the places they send the uplifted don't do them any better than their own homes do.

'Mr Morgan here is a training officer of social services.' Mr Morgan nodded and I pierced my eyes. A pretty name for a person learning to steal kids from his own people. 'He's a fine young man. Top of his class, his professor tells me.'

'Hoi anō: You're too late. The kid took off with the old man ages ago. Must've scared them when you came 'round last time. What's the rules 'bout that anyway? You 'llowed to just chat up any child you like? Doesn't look good given the state's rep, yah know.'

'What poor timing on our part,' the bookish man replied, unbothered by my attempt to provoke him. 'Can you tell me where they've gone?'

I shrugged my shoulders; I didn't expect them to indulge me. Would've thought we'd be throwing hands by now. Even the old lady would've slapped me if I'd said this sort of shit to her.

'In that case then, do you mind if we come in and have a look around? Something inside might tell us where exactly they might have disappeared to. We'll be quick, we assure you.'

'Do whatever you want.'

The bookish man entered first, never taking off his shoes. He hit the light switch and met my eyes when the bulb swinging from the lounge ceiling did not come alive. Mr Morgan entered too, following his lead, breathing in the whole room, a look of sadness falling across him. I resented his emotion. Not all of us were raised in mansions, dickhead. The bookish man looked over the old lady's library, adjusting his glasses as he scanned their titles. 'Best, Smith, Cowan, Grey. A rare collection.' He picked one up, brushed the dust off its jacket and flicked through its pages.

'They cover any of these at university, Mr Morgan?'

'Had one paper that looked at Grey's work in Parliament.'

'Yes, well, I suppose that makes sense. Even so, if you're going to be working with the local Maaris, you'll do well to learn a few of their stories. Helps to keep tensions low.'

They continued speaking as though I weren't in the room and I rolled my eyes at the man who'd never introduced himself and wore his shoes in the whare. One thing to know the stories, I reckon, another thing to understand them. And that's not even mentioning the rep of the authors. None chiefs. None Māori.

They walked through Mum's bedroom and were pleased to see the bed made proper. I told them I didn't make it – I'm one person, I only need one bed – and the bookish man adjusted his glasses as if to say, We'll see about that. He went into the bathroom while Mr Morgan went through the cupboards and they met again in the lounge, standing off in the corner and whispering to each other. Barely any food. Barely running water. They had plenty to talk about.

———

A photo of the flock watched them trade secrets. The church folk stood at the feet of the church, even the stained-glass king looking younger, his hair falling over his shoulders. The minister was a handsome man, his hair slicked back; Tea a little ratbag, his hands folded over his hips, a cheeky middle finger extended; Bent stood at David's side, his teeth as big as his smile; and at last there was the old lady.

The child welfare workers finished their search in the kid's room. I breathed in as much air as I could, praying Plan B would work better than the first one did. They opened the door and the bed was empty, the sheets dishevelled, the duvet borrowed from Mum bulked up in the corner of the room.

Black was buried beneath the duvet. His body lied flat on the carpet, that heavy thing flung over him, one corner scrunched up so he could still breathe. I knew I couldn't turn CYPS away, send them back the way they came like the kid did; they would've surely come back with police. To buy the kind of time I needed,

I had two options. Have them throw hands with me and so stay away out of fear they lose their jobs. Or to trick 'em, believe in their heart of hearts that the kid had taken off and wouldn't return any time soon.

The kid still being sick meant I couldn't move him far. I had to be creative. It didn't matter much anyway; if all those games of hide and seek taught me anything it was to stash yourself where no-one would bother looking. Laundry baskets, wheelie bins. In the mess.

And so, I lay the kid in the corner of the room and buried him beneath the old lady's duvet then roughed up the place. I hung the bedsheet blinds on one side of the sill and pushed the bed a quarter over Black and took all the drawers from his dresser and stacked them near the door. I stole the bulb from its socket and dumped the kid's clothes on the floor and pushed one bedside table on its side, using the other to block the way to the first table, which blocked the way to the kid.

'Is this your room?' the bookish man asked.

'Used to share it with the kid. So yeah, now it's mine, I s'pose.'

'What happened?'

'Last I heard you'd come 'round to see him. Next morning, the old man and Black were gone and my bedroom looked like this.'

'They didn't ask you to go with them?'

'Reckon they already knew what I'd say: Someone has to look after the place. Last time it was left alone some dickheads took our shit like you plan to take the kid.'

Mr Morgan posted himself by the door, content with my answers. The bookish man went on, walking the boundary of one half of the room, checking the state of the carpet and the walls and the windowsills. I acted like I was over the whole thing, leaning my back against the wall and checking my fingernails. A physical you-done-yet? The bookish man pulled a few clothes from the pile and looked them over. Then he went through the drawers, finding in his search the old lady's envelopes. 'You said he'd taken off with Dad, right? Can I ask what happened to Mum?' I replied only with a scowl and we looked at each other for a little while and he resumed his search, knowing from my reaction he'd get nothing more from me.

Some time passed and the bookish man continued. He checked beneath the bed, behind the drawers, opened the window and scanned the world outside. The man had no give in him. He was relentless. A real-deal master of his craft. A true-blue CYPS detective. There was no doubt in my mind at least a hundred others had tried exactly what I was trying now. And few had managed it. To get one by them, I reckoned, I'd have to pull something slick.

'You're useless, aye: spent a good five minutes looking and you haven't even walked this side of the bed,' I said, baiting the bookish man like our tūpuna baited the tuna. A little bit of blood in the water. I shifted the bedside tables and, behind my back, loosened the lid on the small woman's medicine. 'Well go on then. Let's get this shit over with.'

The bookish man ignored me, continuing his search his way. Fella didn't muck around. He was committed to his process. Mr Morgan stayed posted at the door, blocking any quick exit, any chance I had to grab the kid and gap it. The bookish man finished his search on the other half of the room by checking the corners of the wallpaper, noting the way they peeled from the walls, each worse at its bottom corner. He did the first. The second. The third. And at last made his way to the fourth, stepping on the corner of the old lady's duvet.

It was time. I swung my arm and knocked the small woman's medicine onto the ground, spilling the rongoā all over his shirt. He leapt back in a panic, moving as if to wipe himself down.

'Wouldn't do that, bro,' I warned. 'It's a tonic from our tūpuna. Don't want it on your hands, trust me.'

He looked to Mr Morgan for help.

The other fella shrugged his shoulders. Uni don't got nothing on street smarts.

'If I was you,' I said, 'I'd grab a black tee from that pile, run some water over it and dab it up in the bathroom.'

'Are you fricking kidding me?'

'Your gears, bro, up to you.'

He shook his head and Mr Morgan leapt into action, both of them moving with urgency.

'Hey, my bad,' I said with some cheek. 'Fucken thing should've had its lid on.'

———

'Can I tell you what we do at the agency?'

The bookish man had cleaned his shirt and got a fresh one from his car, the hatchback parked parallel to the porch. I'd checked the kid and he was good and I'd checked the tonic and it was all but gone. Split half and half between the fabric of the bookish man's shirt and the carpet. I closed the door behind me and when the bookish man was ready to go, sat to speak with him, knowing that, though the worst was over, things could erupt at any time.

'You mean CYPS.'

He nodded. 'We believe every child has the right to live in a home where they are happy, healthy, loved and looked after.' He paused to make his point, letting his eyes roam the kitchen and the lounge, aware now that the only path to the kid was convincing me that Black was best in their care. 'Where their every need is met. Where their potential is nurtured and they are allowed to flourish – allowed to become productive members of society. Doesn't that sound a good thing to you, sir?'

This was how these types have always dealt with Māori. Played a game of pretty lies and promises of a better future. Learned to do it way back with the Treaty, apparently. I wondered whether they'd try and sweeten this deal too with smokes and blankets.

'Rumour has it the kid's got exactly that already.'

'Our records show he's never been to school. Never even been enrolled. How exactly do you propose he is having his potential nurtured?'

And then when things went tits up, this was how these types have always escalated things. First pretty lies and promises, then threats and intimidation, then big guns and the law.

'The old lady went to school all her life. Finished even, got her School C and everything. Pretty rare for a Māori girl in those days, I've heard. She reckoned she learned nothing 'cept to take a strap, who not to speak the reo in front of and when to shut your mouth.' Same rules the old man played by, now I thought about it.

The bookish man removed his glasses, folding their sides down, and placed them on the table, rubbing his eyes. He was tired, well over justifying his place in homes like this one. To him, it was obvious. Beyond question. School was a good thing. For everyone and in all circumstances. Just think of the doors it'll open, he surely thought, knowing nothing of the doors it'd slammed shut. I looked to Mr Morgan to see if he got it. Wealthy though he was, he was still Māori.

He went to speak and the bookish man went on. 'It has been a long day, sir. A very long day. This is the third home we've been to; it is nearly four o'clock and we still have another one to go. Not to mention the paperwork needing to be completed and logged. Isn't that right, Mr Morgan?' A whole-ass degree and fella wasn't even allowed to speak. Just nod his head when called upon.

'Fuck off and do your work then. I've already told you I got no clue where the kid's taken off to. You scared the poor thing and the old man bolted. Better off asking the stars than me. I wasn't even here when they left.'

'Can I be frank with you for a second, Cody?' 'Course he used that name. 'The phone call we received informed us your father had passed. Furthermore, the person on the phone, a person of great reputation may I add, could also tell us how he passed and when. Now I might have treated such information with some scepticism at the time, but now I've been here, I can be quite sure it's correct. In fact, I could guess the exact spot where he was laid to rest. It's the only raw earth around.' I averted my eyes and swallowed the stress building in my throat. 'So here is what I suspect. Black is still around. Nearby, my instincts tell me. But where precisely, I do not know. If you can't tell me where then Mr Morgan and I will have to keep coming back until we catch you off the wicket.' He placed his glasses back upon his face. 'I don't want to keep doing this. Do you?'

The bookish man leant his head on his hands, looking through me, and the front door swung open and Bent stood there, scanning the room. Immediately, the bookish man changed his tune, leaping from the table and rushing to shake Bent's hand. Even Mr Morgan looked shocked.

'How's your day been, Minister Bent?'

'Good, thank you. And yours?'

'We heard some terrible news from . . . let's just say another member of your church, and we came to make sure everything is okay.'

'And is it, chief?' Both the men at the door turned to me, the bookish man starting to sweat.

'It was 'til these guys turned up. Fricken ballheads have accused me of this, that and everything. Even searched the house.'

'With all the correct papers, I'm sure.' He looked the bookish man in his eyes.

'Oh, it's not like that, I assure you.'

'So that's a no then.'

'We were just completing a welfare check. Making sure everything was okay. Nothing formal.'

'I hope that's all. You know the church doesn't take kindly to your lot taking advantage. We do recall what happened last time, don't we?'

'Of course.'

'Then it's probably time you both head off now.'

The bookish man left with his second, tearing down the dirt track in their hatchback, a cloud of dust following them to the asphalt. I stood on the porch, watching their car disappear into the distance. Bent patted me hard on the back, crossing his arms and looking up and down the photo of the flock. When I went to check him, he asked where the kid was and I told him and he walked into the room and stood over Black still lying on the bedroom floor. Bent placed his hand on the kid's forehead and began to pray, calling for his Lord to bring the boy back to health. He closed his eyes and though his voice rang calm, a pair of tears ran down his face.

I let them have their moment and waited outside looking over the ancient photo and frame I got from Koro. The old lady was a sack of spuds in her mother's arms. The small woman. There was no mistaking it. She wore a long black dress, a tiny handprint of flour on her right shoulder, a silver cross on a silver necklace as tight 'round her neck as the twisted bun on the back of her head. My own nan. Hardly a drive away. I knew why Koro never came 'round, how it'd look if the kid walked in the church looking so much like Bent. But Nan: she lived so close and only came that one time. Abandoned the old lady to her life with Dad. Maybe that old girl was just as shitty a caregiver as the rest of us.

43

We spent the rest of the afternoon in the bedroom with the kid, remaking the bed and fixing the drawers and packing away his clothes. Black stayed still, growing thinner as another day without food and water came to an end. Feeling guilty, Bent and I spoke only a little.

'What happened last time CYPS took advantage?'

'We dragged them through the dirt, lawyers and the media; the whole shebang.'

'But they keep doing it?'

'Some of them, for sure. If they think they can get away with it.'

The only thing left to speak of after CYPS was Koro's tangihanga. Bent didn't seem too fussed about it. Said it was not uncommon to wait a few days before a service was held; said it was the first priority of a preacher to look after the living. David would get it, he thought. And if he didn't, then he said, it didn't matter anyway. Fella was off to see the Lord on High himself.

We sterilised the kid's cut with Tea's vodka then I set off to the city to fetch Nan's rongoā. Bent asked to stay behind and pray for Black, his own brand of medicine. After that, we had to get the kid to a doctor. Bent reckoned he knew one from the church. Pākehā lady but Māori tūturu. Heartie. Went off to study like her old man then came across the statistics on Māori health. Thought it a blight on the whole goddamn country. Turned her whole life around afterwards, apparently: learned the reo while she got her quals then set up a mobile clinic and now does most of her work on pā and in the wops. The white women's Māui Pōmare, Bent called her and chuckled. I just stared at him; I didn't know who that was.

———

The single store was covered by two half-pulled blinds. A weak light shone within, a set of steel shelves barely visible, the rest of the store covered in a coat of darkness. I knocked three times on the door and its sound carried in the air and I waited and saw jack. It was late; Nan had surely gone to bed.

It was a quiet night, the only sound the faraway call of an ambulance rushing off to help whoever was patient enough to endure a five-minute Q&A. I wondered if anybody even bothered to call one for Tea.

Without warning, the door swung open and I jumped and stepped two steps backward and fell onto the road. Nan stood behind the door, fixing her eyes on me. In the soft glare of the streetlights, I doubt she could make out anything except my silhouette. Still, she approached me, reaching her hand and lifting me from the asphalt. 'E tū,' she said and brushed the dust and stones from my sleeves.

At last recognising me, she scowled, twacking me around the ears. 'And why in the world are you out so late, huh? By golly. You gotta know I'm an old woman now. A deaf woman. Can hardly hear the sound of my own voice some days. Oh, you're a sweet thing, e tama. But a gosh darn fool.' She looked me in the eyes and I wondered what she was seeing. 'Hurry now, e tama, tell me what's up. Everything okay at home?'

'We're out of medicine.'

'Already?'

'I knocked it over.'

She screwed up her brow and looked into the night. Nan looked ready to take off, pausing only because she knew her body couldn't carry her this far into the night. The cold. The dark. A plan of sorts was forming behind her eyes.

'Do you have any extras, ma'am?'

She stared into the distance a good while longer. 'None ready right now. But I can have some by the morning.'

'He really needs it, aye. Really really needs it.'

'I know.'

'I just don't know what's gonna happen if—'

'Take a breath, e tama. Slow down. There's nothing that rongoā will do tonight that it won't do tomorrow. The worst thing you could do now is risk your own health running through the night. What if the pirihimana picked you up, huh? Or worse? What do you think would happen to your brother then?'

'But the bro—'

'Is anyone with him while you're here?'

'His old man.'

'Then we're good as gold. We'll see him in the morning. Pono ki te Atua. I'll have the rongoā ready and I'll have sorted a ride and you'll have had a good night's rest and some proper kai in your puku.'

I checked my shoulder, looking into the darkness. I knew the small woman was right, I was just scared.

'Kia tere mai,' she said, her voice knackered. 'Follow me upstairs.'

We walked through the store and climbed a flight of stairs behind a door behind the till. At the top were a short hallway and a door on a chain. Nan worked her magic on it and we strolled into the kitchen and lounge, a brick fireplace and a neat stack of wood standing pretty in the place where those two rooms blended into each other. Her whole place was spick and span, her walls decorated with Māori memories. Tukutuku and a picture of a fantail flying around the thighs of a woman and a greenstone taonga in the shape of a man and a whānau portrait. None of them smiled, none of their necks pictured without a silver chain or chest without a cross. Koro, adorned in a black suit, stood stern over his children, his left hand decorated with a band on its third finger. His wife was small at his side, a long black dress billowing over her and a modest ring unshining on her same finger. The taller of the two kids – a boy close to twelve – looked at me with worried eyes, like he knew how this was gonna go. The youngest sat straight and stoic, bathed in her father's good grace. It looked way different than the ones Bent had given me. Posed and professional.

'The only one I have of them,' she said, flicking her wrist and directing me with her eyes, encouraging me onto a seat pushed in beneath the long table in the kitchen. I sat and she smiled, the small woman finishing her work, warming a copper-bottom kettle on a gas range stove, a fire lashing at its brown metal base. 'It'll whakatau your wairua,' she said, offering me a cup of heated milk.

I nodded and set it down, unable to drink 'til I'd laid out all that I had learned. Said all that needed to be said. And so I spoke of the old lady and Dad, the bookish man and CYPS, Koro and Bent and Tea; of the wops and the pub, the pub and the church, the church and the tagged-up bench and the man in the mobility scooter. As I spoke, the small woman sat beside me, my cup of milk ceasing to steam.

Nan kept composed, even breathed slow, her brown eyes bright and the corners of her lips pulled into a slight smile. She pulled her long-gone-cold milk to her mouth, swallowing only enough down to hold back the sadness building in her eyes. 'E ngā mate,' she whispered, 'haere ki tō maunga, ki te karanga a tō tūpuna.' I mouthed the last part with her. 'Haere, haere, haere atu rā.'

She stared a long moment into her mug, her body frozen with grief.

'What a life you've lived,' she said, at last. 'And after all that, look at you. Walking through the cold and the dark to help your whānau. There's no doubt in my mind, my boy, you're one of the good ones. If only every awa had a piharau like you.'

'A what?'

'A piharau, my boy – an eel, old as the maunga himself. Famous for swimming up waterfalls. Not a bad feed either.' She winked at me.

I laughed through a single breath, my eyes welling with tears. The small woman took my hand in hers, turning it over and cupping it as a fist, running the tips of her fingers gentle over its back.

'I've lived a long life,' she went on. 'And I reckon I know a good deal of its storms. How it rains its waters on everyone. The young always getting the worst. The Lord yet to thicken their skin. I've lived a long life, a very long life, and I've seen a lot. So know, if you don't already, you did good. As good as anyone could hope to do.'

She turned her head towards the lounge. Though I couldn't see what she saw, I knew the look in her eyes well: it was the look of loss. In her pupils, a glossy mirror of the whānau canvas was reflected and her face didn't change, her everything exhausted by years of want and grief.

'If I'd had a heart like yours, my boy, I could've done a lot more for them. For both of my babies. I wish I could say it caught me off guard, that if I knew what was going to happen to them I would've leapt into action. Swam upstream. But I knew. Somewhere deep down, I knew. Between their father and the church and school and the street, they'd been set up to struggle from the get-go.' She breathed heavy through her nose and bowed her head, lifting it only as her breath came to an end. 'I did what was obvious. I kicked in the pub door and dragged the boy out by his ears and I followed the girl all the way into the country and left a key for her there. A few times I even called the authorities. Hoped a night in the drunk tank would scare the boy into sobriety. Hoped a visit from CYPS would frighten your old man into being a better father. I didn't know then he was a state kid. No wonder why he chased them away with such anger. Hoi anō: Seeing nothing for my effort, at some point I stopped trying. Tricked myself into thinking time was all they needed.'

'Can you imagine,' she said. 'Giving up on your own children?'

A feeling of sorrow swelled inside me, wrapping around my throat. To choke it down, I told the small woman I was sorry.

'That's the hardest part, I reckon. Coming to terms with just how much I could've done. And didn't.' The small woman continued with a soft voice. 'Come now, the night is late. Haere ki te moe. Lay down your heavy little head.'

'Nan,' I said.

She met my eyes and hers began to mist. 'In the morning, my boy. In the morning.'

44

My body ached. I clutched my chest and closed my eyes and hoped sleep would steal me. Or better still, a dream. Alone in the quiet dark, the events of the day were catching up with me, burning hot in my shoulder.

Nan tiptoed in through the bedroom door and sat on the corner of my bed. Humming to herself, she combed her fingers through my hair. A vision of Tea stood in the doorframe watching his old lady move with a smile. 'My boy,' the small woman said, her voice trembling. 'You cannot know how long I've dreamed of this day.' My stomach told me she wasn't speaking to me. 'Kua hinga koe.' She pressed her lips to my temple and went on with a whisper, her touch becoming softer, Tea walking away.

I slept and dreamed jack.

When I awoke, the bedroom door was ajar and light floated in from the kitchen. The small woman was at work. I watched her only a moment and turned my head and let my eyes roam the room.

The blinds kissed the windowsill and draped over a pile of books on New Zealand history. The ceiling matched the walls, and a pretty portrait – not heartie but well done – was hanging beside the bed frame. An old painting of a man. Barefoot, dressed in a korowai and crowned with a halo. A good light shone in from one corner of its frame and dulled to darkness in the other, the man covered in colours human and heavenly.

Keen to get back to the kid, I joined the small woman over breakfast. We ate from our plates, drank from our cups and said little. Her silence hid the darkness on her mind. I saw it and said nothing. We finished, cleaned and started downstairs.

'What about the store?' I asked.

'It's not going anywhere.'

The streets were quiet, and the sun hadn't yet risen above the city's silhouette. The occasional car breezed by, going nowhere in a hurry. Wives walked their husbands, strolling lazy and in love. It rarked me up. Did they not know how serial and dangerous life was? I felt the urge to warn them, to tell them everything I'd seen. The piss, the sirens. The gun. They wouldn't walk this way if they knew. Not like this. Not 'round here.

'Love,' Nan said. 'Even in the dark it germinates and grows.'

I thought about it long and hard and Nan knocked on the neighbour's door and the neighbour came out in a singlet, pyjama pants and gumboots, grumbling as she headed down the road to grab her car. We all jumped in, Nan in the front and me in the back, and the neighbour tore down the road. The whole ride she said little, hungover. Nan paid her no mind. Ka aroha was all she said when the neighbour complained Nan couldn't have picked a worse morning for it.

The further we drove, the deeper Nan and I dove into conversation.

'Was it the same way with you?'

'What's that, my boy?'

'Love growing in the dark.'

'Koia,' she said with a smile. 'Took me in its grip and threw me at that beautiful man.'

'Gummon woman,' the neighbour barked. 'Be honest with the boy. That fella of yours was always a dickhead.'

'Ignore that one,' Nan said. 'That big waha of hers is always getting her into trouble. Ain't it just, Jah?'

'Yeah, yeah, chalk it up.'

'Hoi anō,' Nan continued, 'your koro was a man quite different than most men 'round here. He was like a giant, like Tū walking through the street. He had many little dreams, many little ways his ambition manifested. None were more serious than his dream to save this place, though. Heal these people. He couldn't ignore the trouble that possessed them. And so with all that he had he went to work. Marched the streets and read from his book. Offered them a better way. His own.'

'Ain't that the fucken truth,' Jah barked.

'Anyway,' Nan said, ignoring the latest interruption, 'it just wasn't to them what it was for him. "What are you on?" they would ask. "You think that fella in the clouds cares about us. Nah, look around. He don't sweat us, doesn't sweat this place.'"

'Āmene,' Jah added.

'And what could you say to that, my boy? Through no fault of their own, they were born here, on land stolen from their tūpuna, the whole world seeming to conspire against them. Of course they were bitter. What else should a man feel seeing what they've seen?

'He thought to sell them hope,' Nan said. 'And they wouldn't buy it. Thought to sell them hellfire. And they knew it and were unafraid.

'I reckon David just couldn't bear to see his mahi continue to fall apart. He grew to hate them. Came to believe they deserved what they got. It's natural, I suppose. How else was his faith to survive? In the end, he became a callous man. A shepherd, koia, but more an enemy of the wolves than a friend to the flock.'

Her eyes flickered as she spoke, sometimes fiery, though more often than not sad. She scrunched her face and fought for every new thought, the years she was recalling having long passed her by, even the memory of them barely a thing anymore.

'Why'd you stay with him?' I asked.

'Great fucking pātai,' Jah said.

Nan nodded, anticipating the question; she replied with a soft voice. 'Honestly, I couldn't say. I've thought about it for ages but I don't reckon I really know why I didn't leave him sooner. Was always on my mind. Just never did it until I did.

'He wasn't a wholly terrible man, I suppose. There was heaps he did that redeemed him. He was certainly a flawed man – and worse than that, a man not entirely aware of his flaws.' Jah wiri'd one hand at the sky, backing up the small woman. 'Still, he was a man of great conviction, sacrificing everything in the name of the Lord, believing wholeheartedly that He was the way this city would be saved. He truly believed. Like few men. Head and heart and soul.'

The concrete forest retreated into the dirt and a mass of hedges and fences rose in its place. Most paddocks were empty, nursing grass or the remains of a crop. The others were bursting with life. A conspiracy of cows gathered by a corner fence, all fixed on a farmer spraying a field with a mammoth truck. Horses grazed in a field with a duo of lambs born out of season zooming up and down a steep hill, around a trough. They ran and they butted heads and they chased one another, forgetting their partner on occasion, getting distracted by the horses munching. Then it all kicked off again with another butting, their ears pinning back and their front legs lifting off the ground and their wee bodies charging at each other, the winner retreating and the loser chasing her down for her rematch. Utu.

'In another life, I might never have left him,' the small woman continued, speaking more to herself than to me or her neighbour. 'I loved that man. Reckon I still do. But life demanded I make a decision, and I made one. Rightly or wrongly.' She paused, seeming to remember my company. 'Hoi anō: That's enough of that.'

The small woman and I shared a smile, and Jah drove on, flying by Bent's car pushed all the way off the road, and I couldn't help but ask a second something. A question that had been boiling in my throat ever since the old lady turned herself into a tekoteko. 'Do you like your life, Nan?'

She looked at me a long while. Guessing my reasons for asking such a question. 'I suppose so. Most days anyway. There's a lot to like about it, a lot to be grateful for, many things I'd be sure to miss if they were to go away.'

'Like scrounging free bloody rides, aye,' Jah said.

They both laughed and I didn't and Jah soon dropped us off at the end of the road, swearing like hell she wouldn't take her baby down the dirt track. Nan chuckled and said as long as she was back before lunch to pick everyone up again then it was fine and dandy. Jah grunted and said as long as the paracetamol had kicked in by then she'd be here. Would let Nan know by a honk. Won't wait longer then fifteen minutes, though, she said. 'And you're lucky even to get that. My husband only gets two. And I wouldn't give Kuīni Te Atai herself more than twelve.'

So off we went, down the dirt track. The sun rose higher and the earth stayed cold. Nan tried to breathe the whole place in, roaming our paddock with her eyes, her face scrunching at the burned-out stump. I started before she could ask:

'Where we buried him.'

'Your old man?'

'Yeah.'

'He waka pakaru kino.'

She was a different thing in this place, quiet and soft-spoken, listening and watching and trying to make something coherent from the not-so-obviously connected parts that littered the wops. The half-carved gutter and the uneven porch and the ash sprinkled in the grass; the broken hump of the roof and the bedsheet blinds and the wild mix of timber that lined the house; the dead patch of grass and the many-coloured walls and the dry-rotting window that kept the rain but wouldn't keep it much longer; the remains of the corduroy fabric and the still-damp towel that kept the door closed drying on the crooked railing and the mauri of this paddock, death hanging in the air.

Nan's curiosity became concern, anxiety growing in her eyes, as if she couldn't believe what she was seeing. I didn't stop to say anything, and I didn't defend my home; I led Nan the rest of the way down the dirt track and into the house.

Bent met us at the front door, said he spotted us walking down the track. Nan wrapped her hands around his arms, the tall man bending down so she could kiss him on the cheek.

'You okay, young man?' I s'pose everybody was young compared to the small woman.

'Yes, ma'am. I'm okay.'

She smiled. 'And what about my moko. How's he going?'

Bent bowed his head and Nan nodded, walking past him, her and I heading straight for the bedroom, the preacher staying on the porch.

The kid lay still, his blankets hanging off his bed. His breath was shallow and his eyes were closed and his skin an even paler shade of white. When I went to check him, the blankets fell to the floor and piled in an ugly heap, half-looking like a headstone for the bro. The sheets underneath moved with the blankets, exposing his bone-thin body. Bent's medicine had done no more for him than mine and Nan's. He was hour by hour growing more sick.

I wondered how his first night had gone with his old man. Bent holding him and wiping his sweat from his forehead and cleaning his foot with the vodka and throwing prayers like a man throws a rope to tow a canoe back to shore.

Nan placed a loving hand on my shoulder and moved me out of her way, going forward to fix his blankets and tuck them neat around his body. Though she looked to have done nothing different than I'd do, she made a pretty picture of that poor thing. Snug as a bug in a rug, the old lady would've joked, her voice bouncing as she went. Nan made no jokes. There was a loving urgency in everything she did, as if even a moment's pause would be the difference. The difference between what and what, I wondered and thought to know and wished I was wrong.

She gestured to the bedside table and I handed her the silver spoon and she pulled a fresh batch of rongoā from the inside of her coat – she must've prepped it while I slept – delivering it with a whispered word and a kiss on the forehead.

I watched the kid, wishing his nan's touch would prove the difference. She'd healed him the last time she'd touched him, rustling his hair and filling his feet so full of joy he couldn't help but trip over them. I crossed my fingers and hoped she could do the same now.

The light in the room flickered, the shadows in the room dimming and the house growing dark. The wind whistled through the rotted windowpane. The falling-away wallpaper swayed, dancing like branches in a breeze. In between the breath of the wind, the ruru called its name and the pūkeko screamed. And then they didn't. And the light ceased to flicker. And the room stayed dim. The kid coughed and spluttered and rose through his chest, his body lifting like he was being taken away. Nan hugged him down and didn't let him go. The fibred muscles of her arms swelled, raising against her skin and turning her body to concrete. My brother melted in her clutch, his eyes parting just enough to reveal a pink and a red.

———

We stayed at his bedside a long while, hoping and wishing and praying for some change of state. A stir, a murmur. Even a deep breath. All the while Nan studied him, running one hand through his hair and the other over his body. As she watched him, I watched her. When at last she rose from his bedside, she turned to the doorway.

'Let him rest a while.'

'Is he—'

'He'll be okay. The little one can't stay here though. Kāore. We'll have to take him to the city. Get a doctor to have a look. Just in case, you know. Let him rest a little while, recover his strength. Then we'll take him.'

'Bent reckons he knows one.'

'Pākehā lady from the church?'

'How'd you know?'

Nan winked. 'I've been seeing her for yonks.'

We each smiled and there was a long pause and I asked if she thought it would be enough.

Nan answered me with a soft voice. 'Our tūpuna had all kinds of rongoā. Stuff that'd bring a man back from the verge of meeting Hine. The fat of the baby toroa, the stomach of the kererū and the leaves and the shoots and the buds of the koromiko. It didn't work for everything, though. When I was little, the flu swept through the rohe, wiping out a good deal of my cousins before they'd even walked their first steps. Some whānau had an unshakeable faith in the old medicine. Believed between their awhi and their karakia that everything would be okay. And it wasn't. Children died.'

I shook my head. Not in reply. It was a matter of instinct.

'I once read a speech from Māui Pōmare,' Nan continued. 'A local boy, born and bred. The first Māori doctor. "Ka pū te ruha, ka hao te rangatahi." That's what he said. When the old net is laid aside, the new one goes fishing. If it'll be enough, I don't know. But we got to do something different. Lay all this aside and try our luck with a new net.'

The kid couldn't stay here I knew. Between the bookish man and his sickness, this place would be the end of us. Still, I wasn't ready leave the wops. To leave Mum and Dad. Could their ghosts even find me in the city? And what about the river and the ruru – who would be here to hear their music?

Reading me, Nan closed her eyes, breathing long through her nose. 'A lifetime ago, when my babies were little. Aaron would play up. Rark up a teacher or one of the neighbour kids, you know. Every time, your mum would run to the rescue, get in there before her brother would get a hiding.' She smiled. 'It was quite the sight to see, your mum half the size of her brother flying in to save the day. Made me endlessly proud. Aaron would throw his toys out of the cot, of course. Used to feel his mana was being stepped on. Hoi anō: At the end of the day, it was your mother's nature. Wanted or not, she was coming to his rescue.'

Her eyes grew wet with regret, glistening with the early morning light leaking in from outside. 'Well, now I'm taking a page out of her book. And so,' she swallowed a choke in her throat, 'I'm not asking anymore. Kāore. I insist. I'm not going without you. Will stay here if I must, camp out on the porch if you won't have me inside.'

———

Nan looked younger in the wops. Her face scarred with the marks of a long life. A hard-won composure. She didn't shift as she watched me, the whole of her moved in perfect unison, every muscle, bone and joint focused on the mahi at hand.

'Shit, I almost forgot.'

'Language.' Nan looked ready to twack me.

'I mean shoot.'

She laughed and I left her with the kid and darted inside the old lady's room, collecting the coat from atop her bed. 'For you,'

I said returning, a single sleeve of the coat unfurling as I reached my arms. Nan rolled it inside her hands.

'Pae kare. How'd you get this?' she asked, her eyes blinking, soaked in shades of nostalgia.

'Fella left it behind.'

'David?' she asked.

'Tea.'

A silence washed over us. The kid then tossed in his bed and I dropped the coat and Bent rushed to the kid's door, hearing the bedsprings cry out. Nan got low beside him and Bent watched from the doorway and I raced to the other side of the bed, grabbing his hand as Nan cradled her arms around him.

The back of his hair was long and curled, wrapping around his face when he whipped his head, tossing. Wet with sweat, his locks were more black than ranga. Burnt down to ash and charcoal. I'd never seen a head of hair so dark on a boy so pale. Good luck to anyone guessing the sick kid's whakapapa. Poor thing looked more like the old man twisted in the dirt than Mum; more like Koro in the white-fabric box than Bent beside me.

He spasmed again and in waves he looked to get better, his breathing getting deeper and his eyelids opening, and in waves he looked to be getting worse, the whole of him shivering, the kid falling into a kind of fit. I wondered if this was it, Black teetering between this world and the next. Nan called for water. 'Kia tere,' she said. 'No time to muck around.'

Bent stayed where he was, stuck in the mud, and I ran and returned with a rusted bucket and a rag, Nan taking them hard from my hands. She wet the rag and squeezed her hand and pressed it to his forehead, the water running down the kid's temple and soaking the bed beneath him. His eyes closed and his mouth opened. All the while, he continued to shake. Nan held him tight and he hung there, on her arm and knee, his head rocking back and forth, his neck tensed all the way tight, his hands squeezed into soft little fists. His toes pointing and pulling.

My shoulder began to ache. And my legs gave way. I dragged myself to the foot of his bed, feeling his pain as if it were my own. My hands became fists too, my vision becoming blurred.

Gradually, the kid's movement became softer, though not so much as to appear any less desperate. He lied for long intervals without breath. His breathlessness broken only by desperate gasps. The small woman mirrored him, breathing only when he breathed. Their lips were blue and pink and green and made certain this was it. The light and the shadows of the room warred and retreated, dancing over and around him. The winds beat and howled against the house, throwing and shifting the blinds that kept the room.

Nan paid no attention to the rapture raining down around her. Even if the house were to erupt in flames, she wouldn't have noticed. All she was, head and heart and soul, was focused on her moko, wrestling with the power that lifted him from the bed. Ten seconds turned twenty and twenty turned forty and forty turned two full minutes, and the small woman endured. Fatigue mounting. Getting the best of her. The muscles of her arms beginning to cramp. Her hands trembling.

At last, Nan's grip failed. And the kid fell limp. And the rapture came to an end. Time stopped and the world came to a standstill. Death entered like Whiro, a swarm of insects, pacing and stalking and scaling the walls. From every corner, it came together and made itself of darkness. The room shuddered. A light shone. And the new light struck me blind. I turned to see, and I couldn't see. The darkness followed me as I moved.

I gapped it from the room, shoving Bent out of my way. My hands were numb, my legs weak. Nan called to me, her sad voice echoing through the house and I kept going. Bent, waking from his trance, did the same and I stumbled onto the porch, slamming the door on him. On all of them. What could they say that would help me now?

Stuck in a dream, Nan went back to tending to the kid, the faintest echoes of her voice carrying outside the house. For all that she'd seen and suffered, she must've known he was gone. Like her daughter. Like her son.

45

Rangi was grey, his dark coat painting everything above the earth. The sun, the sky, the clouds. The darkest of them fell upon the earth, hanging no higher than the tops of the trees. It was gonna happen eventually, I reckoned, fella fighting back for his place beside Papa. Whether this was it or not, our world was never built to last. The legs of Tāne could never keep the raging heart of his old man away from the one he loved. Fucken toxic though it all was. Husband and wife and child forever fighting.

Blurred by the darkness, the city erupted out of the earth, its grizzly silhouette watching us with a wary eye. I heard its call and didn't hear it. Whatever connection we once shared had died. Time and grief had sobered me.

Bent cradled the kid in the back seat, Black laid across his knees. Nan sat upfront with Jah, and I sat in the back, squeezed in the corner, the kid's head resting on my knees. Nan traced the sky. And I watched her watch it. Her face was knackered, the flesh around her eyes wet and swollen, the lines beside it sinking deep, sitting less like the wrinkles of time and more like scars. Still, she was beautiful. Nothing as ugly as getting old could change that. The kid melted into Bent's arms, the car's every movement rolling him further into his lap.

I turned my body and watched the world through the rear windscreen and though I didn't know what I hoped to see, I didn't see it. A single weed bursting through the asphalt. The maunga buried beneath the clouds. When I turned to face the front again, I saw the first of the sharks, a lady and her lover sitting arm and arm on the steps of an apartment building. She nestled her head in his neck, stroking the top of his hand, her fingers tracing his scarred knuckles, tracing every rise and its misshapen dip.

We drove another five minutes, pulled over on the block before Nan's dairy and walked from there, Jah said she was 'round if we needed anything, her first kind phrase, and Bent carried the kid in his arms. And so, we went on, turning the corner and walking the empty street 'til we stopped below Nan's lopsided banner, the pāua in the pavement refusing to shine today.

Her store looked as we'd left it, the glass cabinets still empty, and we climbed the stairs behind the door behind the till and walked inside her whare. Bent lay the kid on Nan's bed. He bent his body forward, uncurling his arms, the kid moving with him, limp, his farthest arm falling, snapping at the elbow and bouncing. His head turned outward and patches of his hair turned too. What was left was wet to his head with the remains of his sweat.

When Bent had at last lay him down, the kid sunk into the bed, its handwoven linen growing over him like the earth upon the track. The cushion of the mattress, much less soft than the quilt covering him, showed no reaction. A half-week without food and water had robbed the bro's body of its weight. Black had become a child skeleton, his clothes rags. Nan breathed a long breath. She sat beside him, shifting the blankets, hugging them around him, tucking them under his body. She propped his head on a pillow and fixed his face straight to the ceiling. The kid looked no better for it, his eyes sinking into his skull, skin moulding around his cheekbones. His chest was still. His lips were sealed. His mouth was silent. I checked Bent, and he showed no reaction. And I checked Nan and a tired smile stretched across her face. I watched them watch him, their swollen eyes staring through that poor thing buried on the bed.

'Nan—'

'Taihoa. It's been ages since I've seen a face so lovely in this bed.' She pressed her nose and her forehead to his, drawing a breath deep into her lungs. 'Mauri oho. Mauri tū. Mauri ora.'

The bedroom filled with the heat of the fireplace crackling next door. The timber exploded behind a black metal screen, a thousand flames, embers, spinning and dancing up the red brick flue, its crackling quiet compared to the whistle of the copper-bottom kettle coming to a boil in the kitchen, Nan and Bent's soon-to-be cuppas looking on, two square filter-paper pouches on thin white strings sleeping at the bottom of two mugs, Hana Te Hemara pictured on one and Ruapūtahanga pictured on the other. (Both Māori warriors, I'm told.) I could hear the sirens earlier – a drunk couple arguing and a lonely stray barking at a parked car – I couldn't hear them anymore, the crackling fire drowning them out, and now the sounds of the kettle.

It was drizzling outside, the small woman's bedroom window covered with a thin coat of rain, the light twisting and the quiet city blurring into a mess of colours, blue and red and yellow. I focused my attention on the kid butt naked on our nan's bed.

He lied atop two towels, the double bed stripped down to its bottom sheet, the remainder of the bedding folded and stacked on the bedroom floor. He lied unmoving. His eyes closed. His mouth opened. His body still. His wrists limp. The fingers of his hand hanging off the towels. The flesh of his middle caved into the cavity of his puku and his ribs protruded.

Like father like son.

I held the kid's hands with both my own, massaging them with my thumbs. Nan moved over him with a warm wet rag, lifting his frame from the bed and washing every inch of his body.

A glass drum beat through the room, the rain continuing to drizzle, falling sideways on the window face, the quiet city behind it continuing to twist, its light blurring, being stretched thin, the asphalt vanishing beneath long streaks of colour. It could barely be heard above the kettle whistling; its steel case rattled and jumped as its steam lifted from the gas fire's touch. The fireplace exploded on occasion, bundles of burning wood shifting and collapsing, rearranging themselves. It was all jack beneath the sound of the kettle whistling. The high-pitched howl.

Nan continued tending to Black. A subtle change had begun to take place, the skin of the kid appearing to blush beneath the warm wet rag. I couldn't tell if this was real or only my eyes playing tricks, the red light blurring in the window or the shadows of the fireplace dancing across the bro's body. Nan's expression made none of this more or less real, her face fixed, her eyes shifting only as she moved her hands over him. She was down to his feet now, cleaning and heating the rag in the bucket beside her, running the soapy cloth between his toes, over the cut that had scabbed all the way over. I held his hand and loved him, laying my forehead on his arm, the sounds of the kettle echoing, its scream calling visions of the old man and the old lady into the room.

They watched the kid. Their faces a mirror of their living lives, distant and loving and trying and dogged. I stayed where I was. My forehead pressed to Black's.

Eventually, Nan left to wash her hands — that is the tikanga 'round here — and lift the kettle in the kitchen, making Bent and her hot drinks. The sounds of the fire and the rain grew stronger and Bent left too, and I lifted my head and lay my eyes on the bro.

And he lay his eyes on me.

46

A few days passed before Bent came back around.

In the meantime, Nan took the kid to the doctor. He was getting better but still sleeping a lot, she just wanted to be sure. They were away for ages, Bent's friend living on the other side of the city. She had a look at him and ran some tests but had no clue what was going on, figured if he was getting better then he was probably over the worst of it. Said she'd call if something came up in his bloods and to give it some time and if anything changed to bring him back with a quickness. She wasn't a whole lot of help, to be honest, but at least she wasn't a know-it-all.

Black reckoned she was lovely – reckoned she reminded him of Mum. He spoke in short sentences, his body still weak, fighting the sickness. I asked what it was like and he told me 'bout all the crazy contraptions they used, flash-as stuff that checks your blood pressure and another thing that tells you how hot your insides are. Kid even got to hear his own heartbeat.

A little later, when Nan left us alone, he said the doctor asked her about her health. Nan said she was steady but the way she said it made him nervous. Said he looked at the doctor and she was frowning.

'I asked her 'bout it in the car ride home.'

'And what'd she say?'

'Said I should focus on getting better myself.'

'Not a bad idea, aye,' I said, hoping to ease his anxiety.

He looked at me for a long while and I told him to get some sleep, pulling the curtains and flicking off the light and walking downstairs to help Nan in the store.

I'd been doing a lot in the store lately, Nan spending most of her day tending to the kid. Helping him eat and wash, reassuring him that everything was gonna be okay. Running the place was easy once she showed me how the register worked. You push a few buttons and it gives you a number and you take that number in dollars and cents. Done and done. Most of what's left is cleaning, stacking and mihi-ing to the punters as they come and go. You good, bro? Giz us a yell if you can't find nothing. The hardest part is the relay races, someone asking me a question about gardening and me running upstairs to ask Nan then returning to give the answer. Rinse and repeat 'til the stranger on the other side of the counter is good to go.

There's an old Pākehā man who comes in every day for the hell of it. He thinks it's hilarious watching me run back and forth, leaving without even buying anything, a shit-eating grin across his face. First few times it pissed me off. Now I think it's funny too.

''Sup, old man?'

'How are you, youngster?'

'Feeling fast today. If you'd brought your watch, you could've timed me.'

He laughed. 'You listening closely?'

''Course.'

'My dog ate a packet of seeds and I'm worried he's going to grow a lemon tree in his guts.'

'So you want me to ask Nan how to stop the seeds 'fore they grow?'

'Nope. I wanna grow an apple tree instead.'

I put my face in my palms and the fella left, his laugh hiding the sounds of the silver bell on the chain chiming as he gapped it.

———

Bent visited when the store was closed, the kid sleeping, Nan and I having a cuppa with him in the kitchen. He walked here. His waka stuck on the side of the road 'til next week, one of the flock willing to tow the beast just tied up in the meantime.

'How did his tangihanga go?' Nan asked.

'It was packed. People came from all over the country, even a few of the ministers from deep down south.'

'You run the ceremonies?'

The sound of the kid's snoring burst through the walls and Bent turned his head. 'Is that the boy?'

I nodded and the small woman said, 'He's sounding healthy, aye?'

Bent looked at Nan, shifting in his seat as if to ask a difficult question, the small woman shaking her head. I watched them both closely, knowing after my chat with Black that something was up. Nan must've been māuiui too. They drank their drinks and went on, detailing Koro's funeral.

'It would've been nice to have you there.'

'Was looking after the little one,' Nan said. 'And to be frank, after what he'd done with CYPS I don't know that I could've kept my waha closed.'

Bent nodded his head. 'He thought it was best.'

'Silly man thought a lot of things.'

Bent's nose flared. 'He was trying to save me.'

'Save you from your own child, Bent? Come on. You know just as much as I do, he was trying to save the church's rep.'

'Does it even fucken matter?' I snapped. 'Fella's as good as gone.'

Bent reached to touch my hand and I pulled away. A hard habit to shake. He smiled at me, declaring his sympathy, and turned to Nan. 'Yous have a game plan for the whole CYPS thing? I chased them away but that won't be the end of it. Just means they'll play it by the books from now on.'

'I'm going to whāngai them both,' Nan said. 'Even if this one here's grown already.'

My eyes welled up. I didn't cry.

'There's more than a few family lawyers in the church who'd be willing to work pro bono,' Bent said. 'Be good for those folk to get outside the bubble a little and serve their fellow man. You let me know when you're ready to fight the good fight, and I'll put them in contact.' He sipped the tea from his cup and ran his hands along his cheek, the skin still red but less swollen. 'You think you'll come back to church one day, chief?'

I shook my head. 'Not for me, aye.'

He hesitated before he asked his next question. 'Would you . . . would you mind if Black did? You know, if I asked him once he's mended.'

'You reckon that's a good idea, Bent? People might catch on.'

'If you and the old woman are—'

'Excuse me,' the small woman interrupted.

He chuckled. 'I mean if you and the youngest grandmother this side of the maunga are okay with it, I'd like to step up and do what I can for the kid. Might be too late to ever be a real dad to him, but maybe I can be something like it.'

''Course,' I said. 'Can't do any worse than I did. Practically almost killed the kid.' Bent didn't laugh but Tea would've. No end to the dark shit that fella found funny. The small woman smacked me on the wrist, her face frowning. I laughed heartie anyway. Just couldn't help myself. Felt good to play up again. Be a little toe-rag.

47

We buried ourselves beneath our hoodies, tucked our hands in our pockets, bent at the hip and followed the maze the rabbits, stoats and runaway sheep had carved through the gorse. On the other side and over the fence, we walked across the ballhead's paddock, my eyes glued the whole time to the trough and the magpies and just beyond them the place where I watched the kid fall. What a fucken wave the last few weeks had been.

Over the final fence, me and the bro walked down the collapsed cliff, rested upon the rocks and soaked our feet in the water. It took a few minutes but eventually the ducks showed up – haere mai e ngā rakiraki – peeking out from behind a corner then exploding into a flurry and rushing to the edge of the water. The kid threw some bread and we laughed and then we split the loaf we had in half and Black walked a while away so we could feed the ducks separately. Save the poor things scrapping.

When all the bread was gone and the ducks went back to floating up and down the tide, I asked Black if he wanted to do some manus.

'Not really.'

'Your foot still playing up, bro?'

'Nah, not really.'

'What about the rest of you?'

'You mean after my long sleep?'

'Yeah.'

'I'm good.

'That's good.'

'What about you, Kau?'

I got up and stretched and said I wanted to go for a walk and the kid asked if he could come and I said 'course. Chilling was cool and all, but if we come all the way out here from the city we might as well make the most of it. The kid got up and we took off, following the river bend downwards, to where the cliff was uncollapsed. The ducks followed us down the river, probably hoping we were fetching another feed. Gutted for them; the bread was all gone and the kid and I already ate. Pork bones, pūhā and fried bread. Nan was teaching us to cook and wanted to start out easy.

Step 1: Throw everything in a pot.

Step 2: Turn the heat on.

She reckoned if we got as good at dishes as we were at pork bones and pūhā, she'd teach us how to make rēwena bread. The kid was keen as but I didn't know – looked like a whole lot of effort.

And if we got good at that, what would she do? Lady is too full of life to kick back and leave it up to us. And anyway, the more time she spent baking, the less time she had to growl me and the kid. Far as I was concerned, it was a win-win. Nan stayed the queen of the kitchen and the kid and I, long as we cleaned up after her and did our time at the till, had heaps of time left over to muck around and play silly buggers.

Around the corner, the cliff shrunk into the horizon, the white tip of the maunga towering above it, the gorse growing all along its edge, looking over the river bend, crossing its roots beneath the soil, hoping it would get another go at us on our way home. I got the feeling we'd just found our way around the ballhead's paddock, that at last we could rid ourselves of that racist prick and come and go from the water here without even a moment's worry he would pull up in his beat-up ute.

The kid and I walked on, following the cliff until it was flat as a field and even the gorse gave up growing. The birdsongs changed as we marched on, the chatter of magpies replaced by the hooping of a kererū flying backwards and forwards between a pair of trees and a solo tūī singing to itself. I couldn't find the latter for the life of me and so we walked on still, stopping only when we came across a giant of a tree fallen on its side, creating a sort of bridge across the river bend.

The kid's eyes exploded with life and I laughed, anticipating his question.

'Can I?'

'I thought you didn't want to.'

'So I can?'

''Course. Just check it's deep enough first.'

The kid threw his hoodie, socks and shoes off, grabbed a big rock from the riverside and scaled the fallen-over tree on his hands and feet. Following his lead, I threw all my gears off too, ready to rescue the kid if anything went wrong. Above the belly of the water, he stood up and dropped the rock into the river, listening for the sound the splash made. It was hollow as. To our minds, that was as good as a green light and so the kid went through the motions. He squatted, he popped, he stretched while he swung his legs, then just before he touched the water he folded his body into a V, arms over his puku.

The manu was huge. A true-blue bomb. The best he'd ever done. There was no doubt in my mind, the kid was all the way better. No sick kid could do a manu like that. Not in a thousand fucken years.

The kid popped out of the water and I gave him heaps. You're the man, bro. Straight up. You're the motherfricken man. The kid was quiet, just floating there, the whole of him hidden behind a bushel of branches. I waited a moment or two then called to him. Over and again, I called his name and asked if he was all good and he just floated there.

In a full-on panic, I shot into the water, swimming out to him. Seeing he was all good, I punched the kid in the shoulder.

'The hell are you up to, bro? Almost gave me a heart attack.'

'You see it, Kau?'

'See what?'

He pointed with his eyes to a thin rope wrapped around a twig and I stretched my arm to grab it and I snapped the twig and held the thing in front of my face. The rope was waterlogged and frayed but the thing at the end of it looked exactly like it's always looked. The taonga grainy like wood. The whalebone wrapping around itself. More a wave than a fern.

'No fucken way,' the kid said, doggy paddling, the river up to his neck and his eyes starting to tear.

'Language,' was all I could whisper back.

ACKNOWLEDGEMENTS

Tēnei te mihi ki ngā paiaka o te rākau kōrero nei

Tracey Bourke

Darren Ngarewa

Shi-han Ngarewa

Celeste Ngarewa

Waitohu Ngarewa

Haumene Ngarewa

Cayden Tito

Harlen Tito

Ryu Redgrave

Greer Anderson

Kate Stephenson

Tania Mackenzie-Cooke

Suzy Maddox

Melanee Winder

Sacha Beguely

Dom Visini

Stacey Clair

Cyanne Alwanger

Tracey Slaughter

Haoro Hond

Keely O'Shannessy

Mike Wagg

Jeremy Sherlock

NZSA Mentor Programme

Creative New Zealand

Born and raised in Pātea, Airana Ngarewa (Ngāti Ruanui, Ngārauru, Ngāruahine) writes about Māori affairs for The Spinoff. His writing has also been published by RNZ, *NZ Herald*, *Newsroom* and *Landfall*. He won the short story and poetry competitions at the Ronald Hugh Morrieson Literary Awards in 2022.

E kore e kā te rākau rewarewa
E kore e kā te ngākau Ngarewa